Dear Reader,

I started this journey just over two years ago and what you are holding, *Meet me at the Wedding*, is the conclusion of this wonderful journey of friendship and romance and I couldn't be more humbled knowing you have chosen to read it.

Immersing myself into the world of fiction has been both inspiring and cathartic. I had been struggling to find a romantic story that, to me, felt real and captured love in this day and age. I began by scribbling down a plot filled with characters I could both empathize with and identify within my friends and I hope I have delivered.

I have been overwhelmed by the response to all four heroines; Victoria, Malie, Zoe and Lily and the reaction to their personal stories, struggles and overcoming fears in their own way. They are brave, unapologetic and more importantly, true to themselves.

Thank you for your continued support, *Meet me at the Wedding* is such a special book, it is the culmination of four wonderfully diverse stories and I truly hope you have been immersed in a world of romance along the way.

With all my love,

Praise for Georgia Toffolo

'A book with a huge heart, a dreamy location and a fabulous heroine, Meet Me in Tahiti is the very definition of romance. Sweet, funny and full of zest for life – I adored it!'
Veronica Henry, *Sunday Times* bestselling author
of *The Wedding at the Beach Hut*

'Georgia [is] committed to tackling important issues, ensuring representation and writing strong heroines that are in control of their own narrative and sexuality...a must read'
Marie Claire

'Uplifting, romantic and festive – the perfect book to curl up with. I couldn't put it down'
Rosie Nixon, Editor-in-Chief, *HELLO!* magazine

'Totally dreamy, funny in all the right places, and unabashedly romantic. I loved it!'
Laura Jane Williams, bestselling author of *The Lucky Escape*

'The perfect escapism. Romantic, sexy and full of sunshine'
Lia Louis, bestselling author of *eight perfect hours*

'Fresh, fun and full of romance! I loved it!'
Heidi Swain, *Sunday Times* bestselling author
of *Underneath the Christmas Tree*

'A perfect escapist, heart-warming read! I was hooked from the first line!'
Katie Ginger, author of *The Perfect Christmas Gift*

'Unwrap and enjoy this Christmassy treat of a read'
Mandy Baggot, bestselling author of *Staying Out for the Summer*

'A beautiful and heartfelt story of joy and glorious escapism'
Alex Brown, bestselling author of *A Postcard from Paris*

'Meet Me in Tahiti arrived and I promptly devoured it! I fell in love with Finn and Zoe. I didn't want it to end. Each book in this series has gotten better and better'
Sherryl Woods, *New York Times* bestselling
author of the *Sweet Magnolias* series

Georgia Toffolo is a broadcaster and British media personality. *Meet me at the Wedding* is the fourth book of her quartet. It is her fourth novel. She lives in South West London with her dog Monty.

Also by Georgia Toffolo

Meet me in London
Meet me in Hawaii
Meet me in Tahiti

Meet me at the Wedding

Georgia Toffolo
with Pippa Roscoe

MILLS & BOON

Mills & Boon
An imprint of HarperCollins*Publishers* Ltd
1 London Bridge Street
London SE1 9GF

www.harpercollins.co.uk

HarperCollins*Publishers*
1st Floor, Watermarque Building, Ringsend Road
Dublin 4, Ireland

This paperback edition 2022
1
First published in Great Britain by Mills & Boon, an imprint of HarperCollins*Publishers* Ltd 2022

ISBN: 978-0-00-837594-2

MIX
Paper from
responsible sources
FSC™ C007454

Dedicated to the great people of Devon – for your endless inspiration and fortune in residing in the best place on earth.

MEET ME AT THE WEDDING

PROLOGUE

THE WINDSCREEN WIPERS FLASHED back and forth, sweeping the rain from view and strobing the headlights from an oncoming car. BBC Radio 1 was counting down the top ten and the girls in the car were laughing.

'I can't *wait* to see the expression on his face when he sees you, Zo. His eyes will be on stalks!'

'Never mind me, what about V? Looking fiiiinne in that dress. I still can't believe you made it yourself,' Zoe said, switching the conversation to Victoria, who was driving her father's car to the summer ball.

'Thank you,' crooned Victoria, clearly pleased as punch with the praise.

Lily saw the tight outline of Malie's shoulders in the seat in front. Reaching forward, Lily rubbed her arm.

'You OK?'

'Yeah. You know ...' Malie shrugged, the tension still there.

'Your folks again?'

A nod was her only answer.

'You can stay with me tonight, if you like?'

'Thanks, hun, but it's probably best not to rock the boat,' Malie replied with a sigh.

Lily leaned back, catching Zoe's gaze, empathy bright in her eyes.

'Wow. So this is it. End of A Levels, end of school ...'

End of an era, thought Lily, peering through the darkness at her best friends. Hawke's Cove wasn't the smallest seaside village in Devon, but it wasn't exactly a town either and having been in the same class since primary school, they'd always been there for each other. Birthdays, break-ups, frustrating parents, the loss of a parent, first kisses ... Every defining moment of Lily's life had them in it.

'So what are we going to do with the first day of the rest of our lives?' demanded Victoria in a bright voice.

'Surf!' said Malie.

'Sleep!' Zoe replied.

'Work,' Lily grumbled.

They all laughed, as she'd known they would. She loved her job at the Hawkesbury Hotel restaurant, but the early morning Saturday start had been gruelling throughout the whole of her last year at school and would just be as gruelling tomorrow.

But it would be her last shift. Lily had worked hard and saved a lot – enough to pay for culinary school in London. She'd done it. A true independent wow-man. She smiled at the errant thought, catching Victoria's eye in the mirror.

'And what are you smiling at?'

'Nothing. Just thinking,' she said on a sigh. 'I'm gonna miss you guys!'

'Hey, we're not disappearing off the face of the planet.

Besides, you and me are going to London to paint the town red!'

'Not sure where I'll be, but it won't be here, that's for sure,' Zoe chimed. 'But wherever it is, I'll expect monthly visits from each of you.'

'No plans to return to Ibiza then, no?' Malie said, laughing from the front passenger seat.

'Hey!' Zoe cried. 'We agreed! We don't talk about that. Ever!'

'It's not that we don't, it's just that *you* can't. It's not our fault you can't remember what happened … for, like, *three hours*,' Malie replied, quick as lightning.

Lily felt the bubble of laughter rise within the car's interior, taking over all the girls at the same time. But then collectively, as if each one of them realized that this might be one of their last evenings together, the bubble deflated just a little. In the silence, though, it wasn't sadness she felt, but the strong bonds of friendship that would tie them together, no matter where they went. They'd always have this, Lily felt, *knew* even.

Victoria leaned towards the radio and turned the volume down.

'Can't believe you brought up Ibiza,' Zoe grumbled.

Frowning, Lily peered at the road ahead.

'Everything OK?' Malie asked.

'I think so, it's just …' Victoria peered in the rear-view mirror at something, causing both Lily and Malie to turn in their seats, trying to see what she was looking at. 'It's nothing, just the car behind acting a bit weird.'

'Isn't that Claudia and Henry?' Zoe asked Lily.

'How would I know?' Lily replied, cringing at the defensiveness in her own tone which she knew would draw more attention from Zoe.

'I don't know,' Zoe said, shrugging as deeply as the smile on her face was broad. 'You just seem to be quite interested in Little Lord Fauntleroy.'

'Don't call him that. He's my boss's son, that's all.'

'Wish he'd inherited some of your boss's kindness,' grumbled Malie.

'I'd heard they were going out. But I didn't think he'd come back from uni for the summer ball,' Zoe remarked.

Victoria's attention snapped back to the rear-view mirror at the same time as Lily heard the rev of an engine over the quietened sounds from the radio.

Something changed then. Something in the air, a tension whipped tight, like a rope being pulled on either end, an infectious panic spread through the interior of the car, and Lily felt her senses heighten.

'I'm going to—'

Victoria jerked the car to the side.

'What's going on?' demanded Malie.

'She's trying to pass us. Crap, hold on,' Victoria said, casting her eyes quickly back and forth between the road in front and the car behind. Lily turned, to see the car pulling out into the road beside them trying to overtake.

Lily felt Victoria ease off the accelerator to help the car pass them, the pull in momentum drawing the thud of her chest impossibly to her throat. The car had almost passed them when from the corner of her eye, Lily saw the back wheel spin out from underneath it.

'Wait!'

'Brake!'

'Stop!'

'No!'

CHAPTER ONE

Ten years later ...

EVERY TIME LILY ATWELL punched a fist into the icing she was kneading, she imagined Henry Hawkesbury's face.

Every. Time.

He had ruined everything. But she *wouldn't* let him ruin this cake. It was the ninth incarnation of her best friend Victoria's wedding cake. Finally having settled on the sponge – a delicious blackberry and lime – she was focusing her attention on the topping. Torn between buttercream and royal icing, she was trying them both. And resolutely ignoring the fact that because of her, or at least, because of Henry Bloody Hawkesbury, the wedding might not happen. Well, she mentally bartered with herself, it *would* happen, just not the way that Victoria had wanted it to happen. And *that* was unacceptable.

Lily felt the rising panic in her chest and forced a fist back into the firm icing on the smooth metal workbench in the kitchen of her restaurant. How *dare* he come back after ten years and mess everything up. How *dare* he go against his father's wishes and refuse to hold Victoria's wedding at the Hawkesbury estate?

The sudden vibration of her mobile phone, loud and angry, cut through the silence and made her jump. And then, as it vibrated perilously close to the edge of the shelf she'd put it on, she reached up just in time to catch it as it fell.

Lily answered without checking the screen. She didn't need to. Only three people would call her at six thirty in the morning and she'd pick up no matter what she was doing because that's what it was like between Victoria, Malie, Zoe and her. They were her rocks. They'd been there for each other before, during and after the accident ten years ago. They'd cried, laughed and shared everything, but most of all, they'd loved each other unconditionally. And Lily honestly didn't know how she could have survived without them. She wedged the phone between her shoulder and ear.

'Hello?'

'Good, you're awake.' Zoe's crisp voice came down through the speaker.

'Of course I'm awake. What normal person wouldn't be at 6.30 on a Sunday morning? Everything OK?'

'Yes,' Zoe replied in a voice that indicated anything but.

'What's wrong? It's not Finn, is it? You haven't changed your mind, have you?' Lily rushed out as she continued to press into the icing. She'd been surprised to see how the years had turned Finn from an angry teen into the tall, handsome, dark-haired man she'd met only a month ago and couldn't have picked a better man to have captured Zoe's deserving heart.

'No! No, no. Not at all …' And there it was. The faint trace of dreamy wistfulness that seemed to have infected her friends in the last few months. That they had each found their happy ever afters made Lily's heart soar. And even the slight twinge of loneliness she felt being so far from them couldn't take away from her happiness for them. 'Hold on, I just want to get Malie in on this.'

'In on what? Have I missed a Lost Hours? Pretty sure it's too early for V—'

'Nope, just hold on …'

The Lost Hours had become their code for a drop-everything-now-no-matter-what-damn-time-it-was call. A 'break in case of emergencies' – or news. It had saved them, supported them and connected them across continents and years.

'Hola, ladies.' Lily couldn't help but smile reflexively at Malie's greeting. 'Have I missed it?' she asked. As Lily heard a rustling through the phone, she imagined Malie sweeping the mass of her beautiful curls away from her ear.

'Missed what?' Lily asked, confused.

'No, you're just in time,' replied Zoe. 'I'm staging an intervention.'

'Another one?' Lily asked, thinking back to Zoe's last unnecessary intervention *after* Malie had finally realized she was totally, one hundred per cent, head over heels in love with Todd Masters.

'Yes. Because it's been three weeks, Lils.'

Lily's stomach roiled.

'Have you told V yet?' Malie asked gently.

'Told V about what?' Lily replied, folding the icing and punching at it again.

'Lily Atwell. You are brilliant, amazing and beautiful, but also one hundred per cent deep in a river in Egypt!' Zoe cried down the phone.

'I'm not in denial, Zo,' Lily exclaimed, letting out a puff of air as she switched to the rolling pin.

'What time is it, Lils, and what on earth are you doing?'

'It's 6.30 and I'm making icing.'

'Really?'

'Not the point, Malie,' Zoe interrupted. 'Listen. Lils, it's getting serious now. And if you don't fix this, I'm going to come down there and—'

'What, you're going to get on a plane from Sydney and come all this way?'

'No,' Zoe replied after a strange pause, 'Of course not. But this can't carry on. V needs to know that she can't have the wedding at the Hawkesbury estate.'

'No she doesn't,' Lily insisted, which was met by a loud and painfully audible groan. 'She doesn't. Because I'm going to make it happen. I *am*.'

'How, Lils?' Malie asked, the doubt in her tone undermining Lily's determination. 'He's already said no.'

'Well, I'm going to make him say "yes".'

'Have you seen him?'

'Not since ...'

No. Absolutely not! No way.

Henry's last words on the matter cut through her mind, making her want to lash out with the rolling pin.

'Lils, listen. It's not the end of the world.'

'But it's what Blake wanted,' Lily replied both sadly and stubbornly, the ache in her chest expanding once again for the loss of her friend. But he'd been more than that. Boss, mentor ... none of the words seemed to do enough justice to what he'd been to her.

Father figure.

'I know, honey. But Blake isn't here anymore.' Malie's words were said kindly, but they rubbed at a wound not even begun to heal and Lily hiccupped against a bubble of grief. 'Look, do you want me to come back early? I could find someone to cover and—'

'No, Malie,' Lily interrupted. 'Honestly, you don't need to do that. I know you have things to finish up before you come home.'

'Home. I love the sound of that,' she replied, and Lily could easily imagine the smile on Malie's face as she spoke. Lily couldn't wait until Malie was back in Hawke's Cove. Her friend had travelled all over the world making a name for herself on the surfing circuit, before her godfather offered her a job in Hawaii teaching at a surfing school where she'd finally settled.

Then Malie had found the perfect guy – Todd – who didn't try to tame her beautiful wildness, but instead complemented it, pacified some of the white-topped waves that made her a force of nature and gave her a safe harbour when she needed it. And they had decided to return to Hawke's Cove and no one could be happier than Malie's parents at the news, not even Lily. It had done wonders to chase away the shadows that had hung about them since the loss of their son Koa, who had died from cancer when Malie had been sixteen. It had been such a tough time for Malie and her parents, who had turned their grief into a need to protect Malie at all costs, not realizing that they were stifling her so much that Malie had seized the first chance she'd got to fly halfway round the world for her escape.

But soon she'd be back, and would re-open her parents' old surfing business. She'd be coming home. It was everything Lily had always wanted. Her friends, back in Hawke's Cove … And while Zoe was still in Sydney, focusing on her writing, the most that Lily could look forward to was having them all back for the wedding. If there was going to be a wedding.

'Do you know why Henry said no to the wedding?' Malie asked, bringing Lily back into the present.

'No idea.' Punch, punch, roll. The poor icing.

'Maybe you should find out why?' Zoe suggested. 'Then perhaps you could change his mind?'

Lily pulled up short, the rolling pin hovering mid-air. 'That's not a bad idea.'

'OK, it's the beginning of an idea, let's not get carried away,' Zoe cautioned.

'No, I think … I think it could work, right?' Lily said, finally latching on to some plan of action after weeks and weeks of helplessness. 'All I have to do is find out why and then change his mind, offer him something in return.'

'Oh yeah? You planning to—'

'Don't be ridiculous. Just because you're all having sex doesn't mean that—'

'Actually, it might really help take off some of the tension—'

'I'm hanging up now!' Lily cried before Malie could go into any further detail.

'Lils, seriously,' Zoe cut in. 'I love you. Completely. But I'm going to give you a week. If you haven't got him to agree to hold the wedding at the estate, then we're really going to have to let V know. The invitations have been sent out.'

'I know, I know. But don't worry. I'm going to fix it. I have a plan,' Lily said resolutely, half an idea forming in her mind.

'Which is …?'

'Bring him to the table, discuss terms, and get him to agree to the most perfect, amazing, beautiful wedding EVER.'

As she hung up the phone, she thought through what she needed to do. She'd go to the estate and call a truce. And while she was there, she might as well get the herbs she wanted for the evening's service. She hadn't been back there since …

Lily couldn't quite bring herself to say the words in her head. As she leaned in to knead the icing, she put a little more force and determination into her fists. Blake's death had devastated her. It had severed one of the few anchoring points Lily had left.

Fearing that the tears pressing against the back of her eyes might escape, she brushed at her cheek, unknowingly leaving a dusty smear of icing powder in its wake, and gave the white mound a gentle pat before placing it in an airtight box.

She would get Henry Hawkesbury to agree, because she wanted Victoria's wedding to be perfect.

It had to be.

★★★

Despite her thoughts, Lily couldn't help but smile as she pulled her bicycle out on to the cobbled main street that bisected the small seaside town of Hawke's Cove. She loved this time of year. An early summer's sun crested over the hill in the distance, looking out and down on the port town below. The fishermen were not yet back from their morning haul, the tourists were not yet in full flow. It was … peaceful.

She pedalled past the ever-twitching curtain of Mrs Whittaker's house, waving a cheery hand to the local busybody who would be sure to notice Lily's bike ride towards the estate. Especially since it was the first time Lily had ventured back to the estate since Blake's ... funeral.

There. She'd said it.

To herself, at least.

Swerving the manhole that had never caught her unawares since the first and only time it had knocked her off her seat, she took a left at the fork in the road at the top of the hill and cycled along the flat path heading towards the forest that bordered the estate. Each rotation of the wheel felt harder and harder the closer she came.

Blake had been such an important figure in her life. He'd given her a job at sixteen in the kitchen of the estate-turned-hotel and she'd been awed by the glamour and luxury of the grand building, the immaculate restaurant, and the opulence of the rooms she'd been brave enough, at the time, to sneak a peek at. It was a far cry from the small, boxy council house she and her mother had shared on the outskirts of town.

Back then, she'd been trying to save up enough money for the culinary college in London she'd wanted to attend after secondary school, but the accident ... Well, she'd needed an extra year and Blake had not only kept her job open, but also visited her in hospital for the short time she'd been there.

She'd escaped that accident pretty much unscathed, certainly in comparison to Victoria and Zoe. The tiny silvery scars crisscrossing her arms were nothing in comparison to the deeper hurts of her friends. Lily tried not to think about that night, but even now as she pressed on through beneath the thick canopy, memories flashed like shards of light through the leaves, dappling her mind.

A screech of tyres, the blue-and-white emergency lights, the harrowing screech of metal as firefighters sliced through the roof of the car. She shivered beneath the memory of screams of terror, of pain. Of being crushed up against the side door, where she'd had a clear view across the back seats, right into the windscreen of the car that had hit them, bonnet to side, Claudia having recklessly tried to overtake them and spun out of control.

All hell had broken loose. Men yelling, people prodding and poking, making her move when it had been the last thing she'd wanted. She wouldn't leave them – Victoria, Malie and Zoe – no matter how many times the paramedics tried to get her out. She'd gripped Malie's hand beside her, reached for Victoria's where she was stuck in the driver's seat, and stared at Zoe as the only way to reach her. Lily had hung on as if their lives depended on it. They'd held hands like that, locked in some frozen tableau, until she'd been practically dragged from the wreckage.

When Lily and Malie had been discharged after a week or so, Zoe and Victoria had been stuck behind, still needing treatment. She and Malie had threatened to move in, but the nurses and staff at the hospital refused to allow it. Not that it had stopped them breaking in one night, only to set off the alarm on the emergency exit they thought they'd managed to wedge open on an earlier visit.

It had been the only time in the months Zoe spent in hospital that Lily and Malie had seen tears of laughter, rather than pain and sadness in her eyes. To them, it had been worth every reprimand from the hospital.

As Lily continued to pedal, she felt the sensation and ease as something unique and wondrous. Zoe had lost the use of her legs in the same accident that had prevented Victoria from ever being able to have children naturally.

That night had taken something from each of the girls and ten years later, Lily realized that they were still feeling the echoes of that loss. But in the last few months Victoria, Malie and Zoe had each found a way forward from that, with the help of the love and acceptance they had found with their partners. And even the slight twinge of loneliness she felt being so far from her friends couldn't take away from her happiness for them.

Lily resumed pedalling and pushed on into the forest that flanked the border of the Hawkesbury estate, where the dark canopy overhead brought more than shade. It brought memories of Blake. The steady hand the older man had guided her with, the welcome arms he had embraced her with after her return from London. The kind distraction he had offered her aching heart after her ex-fiancé's betrayal. The quiet, sad yearnings he'd had for his son's return … The son who had left Hawke's Cove ten years before and not looked back once.

Until it was too late.

She shivered, the shadows turning her exertions ice cold, as loss entwined with the past to bind her in a sadness she had to force herself to shake free from. Finally, the path emerged from the forest and out into the sprawling open hillside of Hawkesbury estate. The sight of the vineyard spilling downwards in layers from where the old Georgian building stood proud at the top always filled Lily with happiness, even today when it was ringed with the sharp sting of grief. Blake had worked so hard for each and every vine. The pride in his voice and gaze as each harvest had increased in abundance and popularity had been clear to all. His restaurant, naturally, stocked the lion's share of the produce, but in the last three years the estate had been supplying more and more vendors with high-quality wine that was gaining international recognition.

As Lily drew to a halt, leaning the bike and her weight on one foot, she couldn't help but wonder what would happen now. What Blake's son would decide to do with the estate – and everything that his estranged father had worked so hard for.

★ ★ ★

Sorry, mate. Didn't mean to be away for this long.

Hitting send, Henry passed a hand over his face, trying to wipe away some of the exhaustion from gritty eyes. His phone pinged.

No worries. Can just about manage without you.

Although he knew his business partner was being sarcastic, Henry very much hoped that wasn't the case. Their business had been a lifeline over the years and if it hadn't been for Ben, who the hell knew where Henry might have ended up? Probably at the bottom of a bottle. As long as it wasn't a wine bottle.

Seriously, bro, how's it all going?

Henry sighed. Bloody awful?

It's OK.

It certainly would be better now that he'd given the staff four weeks of paid leave. He'd needed some time alone. Just to be. Without hotel guests, or staff members filling rooms that had changed in the ten years since he'd last stepped foot in the estate that had been in his family for generations. The hotel manager had made the calls cancelling the scheduled guests willingly enough, seeming to understand the precarious position they were now all in.

This was the first morning he'd been in the place by himself since he'd arrived. He'd flown into London the morning after his mother had called. Spent a few days with her and her husband in Borehamwood – his mother, sad-faced but dry-eyed, watching as Henry had spent hours on the phone organizing a funeral for a man who he hadn't spoken to in ten years.

He loved you, Henry. But you were both as stubborn as each other.

Henry had made it down to Hawke's Cove in his rental the night before the funeral and stood at the front of the mourners that numbered almost the whole bloody town. He shivered at the memory of casting the dry earth on his father's coffin, still not quite able to believe that he was gone.

The last few weeks had been tough. Tougher than he'd expected. He'd met with Blake's estate lawyers who seemed, if not surprised, then at least satisfied, with his mother relinquishing any rights to the estate from a will that had been made years before.

Henry shook his head and looked, unseeing, out of the window of the top-floor room he'd been using, utterly unable to step foot back in his old bedroom. Blake had left him everything. He'd genuinely expected to go to the lawyer's, sign some piece of paper agreeing to walk away with nothing. And now he was the owner of a five-star hotel, over three hundred acres of woodland and working vineyards, one private beach and nearly thirty employees.

And almost each and every one of them had answered

nearly every question he'd had about the estate with, *Ask Lily Atwell*. A familiar sense of frustration rose within him. He'd had no idea how involved in the estate she'd become in the last ten years.

He'd done his best to avoid thinking about her, or any of the other girls – Zoe, Malie and Victoria – in the years since the accident. Anytime he'd been on the verge of wondering what had happened to them, his mind had done a volte-face, and instead he'd plunged himself into some new project, driven by the demons haunting his past.

But now they, *she* was everywhere he turned. Lily Atwell. The little ball of fiery fury he'd already had one painful interaction with when he'd told her she'd have to cancel her friend's wedding.

She'd changed since he'd last seen her, when they'd bumped into each other, literally, on the steps of the inquest. She'd lost some of the round-cheeked softness he remembered from her teens. Cheekbones had sharpened, but the long dark hair that had escaped a messy bun, tendrils whipping about a strong jawline echoing the outrage practically vibrating from her thin frame as he'd told her no to the wedding, was a richer auburn colour than before. It had made her eyes glow. And clearly reduced him to some kind of simpering fool that waxed lyrical about autumnal colours and innate beauty.

A headache was beginning to form at his temples. Less than two months ago, he'd been in his Manhattan apartment with Ben and his wife Amina, celebrating the end of an investment deal that would finance the latest app to be launched by their company. They'd laughed, still not quite believing how far they'd come from their first contract, scribbled on a napkin, certainly less than legally binding, given half the bottle of SangSom that they'd consumed on a beach in Thailand nearly eight years earlier.

Ben had been bristling with a kind of excitement that seemed, even for him, a little excessive. And that's when Henry had realized. Realized that Amina hadn't touched a drop of alcohol all night. Henry had taken Ben in a hug before he'd even managed to get the words 'we're pregnant' out of his mouth. He'd instantly assured Ben that, of course, he understood they'd be moving to Singapore to be nearer to Mina's family for the birth. And that as long as they built him an 'uncle annex', he'd be fine.

Henry's phone had rung in the midst of it all, but he'd ignored it, focusing instead on Ben, his wife, the baby … But the phone had rung again. And again. It had been his mother. *Darling. I'm so sorry. It's your father.*

Henry loosened his white-knuckled grip on his mobile.

Can you send over the paperwork for the Johnson deal?

Seconds later Ben replied.

You don't trust me?

With my life, mate. But I could do with the distraction.

'Nough said.

Henry shoved his phone into the pocket of his jeans and shrugged on a jumper over his shirt. It might be the afternoon in Singapore, but the sun was rising over the vineyards in Hawke's Cove, touching the fields with gold. Once again, he was drawn to the window that looked over the impressive estate, vainly trying to see what it was about it that his father had loved more than his wife and child.

The early summer sun picked out the dips and troughs of the sweeping hills. Blake's precious vines had tripled in size, winding their way down the bank, and glinting off the glass plates of the orangery at the back of the house.

House. Not home. Not all the things that would be, could be, conjured by the word. Henry longed for the smooth sleek lines of his New York apartment. The hustle and bustle of the noise that hummed constantly from the chaotic streets, tourists and builders flowing forth as if different tides fighting against the other.

The silence here was unsettling. He could lie to himself and put down his sleepless nights to that, but he wouldn't. Because he had stopped lying to himself years ago. When he'd realized that his behaviour had been nothing more than that of a child acting out, resentful of one parent who couldn't care less and one who cared too much. When his behaviour and selfishness had finally tipped to such devastating depths as to irrevocably damage those around him. He cursed loudly into the room where no one could hear. It was too early for the kind of self-recrimination that usually came with a late night and a bottle of whisky. That was what being back here did to him. Turned him back into the angry young boy and away from the calm, professional, successful man he had become.

He was about to leave, when a bright flash of orange caught his eye. Drawn, reluctantly but curiously, back to the window he caught sight of a figure on a bicycle. As the sun glinted off trails of auburn hair held up with what looked improbably like chopsticks from this distance, he realized that there was only one person it could be. The last person he ever wanted it to be.

★ ★ ★

She wasn't going to punch him.

She was going to kill him.

Literally.

She snapped the secateurs repeatedly, her grip firm, as she cast her eye around the herb garden. Lily had been feeling quite positive about the whole thing, hoping to extend an invitation of truce, to start over again, after their last painful confrontation. Until she'd let herself into the walled herb garden and seen …

She could cry.

Weeds had sprung up and were threatening to overwhelm the delicate herbs she and Blake had spent years caring for. The netting protecting some of the now rotting strawberries had torn away and caterpillars had almost completely decimated the lettuce crop.

Rage filled her, hot and scouring and not all of it directed at Henry. A good part, but not all. It had been too long since she'd been here, unwilling and unable to face the new lord of the manor. But now … ohhh. Now she would let him have it.

'What the hell are you doing here?'

She jumped, startled by the angry voice of the man she had been imagining murdering in several colourful ways. Spinning, she turned on him and launched towards him, still snapping the secateurs.

'You!' Lily exclaimed. 'You! How dare you!'

'Excuse me?' His indignant reply burst from lips that were full and that seemed, to Lily, almost carnal. Henry looked utterly devastating in a pair of jeans that clung to strong thighs, topped by a dark blue cable-knit jumper pressing against the outline of a very well-defined torso.

Why couldn't he have run to fat? she internally moaned. Why couldn't he have just become ... *ugly*? It made her even more angry and devastatingly conscious that she had come from her kitchen wearing an old pair of jeans, a loose white V-neck T and a large fluffy orange cardigan.

'How bloody dare you! This place is nearly ruined.'

'Ruined?' Once again, he sounded dumbfounded.

'Yes! Look,' she commanded, waving the secateurs to the left. 'Just look at it. Stinging nettles! We haven't had stinging nettles in here for nearly three years. And the caterpillars!' Lily hated the way she had to crane her neck to look up at him, not realizing how close they were standing.

'That's hardly my fault.'

Lily wanted to jump up and down on the spot and stamp her foot like a child. Of course it wasn't his fault. It was hers. She just hadn't been able to face coming back here since Blake ... let alone wanting to stay away from Henry.

'What are you doing here?' he demanded slowly, as if desperately seeking patience.

'I wanted to call a truce,' Lily practically growled, knowing full well that the tone of her voice suggested anything but. And from the glint in Henry's eyes, he seemed to find it just as ironic.

'And you do this by breaking and entering—'

'*Breaking and*—'

'Causing damage to private property—'

'*Damage?!*' she cried.

'And ... *theft*,' he said, peering into the basket of her bicycle, containing some of the herbs she'd managed to forage before his arrival.

The gall of the man!

Oh, he'd really gone and done it now. Every good intention burned to dust on her tongue as Lily forgot all about Victoria's wedding and her intentions to offer a truce, and instead realized that she was on the verge of being barred from the only haven she had other than her kitchen.

Anger. She latched onto it like a lifeline. She didn't know what it was about Henry, but he was bringing out the worst in her. She was never like this. Never. She was the peace keeper. In London one chef told her she'd be better off in the UN than the kitchen. But the implication that she wasn't wanted there had only made her work harder.

'Henry Hawkesbury, I have been looking after this garden for nearly seven years, while you swanned off around the world with a trust fund in your back pocket, doing God knows what with God knows who—'

'What and with whom I've been doing in the last few years is absolutely none of your business.'

'But this estate *has* been my business. Blake and I built this herb garden together. It's …' Hot tears were pressing against the backs of her eyes, all the anger and grief swelled in her chest, because she'd wanted to say, *it's ours*. But she couldn't do that anymore, could she? Blake was gone. And Lily suddenly realized that all this time, she'd been focusing on what it meant for Victoria and the wedding now that Henry was back. But she had been avoiding how it would affect her.

'Go on,' Henry said, cutting through her thoughts. 'Please.' A wave of his arm gestured for her to continue. 'Please tell me more about how remiss I've been in the last ten years.

Tell me more about the glorious man who turned his back on his son when he needed him the most.'

★ ★ ★

Henry clamped his jaw shut. He'd revealed too much. In that one moment, Lily Atwell had managed to unearth the very thing he'd spent years running from. No. Not her. It was this damn place. A place he couldn't wait to be rid of.

'Henry …'

He looked into large brown eyes that were shining with sympathy. He feared for a moment that she might try and find some kind of excuse for Blake's actions.

'Don't,' he said, cutting her off before she could continue. 'I shouldn't have said that.'

He watched as she bit back whatever words may have been on her tongue and ducked behind the thick curtain of her hair. When she looked up, he noticed a smear of something that looked like flour across her cheek. It made her seem incredibly innocent and his gut clenched.

For just a moment, he'd actually enjoyed verbally sparring with her. Through the last couple of months everyone had been treating him with kid gloves, stepping on eggshells around him. But not Lily. The more he'd needled her, the more outraged she'd been, the more she gave back, and he'd relished it. Fed it even. He wanted that instead of the grief suddenly simmering between them.

Looking about the garden, he honestly couldn't identify the 'damage' she'd identified. It certainly looked better than it had the last time he'd been there when it had been storage for broken bits of machinery older than his own father.

Thankfully she threw the shears into the basket – she'd got a little too close with the sharp edges and he'd been worried for a moment that he'd be forced to take an unmanly step back. They landed beside what looked like half a forestry of herbs, peppered with rose heads, a few handfuls of a strange orange berry, and other bright little flowers.

'What are you planning to do with all of those?' he asked, the sight somehow making this exchange even more surreal.

'A parsley oil. For herb-crusted lamb. And I'm toying with the idea of a sea buckthorn reduction, as we've had such a good crop of it this year.'

'There's a penchant for parsley oil and sea buckthorn reduction in Hawke's Cove, is there?'

'Hawke's Cove might not be London, or New York, or Singapore, Henry, but we do eat down here, in case you'd forgotten.'

'Been reading up on me, have you?' he asked, an absentminded arrogance covering genuine curiosity, because he didn't think it had been a coincidence that she'd reeled off a list of his apartment locations throughout the world.

'What?' she asked as a blush rose to her cheeks.

'You just picked those destinations out of thin air, then?'

'No, your father told me that's where you've been living.'

This time, she looked more defiant when bringing up Blake, but as he held her gaze, her head slipped forward and she hid behind several strands of thick dark hair that had escaped the messy bun held in place by the … yup. Definitely chopsticks.

'And I happen make a very good parsley oil, thank you.' How she managed to sound both prim and defiant at the same time was a wonder to Henry.

He turned away with the excuse of looking around the garden before he could do something stupid, like acknowledge the fact that verbally sparring with her had made him feel more alive than anything else had in the last month or so. But by the time he returned his gaze to hers, he wished he'd already left. Sincerity and compassion harpooned him to the spot.

'I am sorry about your father.'

A sudden and shocking grief hit him square in the chest. Her sentiments lacked the hysteria of others', the almost theatrical display of misery from strangers at the funeral. Those he'd been able to brush off, but Lily Atwell had cut him off at the knees with her simple, honest rendering.

And all the while, he couldn't look away. It was as if she let him react to her words and was patiently weathering the storm they conjured, letting him rage silently. She just absorbed it all.

'You should go,' he managed to bite out.

'Of course,' she said, once again dropping her head slightly as if hiding behind her hair. 'I just need to speak to Annabelle about—'

'She's not here.'

'What?'

'No one is. I sent them away.'

'You did *what?*' she demanded. 'But Henry, this is—'

'What Hawkesbury estate is or was, is none of your concern,' he decreed, trying to understand why he had the strange sense that he was wrong. Very wrong.

'And the guests? At the hotel?'

'Have been cancelled and given full refunds.'

'But what about the estate?'

'What about it?'

'It's a working vineyard, Henry, the vines need—'

'Pretty sure I can handle a few vines, Lily.'

He watched as she bit her lip again to prevent a retort, the angry blush riding high on alabaster cheekbones drawing his gaze upwards from her mouth to her eyes. Eyes that were wide, round and … spitting fire. He could feel the waves of anger rolling off her, breaching his skin like a series of tidal waves. As if by some monumental effort, she released her lip, drew in a jagged inhale, retrieved her bike and wheeled it past him, head held high and knuckles white as they gripped the handles.

He could have sworn he'd heard her utter the words *bloody fool* as she left through the doorway. And he most definitely agreed.

He should never have come back.

CHAPTER TWO

SHE WAS SUCH A FOOL, Lily told herself as she pulled the bike over the gravel driveway. She was supposed to get him onside, not rant at him like a mad thing. He'd told her to leave. She didn't think for a minute she'd be allowed back into the herb garden to repair the neglect from the last month since Blake's death. And without the staff, what would happen to the estate?

As she wheeled the bicycle towards the road, Lily refused to look at the rows and rows of vines gently sweeping down the hill. Would he walk them? Cutting away the ruined grapes, allowing the ones remaining to ripen? Before his death Blake had been worried that the Bacchus might need harvesting early this year. Without John, the estate manager, would Henry even notice?

The wedding. She couldn't put it off any longer. There was no way Henry would change his mind. She had to call Victoria. Now. Because she couldn't keep such a monumental secret from her best friend any longer and she had to do it before she changed her mind. It was tearing her up inside, but she couldn't put it off.

Don't pick up. Don't pick up.

But the moment the phone call rang through, Lily couldn't stop herself.

'He's horrible, V. Just *horrible!*'

'Who is, Lils?' demanded Victoria, just a slight edge of concern in her voice.

'Not Oliver,' Lily replied, knowing her friend was totally loved up and very much in the *everything's-about-my-fiancé* mode. 'Henry,' she clarified.

'Oh. Little Lord Fauntleroy?'

'Yes. No. We can't keep calling him that, V,' she said on a groan.

'Why?'

'Because it makes him sound boyish and harmless. And Henry Hawkesbury is …' *Tall, delicious, hot?* Lily nearly stopped in her tracks, her grip on the centre of the handlebars wobbling a little. Where had that come from?

'Horrible?' Victoria asked.

'Yes,' she said as much to her friend as herself as she resumed her return to the restaurant. '*Horrible.*'

'Do you want a Lost Hours? Should we call in the girls?'

God no, Lily thought. Although she could do with their support, this was something she had to do herself. Victoria was going to be devastated. She heard a rustling in the background and imagined her best friend shifting bolts of fabric and designs. At this time on a Sunday, she'd probably be in her new studio working on her beautiful dresses. She imagined Victoria's long glossy dark hair falling over her shoulder as she sat down at her desk and leaned a head on her palm to focus on their conversation.

'Lils? You still there?'

'Yes, I am. And no, don't worry about trying to get the girls. I can't work out the time differences anyway.'

'You know that wouldn't matter,' Victoria answered.

'Honestly, it's OK,' she replied, firmly putting aside her doubts. Taking a deep breath, she opened her mouth and—

'How's he doing, after the funeral?' Victoria asked accidentally interrupting.

Lily's mind switched back to Henry, half miserable and half thankful for the reprieve. 'I couldn't tell you. He was too busy trying to kick me off the estate. I'm surprised he didn't ask for my keys back.'

'Your keys? Why would he …' She heard Victoria sigh. 'He doesn't know.'

'No. How could he, V? He's had nothing to do with his father for nearly ten years.'

'Oh, honey. The estate has been such a big part of your life. I'm still … disappointed that Blake didn't leave some kind of directive in his will.'

'It's not about that, V,' Lily replied. It really wasn't.

'I know,' she said with far too much sympathy and understanding. Lily couldn't breathe for a moment. Couldn't really believe that she was having this conversation. Because Blake was gone. And her life had irrevocably changed.

'Do you think you could talk to Henry? Tell him how much you've been involved in the estate, the winery?'

'I don't know. There's a distinct possibility any repeat encounter could end up in murder,' she growled, remembering his arrogance, audacity, and she was sure there was another 'a' word there somewhere that would also be appropriate.

'Murder? Lils, are you OK? You're never normally like this,' Victoria replied, her tone wavering into the worried.

'I know,' she groaned. She *really* wasn't normally like this. She was making such a mess of things. She *had* to tell Victoria that the wedding couldn't be held at the estate.

'V—'

'Oh, I meant to say. Oliver's mother has shown the photographer the Hawkesbury estate website and I think she's just about forgiven me for not having the wedding at her village's chapel. Just!' Victoria concluded on a light laugh.

Oh God. Oh God.

Lily knew how much winning over Oliver's parents had meant to Victoria. Nausea swirled in her stomach. She heard Oliver calling Victoria's name in the background and grabbed onto it like a lifeline.

'Lils—'

'It's OK. Go, go, go. Give him my love!'

Lily ended the call before Victoria could say – or ask – anything further. She dropped the phone into the basket beside the herbs as if it were a poisonous snake. She may even have squeaked a little, but thankfully there was no one there to hear the long-drawn-out groan as she rested her forehead against the handlebars.

Stupid. Stupid. Stupid.

She would have kicked the tyres if she hadn't needed to get back to the restaurant. She gulped in a breath of air around the giant boulder of guilt pressing against her lungs. Damn Henry Hawkesbury.

Tall, delicious, hot …

How had that happened? In ten years Henry had gone from the angry, haunted, guilty, too-skinny-teen she had seen on the steps of the courthouse where the inquest into the accident had cleared him and Victoria of any wrongdoing, to a very impressive man.

Yes, he'd been angry, and yes, she might have sworn off men, but she wasn't blind. Her eyes had hungrily eaten up the changes in him. The breadth of his shoulders, perfectly defined in that jumper, stretching across his muscles as if taunting her. The old linseed-coloured leather belt at the waist of his jeans had drawn her unwilling gaze to thin hips and a lean stomach, and she hadn't missed the way that his jeans had clung to his thighs like … Lily Atwell actually growled at herself.

Tall, delicious, hot …

And horrible.

She pulled herself up mentally and literally, swinging her leg over the bicycle. Later. She'd deal with it all later. She'd reached the fork in the path where one would take her back to town and the other would cut through the forest edging the vineyards and down to the estate's private beach.

She longed to take that path. To visit the place that held so many wonderful memories of much, much easier times. She, Victoria, Malie and Zoe had spent almost every day of their summer holidays, and a fair few weekends in between, on that beach. She couldn't help but reach for the echoes of laughter and delight as they would 'borrow' Mr Michaels' small fishing boat from the harbour. Always just a little too late to catch them, he'd yell at them from the harbourside, fist raised and *almost* sincere, if it hadn't been for the smile on his face as he did so. They would row out into the estuary and round the bay, and Malie, always Malie, would jump into the water, and pull the boat up onto the shore.

They would catch mackerel off the high rocks that bracketed the beach, burning empty crab shells on tiny fires made from driftwood watching them turn that incredible vivid pink, dreaming of their futures, of escape from Hawke's Cove, of glamorous lifestyles full of rich, handsome men, of all living together one day. Some of that had happened, some not. And the familiar ache of Victoria, Malie and Zoe's absence from Hawke's Cove felt like a distant drumbeat in her heart.

But Malie was coming back and Victoria was never that far away in London. And just the thought of it chased away the tendrils of sadness, adding a bit more power to her forward momentum. Oh, Lily knew it wouldn't quite be the same as when they'd been kids, when it had been just the four of them. Because it wasn't just the four of them anymore, with each of her friends newly or recently engaged. Lily genuinely wasn't jealous in the slightest, but still she let the bike glide forward for a second and unconsciously shrugged to herself – it wouldn't be the same.

The road beneath the bicycle turned to cobbles and before she knew it, she had pulled up in front of the building that housed her restaurant and her small flat above, just in time to see her mother walking towards her from the harbour, raising a hand and a smile. Lily felt her own wobble a little and desperately needed the hug she reached for.

'You OK, darling?'

'Mmm,' was all Lily could reply as she held just a few seconds longer onto the hug, fearful that if she opened her mouth, it would all come pouring out. Her memories had stirred up more than grief for Blake.

'Do you have time for a cup of tea?' her mother asked.

Checking her watch, Lily realized just how much time had passed. 'Not really.'

'That's usually when we need it most, sweetheart.'

Lily looked up at her mother, the long swathe of white hair, thick and just as glorious as it had been when auburn. Her eyes, kind, the slight lines fanning from the corners, the only real signs of ageing in a youthful face. 'But that's OK. I'm on my way to see Selena and Noel Tayler.'

'Going to the big house?' Lily asked with a smile, thinking of the mansion clinging to the cliff face overlooking the town that Zoe grew up in. It hadn't mattered that Lily had grown up in council housing while Zoe had been born into money. Not one bit. The girls had formed such a strong bond as children that money, continents and years couldn't divide them.

The accident might have stolen the use of Zoe's legs, but it hadn't dampened her determination to get the hell out of the Cove as soon as she was able. Her parents had spent years worrying about their only child, cosseting her to the point of stifling her, fearing for her health. But then the worst thing they could imagine actually happened. And instead of holding her back, it had only made Zoe even more determined. She had left Hawke's Cove to see the world, the blog she had written during those travels leading to a job as a journalist. Not once letting her wheelchair prevent her from doing what she wanted. And although she'd missed her friend so, so much, Lily had understood the need to embrace the freedom she'd found.

Lily couldn't prevent the sigh that escaped her as she realized she'd never made good on her promise to visit her in Sydney. She'd never seemed to have the time. Not with culinary school, then Alistair, and rushing back to Hawke's Cove to lick her wounds when it ended. And then the restaurant. Looking back, Lily realized she hadn't had time for a holiday once in the last seven years and a tendril of sadness wound around her heart. When had she lost sight of the love and exuberance for life that, in Zoe, seemed almost irrepressible?

As Lily jiggled the key in the lock of the door to the restaurant, another large truck passed them heading out of town and a huge gust of misplaced air buffeted against the windows, making them rattle slightly in their frame.

'They must be doing some pretty large renovations at Merrow's Rest. Do you know who bought the property?' she asked, finally pushing open the door and holding it open for her mum.

'No idea,' Marion replied, her eyes just a little too large and round. Lily was about to ask what was going on, when her mother pressed ahead. 'Lily,' she seemed to hesitate. 'Have you spoken to Victoria about the wedding?'

'What about it?' Lily replied, unable to make eye contact.

'That she can't have it at the estate.'

Lily paused mid stride towards the kitchen at the back of the restaurant. 'How do you know about that?!'

'Sweetheart, he's sent everyone home for the next four weeks and cancelled the bookings. It's doesn't take a rocket scientist …'

Lily turned to lean both hands on one of the tables.

Oh God, oh God.

'Breathe, Lily.'

This couldn't be happening. Not really. Her breath became short, her pulse riding loud in her ears. She was halfway towards a panic attack.

'I don't know what to do, Mum,' she said, her eyes shut tight as if she could will it all away.

'You just tell her, sweetheart. She'll understand.'

'I tried. Just now. But she's so excited and so looking forward to it,' she said miserably. 'And of course she would understand. That's what's so awful about it! She was so happy, and dammit, it was what Blake wanted.'

She felt her mother's palm on her back, sweeping gentle circles like she used to do when Lily was little.

'Perhaps it's for the best.'

'How can you say that?' Lily demanded, outraged.

'I just ... I think that perhaps you were putting a little too much focus on the wedding and making it perfect. It's only natural of course, but—'

'What? Why?'

'Well, after your engagement—'

'Don't, Mum,' Lily commanded, pushing up off the table and away from the soft comfort her mother was trying to offer. 'Seriously. Don't. That has nothing to do with this whatsoever.'

The little bell on the front door tinkled and Kate, Lily's manager and all-round lifesaver, pushed through into the restaurant with a large, happy smile.

'If you say so, darling,' her mother replied finally.

'I'll call her tomorrow morning. I just ... Tomorrow. I promise, Mum.'

'Call who about what?' Kate asked as she reached the counter.

'Nothing,' Lily replied, shaking her head trying to extricate herself from the difficult conversation.

'Oh,' Kate said sympathetically, cocking her head to the side. 'Have you not told V about the wedding?'

'Does *everyone* know?' Lily demanded.

'No, darling,' her mother intoned at exactly the same time as Kate said, 'Yup. Pretty much.'

★ ★ ★

Henry hadn't meant to stay in the herb garden. He'd intended to return to the estate and read through the spec pitch for his and Ben's latest app investment, but instead, he'd started to pluck at some of the weeds that had so offended Lily Atwell.

Henry didn't do *weeds*. He hadn't since he'd seen it as his father's punishment for rude behaviour years before. But what had begun in anger and frustration, soon morphed into a rhythm and he'd reached for the gloves and trowel in a little wooden box he'd seen beside the door, getting stuck in and thinking nothing of the damp bite of earth as mud seeped into the knees of his expensive jeans.

Henry was still at it about an hour after she left, when his phone rang, and peeling off the tiny, presumably Lily-Atwell-sized gloves he clamped the phone to his ear to speak to the estate agent managing what he hoped would be the sale of this godforsaken estate.

'Mr Hawkesbury?'

He nearly didn't answer. Mr Hawkesbury was his father. Not him.

'Yes?'

'I have great news,' exclaimed the efficient real estate agent.

Henry listened with only half an ear as the man described a buyer who was apparently very interested in the property and more so in a quick sale. He thought he would be more excited about the prospect. He was, in fact, until the agent explained that they wanted a tour of the estate in a few days' time.

'The full works. And if you could arrange for a tasting, I really think that could swing it in your favour.'

Henry bit back the groan rising in his throat. 'Of course. I'll see to it.'

But when he hung up the call and put the phone in his back pocket, all he could see was Lily Atwell. And how he was going to have to grovel. Hard. And he had an awful feeling he knew exactly what price she'd demand in return.

Having sent everyone else away, she was the only person who might actually be able to give the tour. Instinctively he knew that there was no way he could tell her what the tour was for. He was sure that she wouldn't *actively* sabotage it, but he just couldn't take the risk.

He was absolutely within his rights to sell the damn place and he didn't have to justify his actions to her or anyone. Even if, somewhere deep down, his conscience was chiding him. Warning him that he was sounding a little too much like the old Henry. The Henry who had run from this place and not looked back.

Despite knowing that he would have to see Lily eventually, he put it off. But as he paced between the rooms of the estate, the impressively decorated suits, the large dining area that had once been a grand living room, the entrance hall that had been turned into a reception and on towards the back of the estate, the large gleaming professional kitchen, he couldn't help but wonder just how much Lily had been involved in these decisions.

Had she walked through the same rooms with Blake picking out the décor? Had she been involved in the resolution to convert the east wing entirely to suit paying customer needs? Or had that been just his father? When he looked out of the window as the sun set below the sprawling layers of vines, he asked himself, had *she* suggested expanding their grape variety? Had *she* helped bring Blake's distillery into the twenty-first century, or had it been done so purely for commercial needs?

Never before had he felt the absence of the last ten years so strongly. He hated the fact that she held answers to questions he hadn't realized needed resolving. And still he wasn't sure he was ready to hear them. But just as he'd realized that the fridge was barely equipped with the basics of even beans on toast, he remembered his thoughtless teasing about her restaurant and seized it like a lifeline. Maybe he could find out just how good her sea buckthorn reduction really was and begin a parlay that would see him with a tour guide for the prospective buyers.

★★★

The Sea Rose had surprised him. He vaguely remembered the butcher's that had once stood on the same spot, but as with many of the other shops along the harbour's edge, it was now something completely different.

He'd walked on past Lily's restaurant, curious about the changes to the harbour the last ten years had wrought. And now he'd wished he hadn't. He'd been struck by a kind of seasickness, almost like the opposite of déjà vu, where he'd expected to feel familiarity but didn't.

He'd stood at the bottom of the jetty that struck out towards the sea, the sounds of gulls overhead and water crashing against stone below, and not seen any of the gentrification that seemed to have taken place, despite the large fishing trawlers that still stood sentinel at the edges of the harbour.

Where the new wrought-iron benches bordered the boardwalk, he remembered kicking and pulling at the ancient, sea-soaked wooden benches with his friends, heedless of their mindless vandalism. He remembered breaking onto one of the summer holidaymaker's boats with Claudia and taking it out to sea, getting blind drunk and costing his father nearly three grand in damages and apologies to the owner.

He was so consumed by his own hurt and selfishness that he lashed out at anything or anyone. And it was the promise of alcohol, not food, that led him back to The Sea Rose. At least that's what he told himself as he pushed open the wide glass door to the restaurant at the top of a ramp. Not the determination to prove to Lily Atwell that he was not the careless teen he'd once been.

Until the whole restaurant stopped in silence and looked up at him with shared curiosity and disapproval. And while everything in him wanted to turn around and stalk back to the estate, he didn't. He wouldn't give them the satisfaction.

A small, round-cheeked woman he didn't recognize showed him to a table nearest the counter, affording him a glimpse of the brightly lit kitchen contrasting against the soft dimly lit tones of the restaurant. But if he hoped to be handed a menu to hide in, it had been in vain.

Kate, as she introduced herself, explained that she'd just needed to check with *the chef* about what was left available from the day's menu. Wanting to get their tortuous exchange done as quickly as possible to remove any further interest of the other dinners, he told her he'd have whatever was available. He caught the flash of a young teen, dressed in a white shirt and dark skirt, trying, and failing, to hide the fact she was staring at him. She wasn't the only one.

Left alone at his table, he cast a look around at the other diners, meeting their gazes head on and, one by one, they each returned to their companions. Mrs Whittaker in the corner – also alone – glared at him.

Inexplicably a vision of tiny Father Christmases flooded his memory and he had to stifle a laugh as he remembered once stealing away all the little gnomes Mrs Whittaker dotted about her front garden with such pride and replacing them with the little lit Christmas figurines. It probably hadn't helped that it was the middle of summer. And by the look on her face as she held his gaze now, red-cheeked and wide-eyed with outrage, he was pretty sure she was remembering it too.

He'd copped to the accusation of theft, but drawn a line at assault and battery, and even PC Ellis had had a hard time keeping a straight face as Mrs Whittaker had argued that her gnomes had just as much right to exist without 'molestation' as any human being.

He was drawn back to the present as Mrs Whittaker pushed back from her table with a huff, and marched towards the counter to pay, which had clearly necessitated an imperious glance down her nose at him.

He might have found it funny, if he wasn't already aware that he was very much the focus of almost everyone in the restaurant, *again*. The way their conversations dipped, each person huddling closer to their partner, as if it wasn't patently obvious that he was the subject matter.

Blake, the accident, his wayward teen years, he assumed all were under discussion.

He really shouldn't have come here.

Blocking out the other diners as much as possible, he looked around the room. Much to his surprise, he liked it. The aged oak flooring, a beautiful calming grey tone, was met by white walls and a white ceiling bisected by large oak beams, from which hung baskets with ivy and strings of pearl and hearts pouring downwards from the containers. They picked up the same fresh green colours that dominated the wall behind the worn wooden countertop that looked as if it was made from scaffolding boards. Surrounded by a frame of weathered wood, fresh herbs hung in huge swathes. Oregano and thyme spilled over the frame and downwards, while basil and sage were leafy and full. He thought he could also see beets and Swiss chard towards the edges, bringing flashes of burgundy to the broad leafy mix.

He craned his head, noticing for the first time the skylight that topped the entire counter section, presumably providing light for the herbs and bringing brightness to the restaurant during the day. Turning back to the restaurant, he saw that floating oak shelves were covered in black-and-white pictures but he couldn't quite make them out.

On the tables were old bottles of Hawkesbury estate wine with candles plunged into their necks, dribbles of white wax stark against the dark glass, speaking to long-term use. He frowned, taking in the names of new wines and years, long after he'd left the estate. Ten years ago, his father had only planted the Bacchus and

Pinot Noir. But as he scanned the labels he saw it had stretched to Rondo and Schönburger. His father might have thought he'd not been interested in or aware of the work required for the vineyard, but Henry hadn't forgotten. He hadn't forgotten a damn thing.

***

'You did really great this evening, Kevin,' Lily said to the young KP. 'Really good work,' she added as she started to wipe down the surfaces. The early dinner rush had been quick and intense, but Kev had risen to the challenge. Usually, Vihaan would have been there to pick up the slack, but her chef de cuisine was taking a much-needed holiday before returning the following week so that Lily could focus almost exclusively on … the wedding that might not be happening.

In Vihaan's absence, Kev had really stepped up, the seventeen-year-old flourishing within his new-found responsibility. And the mise en place had been done for tomorrow which meant that Lily didn't even mind that there was a mound of washing-up in the sink. The joy practically vibrating from her KP was totally worth it.

'Thank you, chef.'

It may be a silly thing in a small restaurant currently with a kitchen staff of two, but Lily had insisted on the same formal hierarchy that every restaurant she'd ever worked in maintained. It wasn't for her, but for Kev. If he ever worked elsewhere, that title, that respect and more importantly that instantaneous communication was absolutely vital in running a successful kitchen. A chef didn't have the time to ask if they'd been heard, didn't have the energy to wonder if their orders were being obeyed and didn't have the space for an ego other than their own.

She watched his gaze zone out over her shoulder and didn't have to turn to know that he was once again watching Emma, the sixteen-year-old waitress from the year below him at Hawke's High. Lily tried to prevent the smile from forming on her lips, knowing he'd be mortified to know that she and Kate were well aware of his not-so-secret crush.

'But he's. So. Hot!' Emma exclaimed to Kate, joining her at the pass, fanning herself by way of punctuation.

'He's too old for you,' Kate replied determinedly.

'I'm young, not blind,' Emma replied, rolling her eyes, as Kate unsuccessfully tried to hide her disapproval of the lascivious gaze Emma had unleashed upon the restaurant.

'Who is?' asked Lily, laughing at the exchange.

'Little Lord Fauntleroy.'

Lily's pulse leaped in her throat. 'His name is Henry, Kate,' she chided even as she struggled to focus on dusting the last dessert order with icing sugar and adding a pinch of salt to bring out the sweetness of the caramel sauce. What was he doing here?

'*That's* Henry Hawkesbury?' asked Emma, her voice hush with awe.

'Yes. Though what he's doing here – *at this time of the evening* – is anyone's guess.' The disdain was apparent on Kate's tongue. Lily might have her own feelings about the man but that didn't mean she'd allow bad talk about her customers. She knew what it was like to have the whole village talking about her behind their hands ... not even waiting for her to get out of earshot. She would not have that happen in her restaurant.

'He's probably here to demand payment,' Lily groused.

'Oh really?' Kate demanded. 'And what would that be for?'

'Stolen goods.' She stuck out an elbow towards the herbs and Kate's response was an archly raised eyebrow, having managed to prise the whole sorry encounter from Lily over the lunch service. The woman should be working for MI5.

'He wouldn't.'

'Wouldn't put it past him.'

The simultaneous statements from Kate and Emma blended into one, much like Lily's thoughts crashing about her head and heart. 'Has he ordered yet?'

'I told him I had to check with you first, given the time.'

Lily glanced again at the clock and sighed. Last orders, as everyone else in the town knew, had been over an hour ago. But she had practically taunted Henry with the assurance that they were just as classy as any fancy city restaurant and she doubted that turning him away would do her any favours. But ... maybe this was a sign. Her second chance? If she could talk to him, she might just be able to convince him ...

'Did he say what he wanted?' she asked Kate, mentally running through what was available in the pantry. There might be enough of the lamb left and she could probably pull together—

Kate had gone quiet, and her almost pained expression cut through her thoughts.

'I'm sure he didn't mean it, especially when I said I had to check with you first,' she replied nervously.

'Mean what? What did he order?'

'He said *whatever*.' The words rushed out on an exhale.

A slash of a red-hot anger crashed through her.

'He said *what now*?' Lily demanded.

'He said "whatever".'

'Oh God,' Emma said, literally ducking and disappearing from the kitchen and the firing line.

'I know that look. Please don't give me that look,' begged Kate.

'No one – and I mean – *no one* comes to my restaurant and orders *whatever*,' Lily growled.

'I can see the steam coming out of your ears. Really, I think if you just—'

'We are not a takeaway. We are not a gastropub,' she practically spat. 'And we—'

'Do. Not. Serve. Whatever,' Kate and Kev dutifully concluded.

'Crack open the Hawkesbury Reserve,' Lily ordered.

'I ... don't think that's a good idea.'

'Really?'

'It's just that ... that means you're planning on the salmon as a starter and you were saving that for a special occasion. And you know, it's late and—'

'I can handle it. You guys can finish up and head home. I'll be serving Little Lord Fauntleroy a meal of so much more than *whatever*, he'll never be the same again.'

Kate left the kitchen to the mutterings of *pompous, who-does-he-think-he-is,* and *arse.* Not necessarily in that order.

CHAPTER THREE

KATE RETURNED FROM THE kitchen looking a little pink about the cheeks and presented Henry with a glass of sparkling white which he frowned at, not having ordered either drink or food yet.

'The chef will be serving a fish starter, fish main and a chocolate-based dessert and wine pairings to suit. Do you have any allergies she should be aware of?'

Apart from to the whole of Hawke's Cove?

'No,' he replied instead. 'Is it ... usual not to be told what the dishes are?' he asked, confused as he reached for the thin stem of the sparkling wine.

Kate shrugged her shoulder. 'Menus are ecologically unfriendly and as every plate we serve is seasonal and dependent on local produce, they change daily. But I think we can manage to remember the dishes we serve.' This was said with such an air of defensiveness that reminded him of Lily's earlier response. *London, New York, Singapore.* They might be in a small Devon seaside town, but the pride they both had was as bright as the best of them. But she wasn't done yet. 'And you're not driving?'

At her question, the whole restaurant came to a stop.

Henry closed his eyes on the sudden blank whole that his mind and mouth had become. 'I—'

'We're hot on that kind of thing round here, and if you're going to have wine with each course then—'

'No. Not driving,' he bit out, refusing to acknowledge the other diners who, after a moment, resumed their meals. He could tell that Kate hadn't realized the impact of her question. It hadn't been a mean dig, at the accident, at the past, but something that both he and Lily, and perhaps all the girls – Malie, Zoe and Victoria – still took with them into the present.

After closing down another paying table, Kate returned from the kitchen and placed a small granite chopping board on the table in front of him. The incredible smell hit him like a tsunami. Gin and juniper, sweet and sour, the heady peppery mustard from the dressing struck his nose and made his mouth water. Wafer-thin crunchy slices of toasted rye bread stacked up in a decent pile and the generous portion of cured salmon looked so delicious, he didn't know where to start.

He looked up to say thank you, but Kate had gone. And only now did he realize that he was the last customer in the restaurant. He checked his watch and was horrified to see that it was nearly nine thirty.

Provincial they might not be, but he doubted they were used to serving customers at this time at the night. His conscience stirred his stomach, which growled in response at having thus far been denied the delectation of what was in front of him.

As he arranged a generous sliver of pink flesh on to the rye bread, he dimly noted sounds from the kitchen, a male and female voice departing as if out through the back of the restaurant, just audible over the ambience of softly played music.

And then, all thought stopped. The moment that the salmon hit his tongue, he was in heaven. In the years since Henry had left Hawke's Cove, he'd travelled. A lot. Thailand, Vietnam, Sydney, America, and yes – Lily had been right, he'd had apartments in London, New York and Singapore. And nowhere he'd eaten in all that time had hit him so forcefully. It wasn't just the flavour, the deliciousness. It was that somehow, in one bite, he'd felt thrilled, nostalgic, and hungry for more. He surfed the salty-sweet taste of the freshly caught and cured salmon, yanked from beneath the mouthwatering juniper undercurrents by a slap of peppery mustard and crunchy rye. Before he knew it he'd finished the entire thing.

His eyes, he realized, had widened in awe. And perhaps belatedly only just realized why Lily had been so defensive. He had expected very much less than what this restaurant was capable of. He looked around for signs of life in the darkly lit restaurant and realized that it could only be just the two of them remaining.

He craned his neck through the doorway, behind the counter and into the kitchen. He could just make out the shape of Lily's back, and forearm kneading something with precision and speed that spoke of expertise. He didn't doubt it. Not now anyway.

Without the competing smells of the food from other diners tables, or other meals being prepared, the sweet aroma of crab, garlic and olive oil rose towards him on a bed of steam. At a bit of a loss, he picked up his plate, intending to take it to the kitchen, but stopped as his movements took him closer to the walls and the pictures that, he now saw, were of the townspeople from the last twenty years. Fishermen with their trawlers, children and teens on rides at the town's fête over many different years, some of Lily and her friends, their parents. His eyes snagged on some of his father, standing with his arm proudly around Lily at what he recognized must have been the earliest stages of the herb garden.

As he stood back, he finally noticed how many pictures there were of the estate, not just of his father and Lily, but of the grape harvests. Memories he'd pushed to the back of his mind surfaced. The whole town, it seemed, crowding into the channels between the vines, snipping at pale bunches of mottled grapes – real grapes, not the strange perfect bunches from a supermarket – armed with secateurs and filling plastic buckets. He suddenly remembered following his father, driving the ATV, and tossing bucket after bucket of grapes into the trailer. Back then, Henry had snuck away the first chance he could get, but these pictures of the post-harvest celebrations taunted him. The raised glasses and happy faces of people who had worked hard, and loved it. Sprawled out beneath the trees on the estate, hampers of food, laughter …

He could almost chart the progression of years by the changes in Lily's features, but it was his father that drew him close. The way that his body showed the signs of ageing, the wrinkles, the increasing stoop to his shoulders, the streaks of white in his hair visible in the grey-toned pictures. His fingers clenched around the handle of the granite chopping board, and he was drawn back to the present by sounds in the kitchen.

Pushing the memories aside, he stepped behind the counter and leaned up against the doorframe, oddly content to watch Lily in her element. She was twisting the handle on an old metal pasta machine, gently teasing a wide strip of golden coloured dough out onto a large wooden, floured, butcher's block. As she guided the pasta sheet from where it draped over her forearm onto the surface, without looking, she reached into a small ceramic pot for a pinch of something which she threw into a large boiling metal pot that looked as if it had seen better days.

She wiped her hand on her apron, and pushed back another stray tendril of hair that must have come loose while she'd been kneading the pasta dough with her forearm. Flushed and focused, she looked glorious. Until a brief stutter in movements that had been fluid until now betrayed her awareness of him.

'That was delicious,' he said.

'You sound surprised.'

'Do I? I was aiming for impressed.'

'Aim higher.'

Henry bit his cheek to prevent himself from responding. He quite liked this dismissive streak in her. Over the years his success and looks had brought a wide range of reactions from the opposite sex, most of whom were just as eager to get into his wallet as his bed, but Lily, it seemed, wanted nothing of the sort.

'Yes, *chef*,' he replied with a smile.

Her rich, dark gaze snapped to his, before returning to the pasta machine where she was adjusting the setting. Had he caught a reluctant lift to her lips, or was that wishful thinking?

He cast his eyes around the brightly lit, almost clinical cleanliness of the kitchen until he spied the sink piled high with dishes and frowned.

'Don't you have staff to handle that?' he asked, only belatedly realizing that the question sounded pompous and arsy. 'I didn't—'

'I do,' she said, cutting through his half-formed clarification.

'But he has school in the morning and I am certainly not above washing up a few pots and pans. And Kate's husband is only just back from a two week-long business trip, so …'

He looked at her then, her eyes catching his before turning away, as if she'd given too much away, as if she'd singled herself out as having nothing better to do, nowhere else to go. But he was damned if he was going to sit in her restaurant, alone, with her waiting on him hand and foot. He might have, ten years ago, but he really wasn't that same angry teen.

'What are we having?'

'We?'

'Yes, unless you've eaten?'

'No, I—'

'Then at the risk of almost certain rejection, would you care to join me?'

★★★

The refusal was ready on Lily's lips when her stomach growled in utter horror.

'I think that settles it, don't you? Where are the plates?' Henry demanded, pulling away from where he leaned against the door-frame, as if ready for action.

'*Bowls*. It's *pasta*.' She couldn't help the outrage edging her voice. It was her restaurant, her domain, where everything had to be just right.

'*Bowls* then. I can be your sous chef for the night.'

'Aim lower,' she muttered under her breath and was surprised by the bark of laughter that erupted from the doorway. She turned, quickly, catching Henry mid laugh, the sight of which momentarily stunned her.

'Yes, chef. What's the lowest of the low?'

'Dishwasher,' she said without missing a beat.

He cocked his head to one side, the laughter still shining in his eyes. 'Then I'll get started on that, while you finish the pasta.'

'Henry, you don't—'

'I am more than capable of washing a few pots and pans, and I'll even let you check my work before I'm done.'

The teasing in his tone was too much. It covered too much.

She turned, leaving the pasta on the side for just a moment otherwise it would be ruined.

'Why?'

'Why what?'

'Why are you here?'

She watched as he seemed to pick and discard answers to her question until finally settling on one that felt right. Clearly choosing his words carefully, he said, 'Can we start over?'

Lily took a deep breath. She'd hated the way they'd left things in the herb garden that morning and, despite the fact he seemed to infuriate her at every turn, she knew that Blake would want that. And if she were to have any hope of talking about Victoria's wedding, she'd have to get him on side somehow.

She nodded, finally. At this, he stepped around the kitchen pass and entered her space.

'Hi, Lily. It's good to see you again,' he said, holding out his hand for her to shake. As she tentatively reached for his, warm fingers wrapped around her hand, sending a lightning streak from her palm to her elbow. She flinched, but he seemed to be as momentarily startled as she was and they both released the brief contact as if stung.

Lily turned back to the pasta on the butcher's block, the reciprocal words dying on her tongue as he turned towards the sink. She heard him ferreting out some gloves and soon the whoosh of the tap filled the kitchen. For a while, she lost herself in feeding the pasta through the cutter setting on the maker. She gathered the mound of delicate linguine, teasing it with her fingers to separate the strands, before turning back to the bowl with the fragrant scent of chilli, garlic, lemon and the delicious crab that had been caught earlier that morning. She dipped her little finger into the mixture, checking the seasoning and with a final sprinkle of salt, and another squeeze of lemon, she left it aside and turned her attention to the pasta. She dropped the fresh strands into a furiously boiling pot, reaching for the tongs and ensuring that the fine linguine strands didn't clump together.

Two bowls appeared on the kitchen pass, beside a fork and a spoon, without her even having to ask. She cast a glance to where Henry was drying a large metal pan and shut down the wayward thoughts her mind conjured at the sight of his powerful tanned forearms, jumper and shirtsleeves rolled back.

Stop it! she told herself sternly.

She tested the pasta, knowing full well that it was ready, and moved to the sink where, again, without having to ask, Henry had cleared a space for her to pour away the boiling water.

Frowning, she asked, 'Have you worked in a kitchen before?'

He gazed at her momentarily. 'I spent a bit of time in the restaurant kitchen. Annabelle was hardly reticent about how she wanted it run.'

'I didn't …'

'I was in Borehamwood by the time you worked there.'

It felt strange and wrong to Lily that she felt oddly proprietorial about the kitchen at the Hawkesbury estate. To suddenly realize that he'd once known it as well as she did now. And awkward that he had more right to it than she ever had. No. Not *right*, but …

He held out a colander beneath the lip of the large pan as if worried she might drop the heavy weight. People were surprised by the amount of strength it took to run a kitchen, and Lily had come up against enough male chefs proclaiming the 'weaker sex' hardly up to the task, she didn't need it from Little Lord – *Henry*.

'I could hold this all day,' she said defiantly, refusing yet to let loose the water – even at the risk of ruining the pasta.

'Don't doubt it for a second.' His response was immediate, sincere, and strangely without offence. Most men, like her ex-fiancé, somehow saw the assertion of female equality as an assault on their masculinity.

'I just don't want to ruin the pasta,' she said as she navigated the pasta and water into the colander.

He passed the handles of the sieve into her grasp and Lily was thankful that the steam from the water disguised the blush as the shiver of awareness tingled up her arms again. Ignoring it – and satisfied that she hadn't ruined the pasta while proving a point she evidently hadn't needed to make – she shook the linguine back into the pan and poured over the crab sauce, tossing it together and then into the bowls on the pass. Her eyes on the pasta, she reached for the container of parsley and watercress, and heaped a generous portion into the bowls, before presenting them to Henry. Finally looking up, she noticed the large smile across his features.

'What?'

'The way you move around the kitchen ... it's like ... a ballet?' he said, as if almost embarrassed about his description. But pleasure flowed from within her, because that's how it felt. Knowing that everything was ready, prepared and in position. There was a rhythm to how she moved around the kitchen that no one had noticed before.

He picked up the bowls as she grabbed a bottle of the Bacchus and headed back into the restaurant where he placed them down at opposite settings and pulled out a chair for her. She poured them each a glass of wine, slightly reluctant to sit, to encourage the strange intimacy of being the only two people in her restaurant.

If he noticed, he didn't say, instead inhaling the delicious scent wafting up from the steaming bowl and groaning appreciatively around the large forkful of dinner he'd placed in his mouth. She sat down in the chair with a thunk, trying to dislodge the images in her mind. Images of bedsheets and bodies.

Stop. It!

'So why cooking?' he asked, not even having swallowed.

'Anyone ever tell you it was rude to talk with your mouth full?'

'Multi-tasking. Too delicious,' he said, gesturing to her with his spoon circling in the air.

She smiled and twirled her fork into the linguine. 'I love it. I loved it from the moment that I worked in the estate kitchen. The first time I made dinner for my mum and it wasn't just relief but pleasure I saw in her eyes.'

'Relief?'

Lily sighed. 'It wasn't easy back then, she was working two jobs and hadn't really got the time to do that and make dinners beyond turkey burgers and sweetcorn.'

'Turkey— I haven't ever had—'

'Don't!' she exclaimed, and they both laughed, all the while knowing she would swear on the Bible that she didn't have a box of turkey burgers in the freezer of her small kitchen upstairs, even though she did. 'But yeah,' she shrugged, 'that's how it started.'

'Giving other people pleasure?' Henry queried, something in his gaze making her pulse spike.

'Mm hm,' she said around her own mouthful, not trusting herself to say anything more.

For a moment there was silence between them as they indulged in their meals.

'It really is good, Lily.'

'It's hard for it not to be with such good produce.'

'All of it locally sourced? Kate mentioned about the menus.'

Lily smiled, thinking of the way her friends always teased her about the way she ran the kitchen. 'I have certain philosophies about the restaurant. I try as much as possible to do nose to tail—'

'What is *that*?' Henry demanded, half laughing.

'It's about using everything from the nose to the tail. Whether it's meat or fish, or vegetable, I try to use everything so that nothing is wasted. It's ecologically friendly, as well as challenging. Finding uses for the entire product. There's so much wasted food in this world, which is a crime. We've become so used throwing things away, while there are people who don't have even the barest of essentials. But so much of what we eat, or what we produce, can be upcycled with a bit of creativity.'

'You upcycle food?'

Lily laughed. 'Kind of. My friends have been joking about my recycled mushroom consommé for years.' And then she couldn't help her own curiosity. 'And what about you?'

'What do I do?'

She nodded.

'Apps. Investment, finance backing, development, release, marketing and maintenance.'

'Sounds …'

'Boring?' he queried.

'Involved.'

He laughed. 'It is. But I've left it in my business partner's capable hands for the moment.' At her blank look, he clarified, 'Ben has been with me from the start. If I'm honest, he's the brains and I'm the money. And yes, it *is* more than that and I *am* more involved than that, but without Ben I …' He trailed off for a moment before huffing out a rueful laugh. 'I'd still be pouring salt on old wounds and probably would have run through the entirety of my grandfather's trust by now.'

His honesty surprised her. There wasn't a hint of resentment or anger there, just acceptance. So, so very different from the teen she's once known.

'Where did you meet him?'

'In a bar on a beach in Thailand. I went there after …'

After he'd argued with Blake. After he'd been cut off emotionally and financially by his father. He didn't have to say it. She knew about it – hell, the whole town knew about it.

'You went to London?' he asked, pushing aside his now empty bowl. He'd almost swallowed it whole.

She frowned, not quite sure where he'd got that from.

'Small town. People talk. Even to me, albeit reluctantly most of the time,' he said ruefully.

'Ahh. Yes. London,' she said, trying to keep the bitterness out of her voice. Although culinary college had been everything she'd wanted and more, she couldn't help now but associate it with Alistair, with embarrassment and shame at how he'd run off with their wedding fund and nearly £15,000 of her inheritance from her father.

'You didn't like it?'

His question drew her back to the present. 'I … No,' she concluded determinedly. 'I learned a lot, and it was great living with V for a year before … but it wasn't Devon. There *were* bits I liked. The incredible mix of cultures, the different cuisines.'

'The fact there was more than fish and chips on the menu?'

'Hey – the restaurant at the estate offered more than that and you know it. But yes, Italian, Vietnamese, Indian, Spanish, Thai, Greek, French, Jamaican …' she shook her head in awe, 'it was incredible. But London? Dirty, smelly, busy … Rubbish piled up on streets blackened by chewing gum? Fights every Friday night as the pubs clear out? Yeah, I could do without that,' she said, laughing a little.

'Fair. That's fair. But there's something freeing about being anonymous, about being around people who aren't—'

'Don't say it!'

'What? Provincial and small-minded? You know what I mean.'

'Not everyone is like that round here,' she insisted, despite the fact she really *did* know what he meant and had also been on the receiving end of the village gossips.

'Really? Mrs Whittaker?'

'Is still mad at you for the Father Christmas stunt.'

He nearly spat out his wine. 'You know about that?'

'Henry, *everyone* knows about that.'

He laughed again and the sound washed over her, soothing yet firing something within her. She felt strangely nostalgic for it. Yes, she laughed with the girls during the Lost Hours, but it was different, having someone in person to laugh with. To make her feel funny. Especially when Alistair had always accused her of being boring. Of working all the time.

'So you do something with apps,' she said, smiling as he leaned back in his chair, clutching his hands to his heart as if mortally wounded.

'*Something with apps*,' he repeated.

'That clearly makes you a *lot* of money.'

He raised his eyebrows at this.

'Apartments in New York, Singapore, and London? The TAG Heuer watch you carefully put in your pocket before washing up? The handmade Italian shoes you're wearing under *very* expensive jeans and …' She trailed off at the look on his face.

'Lily Atwell, have you been checking me out?' he demanded, teasingly.

'No.' She blushed, furiously. 'Paying attention. That's all.' Doubting he would believe a word of it. She certainly didn't.

He topped up the glass she had barely noticed finishing before filling his own.

'I don't think I realized how hungry I was,' he said.

'Wasting away now there's no staff on hand to feed you?' Lily winced at the bite to her words, hating how quickly she had drawn that hurt to the surface and hating how his head jerked back as if slapped.

'Look, I sent them away because ... because I just needed some time. Some space. All those people ...'

'I understand,' she said into the silence he had withdrawn into.

Dark fury tinged his eyes. 'Just because you were close to Blake—'

'I *understand*,' she repeated, placing weight on the last word because it hadn't been Blake she'd been thinking of.

In an instant the fury disappeared, wiped away by the hand rubbing across his face.

'Of course. I'm sorry. I—'

'It was a long time ago. I was seven and ...' She struggled to find the words that would join them in their grief. 'Very different circumstances,' she shrugged.

★★★

Henry felt like a complete arse. He'd spent the last few days rolling his grief around an empty estate as if he was alone in that experience. As if no one could or would understand. Lily was right, it was under very different circumstances but it didn't lessen, or take away from the loss of her own father.

He remembered the fishing accident that had taken Anthony Atwell's life and devastated the small community of Hawke's Cove. The vigil that had been held that morning, the sun not even broken over the horizon, as the entire town came down to the harbour, bundled against the frigid cold of the winter's morning, with candles and a grief-stricken silence. He remembered watching the way that the people had parted, allowing Marion

Atwell and her young daughter through the crowd to stand at the foot of the harbour, waiting and hoping to see who came back. The jagged sobs that had wracked Lily's mother's body as she'd taken one look at the captain's face and crumpled onto the floor, while the people nearby had tried to help hold her up.

Grief, aching and hot, surfaced in his chest and horrifyingly he felt the hot press of tears against the back of his eyes. For himself. For her.

She placed a hand on his arm, then reached for the bowls and retreated to the kitchen while he got himself under control. It was too much. Too close and he forced himself to remember why he was here.

By the time she'd returned, he'd taken a large mouthful of the not-surprisingly-delicious wine and swallowed his grief.

'So, are you up for dessert?'

'Actually, I had a proposal for you,' he interrupted, desperately attempting to get his plans back on track. To break the strange, awkward connection that seemed to be slowly forming between them. To get her on side, so that he could eventually leave. Return to New York and leave this all behind.

'Oh?' she asked, her head cocked to one side.

'Yes. Ah, it seems,' he said, trying to blag his way through this, 'that there is a tasting tour that I wasn't able to cancel.'

'VIPs, huh?'

'Yup. That's it. Very important.'

'And you can't ask John because—'

'I sent him away.'

'Actually, I was going to say, because he's in South Africa visiting family. But yeah, sent him away would just about cover it.'

'And Annabelle is—'

'Back up in Yorkshire with her friend Betty,' Lily concluded almost gleefully, as if realizing full well what this meant.

'So you're my only hope,' he said, his tone so near begging it was almost embarrassing.

'Mmm,' she hummed, shrugging her shoulders.

'Oh, come on.'

'Really, Henry, I'd *love* to help. But I'm just sooooo busy.'

He bit his bottom lip. There was literally no one else who could do it. He knew it and more importantly she did too.

'OK. Out with it.'

'Out with what?' she asked, all mock innocence. It might have worked, too, if she hadn't been practically bouncing in her seat. Her features had come alive, excitement sparkling in her eyes, and he was struck by wave after wave of beautiful glee.

'What's it going to take?' And before she could plead any more unnecessary ignorance, he pressed on. 'For you to do the wine tour.'

Once again he felt harpooned by her gaze. One that seemed to block out all else from his mind. He almost smiled that the sheer joy vibrating from her, it was oddly infectious.

'Just a teeeeny, tiny, little thing.'

'The wedding,' he concluded.

'Mm hm.'

'Lily, that's neither teeny, tiny nor little!'

'Such a shame. I really would have loved to help with your VIP tour that's happening …' She left it hanging in the air.

'Two days. It's happening in two days,' he replied through gritted teeth.

'Two days. Ouch.' She grimaced, before plastering on a deeply insincere smile. 'I'm sure you'll find—'

'OK, OK, fine,' he said, holding his hands up in surrender. 'The wedding for the tour.'

'Really?' This time she seemed genuinely shocked. 'Really, you'll do it? You won't back out or change your mind?'

'No. A deal's a deal.' He held out his hand and she grabbed for it, shaking so hard, it nearly dislodged his shoulder. 'You want to jump up and down, don't you?' He grinned.

'Nope. I'm good,' she replied, the lie obvious to his own ears.

'You sure?'

'Yup.' This time she was biting her lip, the one that was trying really hard to pull into a smile from where her teeth anchored it in place.

'I'm going to go before I have to agree to anything else,' he said almost reluctantly. He was still smiling as she ushered him out of the door with promises that it would be the best wine tour ever. The bell tinkled as the door closed behind him and he looked out at the night sky above the harbour and sea beyond, taking a deep breath of cool hair.

And then nearly choked on the laugh that erupted in his chest as he heard the high-pitched squeal of glee coming from within the restaurant behind him.

'You know I can hear you, right?' he called through the glass.

'Don't care,' she called back. 'Yes!! Yes, yes, *yes*!!'

He could see the shadowy outline fist-pumping the air behind the curtains and for the first time he could remember, he returned to the Hawkesbury estate with laughter in his heart, feeling lighter than he had done in months.

CHAPTER FOUR

It's on, ladies!! Lx

Thank God! Mx

AMAZING!! How? Zx

Did you have to offer him your firstborn? Blood sacrifice? Mx

No, just a wine tour. Lx

Really? That easy? Zx

Apparently so. Lx

Don't question it, just do it! Bloody brilliant, Lils! Mx

I thought he'd cancelled all the bookings. Zx

So did I, but as Malie said, I'm not questioning it. Lx

Lily looked over the text exchange with Malie and Zoe again and for the first time in weeks, breathed a sigh of relief. It wouldn't be long before Vihaan was back and she could focus almost exclusively on Victoria's wedding.

She did a little dance in the living area of her flat. Clothes were tossed about on the bed that was tucked away in the corner of the living space, beneath the window that looked out over the harbour. The small kitchenette that had been part of the remodel was tucked under the eaves of the sloping roof and fit for the most basic of her needs. Anything else could be done downstairs.

She walked over to the clothes rail, usually so neat and ordered – in ascending colours of the spectrum – hanging from old plumbing piping and secured into the ceiling. The weather report had promised heat and blue skies and as her fingers tripped over the coat hangers she came to a dress that Victoria had made for her nearly two years ago, and was as yet unworn. It was beautiful. Bohemian in style, the neckline dropping to her sternum but not overtly revealing or indecent, the long filmy material would cover her arms from the glare of the sun. Something unfurled within her: the desire to step outside the long-sleeved tops and trousers that had become her chef's uniform. The want to … to look pretty. And a wave of excitement crashed over her as she reached for it, telling herself that she wasn't wearing this for Henry. Not. At. All.

She opened the door to the bathroom, where the floor-length mirror had been hung, and looked at herself.

Was that really her?

The dress hung beautifully from her shoulders, clinging to her torso and flaring out from her hips. Her cheeks seemed slightly flushed, her eyes bright with excitement. No. It was satisfaction, she chided herself, that she'd managed to get the wedding back on track. It had nothing to do with the idea of seeing Henry again. Nothing whatsoever! It was only when she reached to pick up the towel from where it had dropped on the floor that she noticed the thigh-high split in the material, making her baulk. She checked the clock on the wall. It was too late to change now.

She grabbed her keys off the small side table where the picture of her, Victoria, Malie and Zoe sat. It had been taken barely an hour before the accident. She knew that most people would have thought it strange – would have seen it as a reminder of the awfulness that followed – but she didn't. None of them had. It was a bright point in their lives, one that had drawn them through the darkness, showing them that they were stronger together. Always.

Downstairs, she retrieved the basket she had prepared last night from the walk-in fridge at the back of the kitchen, and strapped it to the pannier of her bike and with a silent apology to Victoria, tucked the beautiful silky skirts of the dress out of the way of the wheels, hoping not to crease the material, and pushed off towards the Hawkesbury estate.

Lily couldn't help but smile as she pulled out onto the cobbled main street that bisected the small seaside town. She loved this time of year. The summer's sun crested over the hill of Hawkesbury estate, looking out and down on the port town below. The fishermen were not yet back from their morning haul, the tourists were not yet in full flow. It was … peaceful. It was home.

By the time she knocked on the door to the estate she felt as if everything was falling into place. A thread of excitement and glee wound through her so much she felt she might burst. So when Henry opened the door, bleary-eyed with only one arm shoved through the sleeve of a shirt, it wasn't the frown of faint annoyance that her gaze latched onto. It was his abs. Honed, perfect and, she sighed, *delicious*.

'Excuse me?'

Had she said that out loud?!

'Cheeses! I brought cheeses,' she finished lamely, holding out the basket before her, trying to cover the sudden tension between them.

'Cheese? Lily, you're an hour early.'

Reluctantly dragging her gaze away from … *mmm*, she finally caught his expression. He looked awful.

'Are you OK?' she asked, worried by the shadows in his eyes and the dark smudges beneath them.

'Not sleeping. What are you doing here?'

'The tour?'

'Is not for an hour. As I said.'

'Yes, but we need to open the reds, make sure the whites are chilled and I need to get the—'

'Cheeses?'

'Yes, they need to breathe.'

So did she. Taking a deep breath she tried not to inhale the scent of freshly showered male as she stepped past him into the foyer of the estate.

'We also need to talk through a few things. The tour will be about two hours, one for the estate, one for the processing and tasting and any questions. But,' she said turning back to where he still stood in the doorway, the shaft of sunlight falling behind him, casting him in shadow, 'I was hoping that I could also talk you through the wedding?'

'Why would I need to know that?'

She frowned. 'Henry, it's happening on the estate, and the staff …' Unease swirled through her. 'You do know that the staff will need to come back for it? All of them?'

He wiped a hand over his face as if trying to rub away some of the tiredness he clearly felt. 'Coffee,' he groaned.

Lily smiled gently. 'Come with me.'

She led him down the foyer and through the dining room she

was used to seeing dressed and full of guests, towards the counter
area where the coffee machine was. She switched it on, knowing
it needed a full five minutes to warm up, then turned towards
the small alcove to the left where a selection of the estate wines
were housed for dinners and tours.

She cocked her head to one side, checking the years, and grapes
and started pulling some of the reds from their slots. By the time
she'd finished she had three reds, two of the Estate Ruby from
six years apart and the Merlot, and had checked the fridge behind
the counter for the vintage Reserve, the Bacchus, the rosé and
the Estate Nectar – a dessert wine that would pair beautifully
with the fruit tart that—

'Hey!' she said, slapping Henry's hand away from the fruit tart
he'd unearthed from the basket. 'Not for you. Not yet.'

He pouted like a sullen child. Only it didn't make him look
like a child. He looked … good.

'Coffee,' they both concluded together.

She returned to the machine and set it to make two espressos
and passed one to Henry, before bringing out the pastries she'd
tucked into the basket just in case.

'Almond croissant?'

'Home-made?'

'Of course,' she replied, indignant at the suggestion they might
be anything but.

'You are a goddess.'

Lily's cheeks warmed at the compliment and the look of sheer
delight that had chased away the earlier shadows as he bit into
the flaky pastry. And the moan that he emitted made her mouth
water. For the croissant.

She hid a small smile beneath her own pastry as she took a bite.

With the last mouthful consumed and the coffee cup empty, Henry turned to Lily and sighed.

'The wedding. Just ... hit me with it.'

'You sure?'

'Yup. Though I have an awful feeling that I made a deal with the devil.'

'Thought I was a goddess.'

'They are not mutually exclusive,' he grumbled as she led him out of the side exit of the estate.

'OK. So there are going to be eighty guests. The wedding ceremony will start at two and be held on the south lawn, facing the sea. Chairs, decorations, a wedding arch,' she said, gesturing to where it would take place. She was giving him the bare bones, not because she couldn't imagine how beautiful it would be – she had it all clear in her mind – but she didn't want to overwhelm him. It was going to be a massive undertaking and he clearly didn't know what he'd signed up for. 'Photographs and canopies, from three until four thirty when the wedding breakfast will begin in the orangery.' She walked him through to the long glass-panelled orangery. The dark iron latticework gave it both an aged and industrial look. But the wooden-beamed dining tables counterbalanced the effect beautifully. 'First course will follow the speeches, then mains and desserts will be served before the party moves into the dining area which will be prepared for dancing and the bar will be—'

'Paid for by?' Henry suddenly looked slightly concerned.

Lily bit her lip. 'Blake had offered ... He'd ...'

Henry winced.

'He'd been putting bottles aside since Christmas and—'

'Fine,' he said, looking out at the orangery.

'Really?' Lily asked, surprised.

'Yes, Lily,' he replied drily. 'I'm not a complete monster, you know.'

Lily shrugged.

'What?'

'I had you down more of a beast,' she teased. 'Looking down at the villagers from his estate high up on the hill?'

'I guess that would make you Beauty.'

★ ★ ★

He hadn't meant to say it. Not really, but the moment the words came out of his mouth, Lily had blushed and he realized that he liked that look on her. It was different to the calm control he'd seen from her in the kitchen or the fiery anger sparking gold-coloured daggers in his direction. It made her look ... younger. Happier.

He really didn't care about the estate providing the wine for the wedding. Or taking the hit on the cost of the staff. He'd read enough of the email exchanges back and forth between Lily and his father as they'd discussed Victoria's wedding to know how much was being fronted by the estate. It wasn't about the money – although he could imagine that was why Lily had thought he'd cancelled the wedding in the first place. It wasn't as if he needed it. He'd already decided that the money from the sale of the estate would be put into the running of the Aubery App. He could see, now, that it looked petty and mean. But it hadn't been for any of those reasons that he'd cancelled it. It was that he hadn't wanted this. Hadn't wanted the involvement of it. Hadn't wanted it to become part of his memories of the place. Memories that were – for the most part – not bloody great to say the least. In truth, he hadn't wanted to be, once again, on the outside looking in.

Clearing his throat and the thoughts from his mind, he turned towards the counter for another coffee, knowing it would ruin his chances of sleep again later that night, but not caring.

'So, I'm assuming that you've just given me the bare bones,' he judged as he took a mouthful of the dark rich liquid.

'Of?'

'The wedding. Surely there's a lot more *fancery* going on.'

She smiled ruefully. 'But you don't need to worry about that. The flowers, the decorations, the photographer, the band—'

'There's a band?'

'Are all sorted, as is the food, which Annabelle and I are going to cover,' she pressed on.

'So where's the mood board?'

'I don't have a mood board.'

'I don't believe you,' he teased.

'OK. Maybe I do have one … but this wedding is important, Henry.'

'I get that. But don't they have a wedding planner?' he asked, a bit in awe of just how much she'd taken on, especially given the time she needed to put into her own restaurant.

'Yes, but she's based in London and doesn't know the estate.'

'I'm not sure that I agreed to all this.'

'You did!'

'It sounds like,' he was going to say a bloody nightmare, but the look in Lily's eyes was so damn hopeful. 'It sounds perfect for Victoria and Oliver Russell.'

'Not to your taste, then?'

'What, a wedding?' he said, nearly choking on the coffee. 'Nothing, ever, would induce me to do that. Ever.' Something passed across her eyes that prompted him to ask, 'What about you?'

She ducked her head, hiding once again behind her auburn hair. 'I'd ... thought about it once. Was engaged.'

'Really?'

'Don't sound so bloody shocked, Hawkesbury.'

'What happened?' he asked, aware that there was no ring on her finger, though when he'd noticed that precisely he couldn't say.

'He ran off with £15,000 of my money.'

'What?' he'd almost yelled it and straight away wished he could have taken it back when she'd flinched. For a moment she looked as if she might try to explain, but the sounds of the doorbell cut through the awkward silence and in an instant she rallied, a broad fake smile painted on her lips as she said, 'Showtime!' and she escaped to answer the door, while Henry was left reeling.

Nothing about Lily's behaviour towards the prospective buyer, Mr Jameson, his wife Natalie, or his assistant Ian, showed any sign of the hurt that he'd seen in her eyes just moments before they arrived. She was all smiles, welcoming greetings and full of explanations about how the day would be run and there he was, left to follow in her wake, warring with his conscience. He really should have told her about the purpose of the tour. He should have told her already about his plans to sell the estate because he could see the moment that Jameson would say or do something that would reveal the sale but could do absolutely nothing to prevent it. It was torture.

'So I thought we'd start with the vineyards, especially before it gets a little too hot out there, and then move on to the distilleries in the barns, a tasting and then a quick tour of the cellars, if that suits?' Lily asked.

'Absolutely,' Mr Jameson replied, and although his wife seemed a little more interested in the tasting portion, she put a brave face on the walking part, despite the way her five-inch heels plunged into the soft earth and occasionally got stuck.

Lily led the small group out into the sun and the grounds at the back of the estate towards the vineyards.

'The estate has been in the Hawkesbury family for almost twelve generations, but it was Blake Hawkesbury who introduced the first vines to the acreage in the early 1980s. The land benefits from the location in the warm weather – with Indian summers allowing for extra ripening – and in the winters, which provide the colder temperatures to gently settle the wines without needing electricity to chill them. This means that we don't have to rush our winemaking. But also important in allowing us to grow the grapes we do – and what makes our wine taste the way it does – is the quality of the soil. When Blake first planted the Pinot Noir and the Bacchus, he chose land that had been primarily used for grazing for at least thirty years at that point.'

She led them down towards the vines, the sun beaming onto the large green leaves and pearling over the ripening bunches of grapes. Henry couldn't remember the last time he had walked amongst them – the way the vines had expanded in the last ten years was nothing short of startling. He looked down the south-facing hill, rows upon rows of vines reaching nearly down into the Bristol Channel and the Celtic sea below.

Henry only half listened to Lily describing the types of grapes grown and how they benefited from the streaks of limestone in the soil. He half followed along in the present, and dwelt half in the past as he remembered Blake's words describing his endeavours, remembering the bitterness and resentment that had poured through his young veins wondering why his father didn't realize that he couldn't have cared less about the grapes that seemed more important to him than his wife and his son.

'Do you use pesticides?' asked Jameson.

'Although we're not an organic vineyard, we have virtually stopped using any weed spray, which is great news not only for the vines but the wine too. We make sure that any machinery we use has a limited impact on the soil in terms of compaction and only in extreme circumstances is insecticide used – though to be honest, we haven't had to use any in the last ten years.

'Our wines are made exclusively from our own grapes, which means that we have full control of the product, from planting, to harvest to when they are released. Which is only when they are absolutely perfect for drinking,' Lily concluded with a smile.

'Speaking of which …' Natalie interjected.

'Of course, shall we?' Lily gestured for the small group to head back up towards the estate, and Henry reluctantly followed. He'd forgotten how … alive it felt out amongst the vines. Vines that, even if not his, not really, filled him with a sense of industry that could be touched, grown, harvested. It occurred to him then that there might be similarities with developing a final product from the seeds of an idea, nurturing it to its full potential, weeding out the kinks in the codes, supplying a demand that either was present or could be created within a customer ... but there was no comparison. It was sterile. Cold. Ones and zeros on a coding screen, in development or in the bank. But being out here, smelling the salt on the air, the heat of the sun on his skin, it felt like ...

He shut down his thought process before he could say the word. The one that taunted him late at night. The one that had, until now, really only been significant in its absence. In his exile from it. The sooner he was done with this place, the better.

But as he followed Lily, still reeling off information about the estate, he realized that she was in her element. She had the same look of pride and joy about her that his father used to get. It was the way she was in the kitchen. Confident and assured. Her eyes were bright and she glowed in the midday sun. He realized for the first time that the dress she wore – while not showy or revealing – swirled around her long legs, and clung to her frame. And he could no longer deny that he was attracted to her. That she called to him like a siren. And if he wasn't careful, he'd dash his whole damn life on the rocks for her.

They entered the estate through the door beside the orangery and suddenly Henry knew where they were going. Instead of peeling off towards the barn where the distillery was, Lily led them to the wine cellar.

Dark shadowy stone stairs were illuminated by dim ochre-coloured lighting. The temperature was cool against his heated skin – the sudden drop bringing out goosebumps on his skin.

'So here we have the true heart of the winery,' Lily said,

bringing the group into the large cavernous space that stretched beneath the entire estate.

Frowning, Henry looked around, orientating himself against the changes since he'd last been down here. He could have sworn that there were more rooms shooting off the central area now. It was clean and dry, no sense of the damp he'd remembered from his childhood.

'For years, this had been used for the estate's storage – the machines and other equipment needed when it was a working farm – but the farming petered out some time in the Sixties.'

'Sixty-eight,' Henry supplied.

Lily looked up at him in surprise. It was the first time he'd interjected on the tour.

He smiled ruefully. 'My grandfather was quite a character, but a farmer he was not,' he said of the man he vaguely remembered as a child. 'He was much more interested in spending money than he was in making it and let the farm slide to the point of no return. My— Blake had grown up with my great-grandfather's mentality and saw the estate not as a cash cow, but as a beacon for the whole surrounding area. He realized that he could combine his love of wine with his love of Hawke's Cove and after a not inconsiderable argument with his father, he invested heavily in the work needed to develop vineyards. *Before* they were trendy in the UK.'

'I love that,' Jameson gleefully proclaimed, as if the personal touch was greater than the sum of all Lily's explanations so far.

'Of course,' Henry pressed on, 'his first bottle of wine was terrible. He'd made twelve bottles and instead of being put off by the fact he'd produced the most expensive bottle of vinegar ever known to man, he was determined to get it right.'

'That sounds like Blake,' Lily asserted with a smile on her face, as if he'd given her something, a gift, a piece of information about the man she clearly cared for and respected. 'In fact,' she said, walking down one of the dark corridors, the small group following in her wake … 'Hold on.' She came to a stop at the end, reaching a wall completely covered by a full wine rack. 'Does this look like the one?' she said, gently retrieving a dusty bottle. The cork, long since seeped in red wine, was mottled and the label yellowed with age.

Henry let out a half laugh mainly full of air. 'Well, it was before I was born, but yes. That looks like the one.'

'Do you think we could open it?'

'Not if you value your life and taste buds,' Henry assured Jameson. He looked around the space and noticed a slightly out-of-place mahogany chest. Natalie observed that his attention had wandered and came to stand beside him.

'What's in there?' she asked.

But Henry shrugged. 'I don't know. I've not seen this before.'

'That's the … it's the family's private collection.'

Frowning, he turned to find Lily avoiding his searching gaze.

'That must have some pretty special bottles in it.'

'It does,' she confirmed with a sad smile.

'Can we see?' Jameson asked.

'I'm afraid not. It's a personal collection.'

Jameson turned to Henry, 'I'm sure we could—'

'No. We don't have the key,' Lily interrupted, making Henry frown even more. Why was she being so secretive about it?

'Oh.' both Jameson and Natalie's expressions conveyed disappointment.

'But we do have some rather lovely wines set up for a tasting outside the distillery, along with a small spot of lunch, if you're ready?' The brightness had returned and Lily's enticing offer managed to chase away everyone's disappointment, aside from Henry's.

She led them back up into the light and to the old wooden benches in front of the distillery barn. The doors were wide open so that the tour party could see inside, before she disappeared back into the main building to retrieve the wine and the basket of food she had brought with her.

Henry let the group talk amongst themselves, noticing the hints of excitement through the hushed whispers. Lily had done an amazing job so far and he knew that Jameson was already half in love with the place. If he made an offer, Henry honestly couldn't see why he would turn it down, but he could also just as clearly see the hurt that would be sure to be on Lily's face. His conscience bit more painfully than the pang of hunger in his stomach.

Lily returned with a small trolley that contained the wine glasses, water, the bottles and the food. It looked like the best picnic anyone could imagine.

Moments before, Henry would have sworn that he'd not be able to taste anything above the ash of his conscience on his tongue, but as Lily talked them through the sparkling, the whites, the rosés and the reds, Henry was astounded by just how far the wine had come in the last ten years. In complexity, in taste.

Jameson had explained that he knew about the winemaking process, so instead focused on astute questions about their equipment which Lily seemed utterly unfazed by. Especially since Natalie interspersed the questions with praise and sighs of appreciation not only for the wine, but the food too.

★ ★ ★

Lily had enjoyed herself this afternoon. It had been strange, but good. It had felt, for a moment, down in the cellars as if she and Henry had been working together. Part of a team, even. And she couldn't remember the last time she had felt that way. Yes, she worked with Kate and Vihaan, but they were her employees. No matter how friendly, there was a hierarchy there. But with Henry it had been different.

She'd done estate tours before, when Blake wasn't able to. Especially in the last few months, when he'd been fighting a pain she'd insisted he went to the doctors about, which he'd resisted. But those tours had been large, groups of nearly twenty on some weekends. This had felt more personal. Especially when Henry had been able to fill in some of the history of the estate and Blake's choices. She smiled as Natalie finished the last forkful of the fruit tart she'd made that morning.

'That was delicious. All of it!' she exclaimed as her husband answered his phone and stepped away from the table. 'And you made the food yourself?'

'Yes,' Lily said, returning her smile.

'Even the *cheese*?'

'We do have great local produce in Devon, but I've been experimenting with vegetarian rennet and—'

'Oh, here we go,' Henry teased. 'Don't get her started on food. Lily owns a restaurant down in the harbour that is truly excellent.'

Lily blushed, touched that he would say such a thing and feeling slightly awkward for the praise. She'd always hated the spotlight.

'And, I know this is so silly, but I absolutely love your dress.'

'It's not silly, it *is* a lovely dress made by my friend Victoria.'

'Is she here too? I'd love to go to her shop.'

Lily let out a small sigh. 'Sadly not. She's in London, but she is working on her first collection for Russell & Co's department store.'

'Wow, that's pretty amazing.'

'Yes, it is and she is,' Lily replied proudly. 'The collection will be under Victoria Scott, just in case you're interested.'

'I am! Very,' she said, eyeing up Lily's dress one more time as her husband returned to the table.

'I'm afraid that's us, darling,' Jameson said to his wife. 'We have to be getting back. But it's been a real eye-opener, let me tell you.' He turned to Henry. 'It's a really great set-up here and I must say, I'm very interested.'

Lily frowned, not quite sure what Jameson was interested in.

'And,' he said turning to Lily, 'it was a pleasure to meet you. I don't suppose you're included in the package?' he said, laughing to himself. Not that Lily could see exactly why he was laughing. She cast a glance to Henry, who had turned to stone, the colour draining from his features.

'What package?' she asked, smiling despite the way nausea was swirling in her stomach, not yet sure what he was talking about, but instinctively knowing that she wouldn't like it.

'The sale package, of course. For the estate. It really has been so lovely,' he insisted, taking her hand and pumping it in a strong shake, seemingly unaware of how the bottom had just dropped out of Lily's world.

She glued her gaze and smile in place to the retreating backs of Jameson, his wife and his assistant. She was even aware that she had raised her hand to wave off the group as the doors shut behind them on the sleek black saloon. She stood there, hand still raised in a wave, as the car disappeared down the drive and then from view. She stood for just a moment, shock and fury raging within, competing against the sheer speechlessness that prevented one single word or sound from erupting from her throat.

'Say something, Lily. Please,' Henry begged from behind her.

She spun then, turned on him.

'You bastard.'

CHAPTER FIVE

'YOU COMPLETE AND UTTER—'

'Stop, Lily. Just stop.'

'How could you?' she yelled, fury and betrayal fighting to come out. But underneath it all was complete devastation. She should have known better. Men were all the same. Well, the men she met anyway. They lied and took what they wanted, uncaring of who they hurt in the process. She stormed past Henry, who was still yet to say another word.

She reached her bicycle from where it leaned against the side of the main house, briefly considering the basket, and choosing to leave it. She had to get out of here. Before she killed him. Because she really, *really* wanted to kill him this time.

The dress swirled around her legs and she bunched the silky material in her fist as she swung her leg over the seat, heedless to any possible damage.

She was *such* a fool. How could she have trusted him?

As if her actions had spurred his, he ran out in front of her, sliding to a halt on the grave, but she didn't care.

'Lily, wait. Please, let me explain?'

'Look,' she said, pressing down on the pedal and launching

the bicycle forward. He took hasty backward steps. 'You want to sell the estate? Fine. It's yours to do with as you wish, Henry. But you used me! You lied to me!' she cried, as she pressed down again on the upward swing of the pedal, before he grabbed the centre of the handlebar and halted her progress.

He was straddling the front wheel and their faces were almost inches apart.

'I didn't think you would help,' he rushed on an out breath.

'Of course I wouldn't have bloody helped, Henry. You know what this estate means to me,' she said angrily.

'No, I don't,' he almost shouted, causing her to flinch a little in the seat, putting one foot down to steady the loss of his grip on the bike. 'I have absolutely no clue why this estate is so important to you. I have absolutely no comprehension as to why every time I have a question about this place, I'm told to ask Lily Atwell. Or every time I try to make a decision I get this blank stare and I'm told to … *ask Lily Atwell*. So tell me! What on earth do you see that I don't?'

She saw anger in his eyes, but she also saw confusion, and hurt. And that she understood. Not just because that was precisely what she was feeling, but she had seen – could still see – that Henry was wrangling with his feelings.

She shook her head and shrugged, trying to ease the words into her mouth that had blocked her throat to almost choking point.

'I see …' *so damn much*. She tried again. 'I see the place where Blake brought me after the accident. A place I could be while my mother was forced to go back to work, unable to take any more time off. A place I could escape to when things became painful, when Victoria was told she couldn't have children, and Zoe was told she wouldn't walk again. I see the walled garden Blake asked me to help turn into a herb garden. The fruits we planted, the herbs, the bay trees, and blackthorn. I see the place where I earned the money that went to pay for my culinary college in London,' she said, drawing in a breath while memories and images flashed through her mind.

'I see a home, Henry. A safe haven. One that looks over and after our town. I see a place where people come to visit and fall in love with everything that is Hawke's Cove and come back the year after and the year after that. I see the land that was cared for by a man who helped nurture me back to my sense of self ten years ago. I see him walking amongst the vines that he loved. I see the pride that Blake felt when he produced an award-winning wine. I see how much hard work he put into this estate and the joy that he brought the people of this village when they also reaped the benefits of his hard work.'

★ ★ ★

Henry hated the sincerity ringing her tone, it was almost righteous and each and every word struck him like a knife.

'Yeah, well, you know what I see, Lily? *All* I see? Reminders of the same man who lost himself so much in this damn estate he forgot about his wife, he forgot about his son. A son that he later exiled. A man who instead of asking his son what was wrong, chose to invest his time and his care in you! Because he wasn't ashamed of you, was he? No. You were completely innocent and I was to blame for the accident that took Claudia's life.'

This time it was Lily who looked as if she'd been struck. Eyes wide and glistening with unshed tears, he almost hated himself at that moment.

'Henry, that's not how he—'

'Of course it was,' he growled. 'Because if not, then why didn't he reach out to me? Ten years, Lily. Ten damn long years and I never heard a word from him. So yes, you might see all the things that he wanted you to see. A home, a thriving business, his precious vines. But for every single thing you see, I see what I didn't have. Even before the accident.'

He could hardly see her anymore. The estate dropped away, the vineyards, the summer's sun and instead he was transported back to the dark, angry ache of his childhood.

'Did you know your precious Blake missed my fifteenth, sixteenth and seventeenth birthdays? That on my fourteenth, my parents argued for four hours and the last thing I heard was my mother demanding a divorce?'

He could still remember the fight now. The agony and pain in his mother's voice as she begged him, begged her husband to change, to just spend one night with her and their son, instead of out on the fields with the harvest. Instead of rushing off to some other town affair that couldn't be handled by someone else.

'That's why she left. That's why she took me with her. Because he couldn't once look up from this place. Its small town, gossipy mentality where people aren't allowed to get over their mistakes, where nothing and no one is more important than the Hawkesbury bloody estate.'

He was breathing hard now, the effort and energy expended in opening up his hurts, his past, almost a physical thing.

'Do you know what the last words he said to me were? That

until I learned to be less selfish and think of others, I wasn't welcome back. That he didn't want to see me again.'

Lily's eyes grew even larger and rounder and he cursed himself for causing the pain and hurt he saw there.

'I'm pleased that he was there for you. I am. You deserve it so much more than I ever did. And it made you happy and that's wonderful. But that's not who he was to me. That's not what this place is to me. And I can't stay here.'

With that he walked off, before she could reply. Before she could lessen the hurt that he wanted to pull about him like a shield. Because it was so much better, easier even, than the sheer avalanche of grief he was trying to hold back.

★★★

Lily cycled down the path to the road and on to the town with tears in her eyes and an ache in her heart. For Henry, for herself. For Blake. As she rounded the corner into her mother's road on the outskirts of Hawke's Cove she saw her through the bleary sheen of tears, standing in the garden in front of her small cottage. Lily practically dropped the bicycle on the ground, stepping over it, and rushed into her mother's widespread arms.

'Sweetheart, what's wrong?'

'I didn't know, Mum. I didn't know.' She collapsed into the embrace as great sobs wracked her chest.

'Didn't know what, my love?'

'I didn't know how badly Henry was hurting because of Blake.' So much hurt it nearly crushed her – she couldn't imagine what it was doing to Henry.

Marion gently pulled out of the embrace and levelled her with a look, as if she could fathom all that had happened from Lily's gaze.

'Come on, let's go inside and get that cup of tea.'

As Marion flipped the switch on the kettle, and set about making a pot of tea – her mother was fond of calling people without teapots heathens – she made Lily tell her everything. She was silent from the beginning to the very end, but seemed neither as shocked nor surprised as Lily had been.

'Mum, can I ask you something?'

'Of course,' she said, with a gentle laugh.

'What was the last thing Daddy said to me?'

Marion bit her lip, smiled a little sadly as she always did when they talked about Lily's father. She nodded, as if to herself, and stirred her tea before finally looking back up.

'Every morning, before he left for the trawler, your father would look into your room. If you were asleep, which was most of the time, because honestly, Lily, as a child you slept like a log, he would sit on the side of your bed, lean in and kiss your forehead. Then he'd whisper that he loved you and that he'd be back because now you owed him one.'

'Owed him?'

Marion smiled at her confusion. 'Yes. He did the same thing to me, every morning too. He'd say that if he went to sea nothing would keep him from coming home for those two kisses he was owed.'

Lily gripped her mother's hand, the fine smooth skin against the fragile bones in her fingers, tears once again pressing against the back of her eyes, as each drew strength from the other and their love of Anthony Atwell.

'Lily, your father loved you so much, just like Blake loved Henry. But Tony died when you were so young. There was no time for the big messy arguments, no time for great disappointments.'

'What?' Lily replied, shocked.

'No, I didn't mean you, sweetheart. I meant that he never got to disappoint you. Parents, like it or not, are fallible. We make mistakes. And Blake, well, he was a lovely man and I'm sure that he very much intended to make amends with Henry, but he didn't get the chance, and that kind of pain ... it's a hard one. It's a deep one.'

Lily took her mother's words into her heart. Felt them settle about her shoulders as she began to see it all through Henry's eyes.

'It was wonderful that Blake was there for you,' Marion said, 'but for Henry, that might be a bit difficult for him to process. So perhaps it's understandable that he might not want to keep the estate.'

And suddenly Lily felt guilty, adding heat to the feelings filling her chest. 'I ... I feel like I stole something from Henry.' Her mother looked a little confused. 'His relationship with Blake.'

'No, sweetheart, you didn't. But he did give you things that you can share with Henry now.'

Lily hiccupped around the grief in her throat, a half laugh, half gasp. 'When did you get so wise?'

'I've had a few years to practise,' she teased. 'And yes, the Hawkesbury estate was – is – important to you but perhaps ... Perhaps the time you had there with Blake was a gift and valuable for what it was. It helped you, gave you an outlet. But look at you,' her mother exclaimed, taking both hands in her own, 'you have the restaurant, which is doing so well. Malie's coming back. Maybe it's time for you to think about what else you could be doing?'

'Well, I have the wedding—'

'No. *After* the wedding, my love,' she prodded gently. 'There's a big wide world out there. And Vihaan is back in a week, maybe you could take some time off? Maybe you could go and visit V in London for a day or two. Or maybe even do a bit of travelling, like Malie and Zoe. I've always thought ... No. I ... it's OK. I've said my piece,' her mother concluded cryptically.

There wasn't much to be said after that. Marion had to head out, although Lily genuinely couldn't imagine where her mother was going with a paint roller, and all the other DIY stuff she'd put together in a package by the front door. She'd been practically pushed through the hallway and back out into the street.

An old lady needs her secrets, she'd said.

As Lily had retrieved the bicycle from where she had dropped it, a large, sleek black SUV pulled into the road, slowed, and then sped off. Which was strange. Not the SUV – they'd been slowly filling up the roads around Hawke's Cove for the last few years – but Lily could have sworn she'd seen Zoe in the brief glimpse of the passenger seat. Which she couldn't have. Obviously. Zoe was in Sydney with Finn and wasn't due back until a few days before the wedding. She shook her head, trying to order the confused thoughts in her mind.

Henry. The sale of the estate. The wedding. Henry.

They were all spinning around together like clothes in a washing machine. She had meant what she'd said to Henry and to her mother. It wasn't about the estate. She knew that, as much as she felt an emotional claim to the place, it wasn't hers. It never had been. It *was* Henry's to do with as he wished. And although it would have a ripple effect on the town and its people, the Jamesons had seemed nice. They had. It was Henry that she kept coming back to.

Because in her heart of hearts, she knew that Blake had loved his son. But her mother had suggested that she could give something back to Henry. And Lily realized she held the key. Literally.

* * *

Henry had spent the rest of the day turning his conversation with Lily over and over his head. The documents sent over by Ben had gone untouched. The calls on his phone had gone unanswered, and at some point, though he couldn't say when, dusk had fallen over the estate.

He regretted it. The argument with Lily, the things he'd said to her. He'd seen the hurt, felt his own, and it was all too much. So when the doorbell rang and he pulled it open expecting to find her standing there it took him a moment to understand what he was seeing.

'Don't suppose you have a room for the night?'

'Ben?'

Over Ben's shoulder, he could see Amina standing behind Ben, a smile on her face that wobbled every time she shifted her weight back and forth between her feet, her stomach round and *very* pregnant.

'Are you—'

'I *really* need to pee,' she exclaimed. '*Really.*'

Genuinely concerned that it might cause her to explode, he stepped back for the door and gestured for her to enter. 'Second door on the left.'

'Thank you,' Amina replied at a startlingly high pitch as she rushed past him.

Ben raised his eyebrows. 'The perks of being pregnant. So, room at the inn?'

There were two small bags on the floor by his feet, and a bottle of SangSom in his hands.

'Where did you get *that*?' Henry couldn't help but ask.

'I have my ways. Come on, keep me standing out here and I'll need the toilet too.'

Henry couldn't help but smile. He'd missed them both so much and just hadn't realized it until this point.

'Come on, I'll give you the grand tour.'

'Later. The drive up from Newquay was insane after the flights.'

'Flights?'

Ben pierced him with a look. 'Have you already been drinking?'

'No,' Henry defended. 'Have *you* been drinking? How did you get here?'

'Singapore, via Heathrow, to Newquay. Amina has one last meeting in Lyon tomorrow before she's going on maternity leave.'

'You came all this way for a night?' Henry asked, thinking that his friend might have lost his mind completely.

'No,' Ben assured. 'I came all this way for my best friend.'

Something inside Henry shifted and he grabbed his friend in a hug, no back-slapping, no awkward jokes. Just a proper old-school hug.

'Am I interrupting?' Mina asked from over Henry's shoulders.

'He was mine first, you know,' Henry teased.

'Finders keepers,' she replied without missing a beat.

Henry let Ben go, not before his best friend levelled him with a look. 'You OK?'

'Not really,' Henry admitted for the first time.

'Didn't think so.'

'Yeah, OK, smarty pants. No need to rub it in.'

Henry turned to Mina and was shaking his head at all the changes to her body in the last few months. 'Hey, gorgeous,' he said, and welcomed her warm smile and embrace just as much as he had Ben's.

'Hey, that's my pregnant wife you're talking to.'

'You know I saw her first too,' he said to Ben over Mina's shoulder.

'Possession is nine tenths and all that.'

'Possession?!' Mina demanded, pulling out of Henry's embrace to glare at her husband.

'Not what I meant, my love.'

'Better not have been, or you'll be sleeping on the …' Mina stopped and looked around. 'Just how many rooms does this place have?' she asked, unable to keep the awe from her voice.

★ ★ ★

After showing them around the estate, they retired to the private living room in the west wing where Henry had set a fire in the fireplace, taking the edge off the cool of the night, despite the summer's heat.

'It really is beautiful,' Mina said again with an appreciative sigh, settling back into the sofa and gently smoothing circles around her large bump.

Henry couldn't help but smile. 'It suits you.'

'The bump? Don't let Ben hear that, or he'll have me knocked up again in no time.'

'That's the plan,' Ben said smugly.

He'd missed them. He'd missed the banter, the friendship, the familiarity of them. The last few months he'd spent at the estate, he hadn't realized just how isolated he'd made himself. Rarely going into town where people would stare, just about stopping themselves short of actually pointing. He'd sent away the staff so that he could have time to think, to process, and to decide what to do, but …

'It's really good to see you,' Henry said into the companionable silence.

'Don't go soft on me now.'

'I wasn't talking to you, Ben.'

He snorted. ''Course not.'

Henry peppered Mina with questions about the last meeting she had in France, about the apartment that they'd found in Singapore, and how excited her family were to have her back home and looking forward to the baby. Ben seemed content to let his wife talk away the hour or so but Henry wasn't fooled. The clock chimed eleven, 'And that, gentlemen,' Mina stated, 'is my cue. Bed calls.'

She placed a firm kiss on Ben's lips, laughing as he tried to affectionately grab her arse.

'Get a room!' Henry admonished.

'That's my intention, Hawkesbury.'

Hawkesbury. Lily had called him that. She was the only person apart from Ben and Mina who had.

'I don't want to see you until that bottle is done,' she commanded.

Henry frowned. 'What? You actually expect us to—'

'Finish every last drop. I need my man hungover tomorrow, because it's the only thing that makes him manageable on a flight. Otherwise, he'll be crawling into the cockpit and trying to convince the pilot to let him fly.'

'Hey, I've got over—'

'Twenty hours of flight time under your belt. Yeah, we know. The guy living down the road knows too,' Mina concluded.

'My wife, ladies and gentlemen,' Ben exclaimed to the room. 'Such a delight.'

'I usually just slip him some Valium,' Henry joked to Mina.

'I'm saving that for the birth,' Mina said, waiting for Henry to stand for a hug.

'Fair,' he replied, pulling himself out of the chair and taking her into his arms, a slightly awkward fit around her bump. 'Thank you,' he half whispered.

'Anytime. Seriously, Henry. Anytime,' she said, smiling up at him. 'Sweet drinking, boys.' With that she disappeared from the room.

Ben walked over to the side cabinet, withdrew two crystal cut tumblers, and placed them on the table in front of the sofa. He screwed off the cap of the bottle and poured two distinctly unhealthy shots of SangSom.

'You're not messing around,' Henry exclaimed.

'Neither is my wife. She wasn't joking about the hangover.'

Henry took the glass when offered and inhaled the sweet scent of rum, so familiar and so much more welcome than all the wine in the estate.

Ben watched him over the rim of his own glass.

'How's the office?'

'Don't give me that crap,' Ben replied without malice.

Henry sighed.

'What's going on?'

'I'm selling the estate.'

Ben raised his eyebrows and nodded. 'OK.'

'Just like that?'

'If it's what you really want.'

'Of course it is. Why the hell would I want to stay here? Why on earth would I want to keep the one place that—'

'Was your home?'

Henry glared at his best friend.

'Look, I get it. I do. There's a lot of bad memories and mojo here.'

'That's putting it mildly.'

'There are no good ones? Really?'

Henry was about to shake his head but stopped. Inexplicably, Henry saw Lily, walking amongst the vines in the sun, turning to smile at him over Natalie Jameson's shoulder, a soft light in her eyes. He remembered how she had slapped away his hand from the basket, and how she had teased him in the restaurant, telling him to aim higher. And then, from just a few hours ago, how he had felt to see Ben and Mina at the door, the teasing banter filling the rooms with new memories. New memories that had him shaking off his friend's question. A friend that clearly saw too much.

'Anyone I should know?' Ben asked.

He never could really get anything past him. 'She's … someone I used to know.'

'Spill,' Ben commanded, and he did. Henry told Ben everything. From the first time he'd cancelled Victoria's wedding, to the encounter in the herb garden, the meal at the restaurant, the proposed sale of the estate, the tour … It didn't exactly relieve the ache in his chest, but it had at least shifted slightly.

'Man, you shouldn't have lied to her.'

'I didn't lie,' Henry grumbled. 'I just didn't tell her what was going on.'

'Semantics,' Ben said, reaching over to pour the last couple of inches of SangSom into their glasses.

'Does she know about the app?'

Henry frowned. 'What has that to do with anything?' he asked, not needing to question which app Ben was talking about it. He meant the *first* app. The one that they had talked about on the beach in Thailand. The one that had started their business venture and friendship.

'I'll take that as a no.'

'She doesn't need to know about that.'

It was Ben's turn to frown. 'What is it that you want her to think of you?'

'What do you mean?'

'I mean, it seems as if you're letting her think the worst. Letting the whole town think the worst of you when that's just not the whole story. You're not that angry teen anymore.'

'I know that,' Henry bit.

'But you don't seem to want *them* to know that.'

'Them?'

'The locals.'

Henry grimaced. 'Lily called me a beast.'

'I take it she's pretty?'

'Putting it mildly,' Henry replied ruefully, thinking of the way she blushed, the way her eyes lit up when she was teasing him or telling him off. She was truly beautiful.

'Well,' said Ben assessing him through squinted eyes, 'you haven't grown horns in the last few months.'

'Horns?'

'Every fairy-tale villain needs horns.'

'Something you want to tell me, mate?' Henry asked, unable to keep the amusement from his voice.

'Henry,' Ben's voice was suddenly grave, 'when you get married, these wives ... they force you to watch these films. Cartoons. Things that men shouldn't—'

Ben's words were stopped short by the cushion Henry chucked at him.

'What can I say?' Ben exclaimed, laughing and shrugging. 'Mina likes fairy tales. So I've seen quite a few. And yeah, I'm not surprised Lily called you a beast. I can see similarities.'

'What do you mean?'

'Sending the staff away, holding up in your rambling estate—'

'Being lynched by the villagers.'

'Enticing the local village girl.'

'Yeah. I don't think she'd see it as "enticing".'

'You like her?'

Henry took a mouthful of rum, while he considered how to answer that question. He did. He knew himself well enough, and there was genuinely very little about Lily Atwell not to like. She was kind, generous, and her laughter could light up Manhattan, and had even – for a brief moment – lit up the Hawkesbury estate. Before he'd ruined it all.

'Yes. I do. Not that it matters.'

Ben exhaled through pursed lips. 'Of course it matters.'

'Ben, in two months' time, I'll have sold the estate and moved back to New York, be knee-deep in the latest investment and Lily Atwell will still be here, working in her restaurant and hating my guts.'

'Or not. It's really up to you.'

'The decision was made years ago. I was never supposed to come back. I shouldn't even be here now.'

'Yet here you are.'

Henry nodded. *Yet here I am.*

The clock chimed twice.

'Right. That's *my* cue. I think I'm suitably sloshed enough to be devastatingly hungover tomorrow thereby requiring me to sleep the entire way to France. My wife thanks you,' Ben said, saluting at Henry with a smile.

'What time are you leaving?'

'Eight. Don't worry. We don't need an alarm. Mina's up before 6.30 like clockwork. Something to do with babies pressing on bladders.'

'Too much info.'

'Just you wait. One day it'll be your turn.'

'Doubt it,' Henry called after Ben's retreating form, to the answer of, 'yeah, yeah, whatever.'

And if pressed, he'd have lied on the Bible, and sworn that he didn't suddenly see an image of Lily Atwell, pregnant and beautiful with it, flashing through his mind.

CHAPTER SIX

OVER THE NEXT FEW days, Henry found himself returning to Lily's herb garden, because that's how he thought of it now – Lily's – working away at the weeds. There was something peaceful about it. He might have left the estate ten years before, but the skills that his father had taught him as a child – to tend to the land and care for its produce – had never left.

He'd heard back from the estate agent who had assured him of the Jamesons' interest and had told him they were putting together a very competitive offer. Competitive to what, Henry couldn't guess, because there had been no other interest in the estate from what he could tell.

Which was why his work in the garden seemed pointless. It wouldn't be his, and he doubted the new owners would allow Lily to maintain access to the place. But he couldn't help himself. He'd cleared the four beds of weeds and replaced the netting over what he'd been able to salvage from the strawberries and the other fruit. Half of the stuff he couldn't identify, but he carefully pruned the bay tree back to some kind of round ball-like shape, which he'd been surprisingly proud of.

He reached for the mug of coffee steaming in the soft summer air of the late afternoon and took a large mouthful. He still wasn't sleeping properly and was almost sure that he wouldn't until he was finally rid of the place.

He heard the crunch of gravel as footsteps approached the garden and turned as if he'd been waiting for her. Perhaps he had.

Lily stood, framed by the doorway, looking stunning. Her hair was down again, falling around her shoulders in waves. She wore low-heeled boots, her legs were encased in jeans that clung lovingly and a loose pale pink T was half tucked into the waist, covered by a long, calf-length olive green cardigan.

'Hi,' she said gently, her eyes not on him but scanning the garden.

'Hi,' he replied lamely. She raised her eyebrows and he shrugged in response.

'I think you missed a bit,' she observed ruefully.

'I think I missed a whole lot of things.'

She exhaled, but in relief or exhaustion, he couldn't tell.

'I brought you something,' she said, swinging the bags in each of her hands.

'Please tell me that's food. Please,' he begged as his stomach rumbled angrily. He'd run through what little there had been in the fridge and had not yet had the wherewithal or the energy to attack the freezer.

Lily laughed and blushed prettily. 'Just something I threw together.'

'Yeah, right.'

'I considered you worth about half an hour of prep.'

He levelled her with a direct gaze. 'I'm not sure that I deserved that much, Lily.'

'Good thing it wasn't up to you then, or you'd be dining on a boiled egg.'

Henry couldn't help but smile. 'I'd have taken it anyway.'

'I ...' She hesitated. 'I also brought you something else.'

He couldn't help it. He closed the distance between them, wanting to be closer to her, needing to be. What was it about her that chased away the darkness?

She reached for her back pocket and produced the smallest key he'd ever seen. It was perhaps less than an inch long.

'What does that open?' he asked, curiously staring at the small rusty key in the palm of her hand.

Lily seemed to wince slightly. 'Quite possibly a bit of hurt. But hopefully also a bit of healing.'

★ ★ ★

Lily led him back down to the cellar they had visited only days before, hoping beyond all hope that what she was doing was right. She'd wanted to come sooner, but the restaurant had taken up all her time. Vihaan had returned from his holiday and had needed a couple of days to get back into the swing of things – and to see how much Kev had developed in his absence. Enough to step up so that she'd have more time for the wedding.

But before she could do that, she needed to do this. For Henry. For herself.

Henry hadn't questioned her about where they were going, he seemed to follow her with a trust and acceptance she wasn't sure she deserved. This was either going to work or it wasn't. But she would at least have tried. Lily had resigned herself to the fact that he was going to sell the estate, but the conversation with her mother had repeated in her head and, having lost her own father, she knew how important that relationship was. She wanted to give Henry something of that back. Not because she was going to get anything out of it. But because he deserved it.

She turned on the light, thankful she was wearing her cardigan, as the cool dry air of the cellar bit a little in contrast to the heat from the summer's sun. She drew him towards the mahogany chest.

'This is yours,' she said, giving him the key.

'Why do you have it?'

Henry was shrouded by the shadows of the alcove in the cellar so she couldn't quite see the expression on his face but noted the curiosity in his tone.

'Blake was worried he might lose it. He was always losing things. And … it was important to him.'

Henry took the key, but held it in his hands for a moment as if unsure as to whether he wanted to use it or not. She nodded to herself and turned to leave.

'Can you stay?' he asked.

'Are you sure? I—'

'Please.'

'OK,' she replied. Henry held her gaze and she wondered what he saw. Because for a moment, they were there, together, and the moment that he opened the chest … She wanted him, needed him, to see that she wasn't intruding.

He turned to the chest, breaking whatever strange hold that moment contained, and placed the small key in the lock and turned. One large mahogany swing swung open to reveal a wine rack with twelve bottles on the shelves and a series of drawers beneath.

'The drawers have Blake's diaries in them. Decisions about the vineyard, descriptions about the grape varieties, when planting worked, what seasons were good. That kind of thing,' she explained.

'And these?' he said of the wine bottles.

'Take a look,' she directed.

He retrieved the first bottle from its storage and an envelope came loose from beneath it, falling towards the floor, but Henry caught it just before it could land.

★★★

Henry peered into the gloom at the aged white envelope with a handwritten date in the corner. He frowned, seeing his birth date on the envelope, and looked back at Lily.

'What is this?'

'Take a look,' she said again, with a gentle smile.

Rather than opening the envelope, he placed the first bottle – the label proclaiming it to be of the same vintage year as his birth – on the floor. He gently half prised another bottle, checking the label's date, then the next and the one after that. Each of the bottles had a similar envelope wedged beneath them. But his mind was on the dates. He hadn't missed how they were from specific years in his life. His birth, his eighteenth, his twenty-first.

Towards the bottom of the shelves, he could see the distinctive larger shape of sparkling wines and he half feared what they were to represent. With a clenched jaw, he peeled open the envelope in his hand and withdrew a thin sheet of paper covered in his father's handwriting.

Dear Henry,

Today you were born. It was about as dramatic as one could have imagined, though also completely unimaginable. You'll know one day what it feels like to hold your firstborn in your arms, God willing. But I was utterly unprepared. As a parent you think that you'll be the teacher. But today, Henry, you taught me what it was to love completely, wholly, overwhelmingly and unconditionally. And I'm honoured that I get to see the man you will become. I only hope that I can be the father you deserve.

With love,
Your father

Henry's hands were shaking by the time that he finished reading the letter, his throat was rough and he realized that he must have read it out loud, because the look in Lily's eyes, the sheen of tears, told him that she knew. That she understood.

He went back to the shelves and crossed to the last few bottles – each had a date from every year of his life, and the last few were from years that were still yet to happen. Henry shivered. All this time, he'd thought his father had forgotten him, or rejected him like a dirty secret or source of embarrassment and shame. He'd thought his father had exiled him from his mind as much as from his estate. But here was evidence to the contrary. That each and every year his father had bottled a wine for him and written him a letter.

He peered beneath the sparkling wines, not wanting to disturb the precious alcohol. The envelopes bore the headings, 'On your wedding day', 'On the birth of your first child', second and even a third. His father had imagined him having three children?

'He might not have been present with you, Henry. But he never once stopped thinking of you. He was proud of what you had accomplished and felt shame and guilt about how you'd parted.'

Henry nodded in the darkness, against the weight of the pressure in his chest, ache and guilt swirling in a heady combination.

'My eighteenth … Blake had wanted to show me something in the wine cellar. And all I could think of was that I didn't want anything more to do with his damn wine. All that day my father had said nothing – no happy birthday, there'd been no card or present – and I genuinely thought he'd forgotten it and I stormed out.' He felt tears press against the backs of his eyes and he clenched his jaw, trying to stop them. Trying to hold on to it all. 'I think … I think he wanted to show me this.'

He felt Lily's warm hand wrap around his, their fingers intertwining, and he clung to them as if they were a lifeline. Her understanding and compassion were almost his undoing. For a moment, he just stood there, drawing strength from her, allowing her to anchor him. Finally getting himself under control, he reluctantly released her hand, reached for two of the bottles, snagging their envelopes with his finger and turned to Lily.

'Up for a drink?'

★★★

Henry emerged from the cellar into the setting sunlight and stopped. It was as if he were seeing the vineyards and the estate grounds with fresh eyes.

I only hope that I can be the father you deserve.

He would have rubbed a hand over his face, but he was still holding the two bottles. And the envelopes. Lily had gone back inside to retrieve the bags of food she'd brought and to find a bottle opener. He'd needed it. That moment to himself. Just to lean into the feelings that had been almost overwhelming in the cellar, but were now soaring free, the tightness in his chest easing.

Quite possibly a bit of hurt. But hopefully also a bit of healing.

That's how Lily had put it. She'd been right. On both counts, he realized as he wondered at how something could both hurt and heal at the same time. She had given him this. And he had only taken from her.

He walked towards the benches just outside the barn that contained the distillery and placed the two bottles on the table. He stared at the envelope from his eighteenth birthday, half fearful of what he would read. He had argued with Blake that night, hurling words of anger and resentment at him like missiles.

He felt, rather than heard, Lily's return. She approached him cautiously, but she needn't have. He welcomed her presence. Wanted it. She placed the bags of food and retrieved two wine glasses she'd nestled within them and rested them on the table, passing him the corkscrew.

She sat at the bench and turned her face into the setting sun, letting him uncork the wine and pour the full-bodied alcohol into their glasses. She inhaled the aroma appreciatively.

'You didn't let it breath,' she accused lightly on her exhale.

'Shut up and drink your wine,' he replied jokingly.

'Which one is this?' she asked.

'My eighteenth. I'm surprised it hasn't turned to vinegar.'

'I'm not,' she replied, almost serenely. 'Blake knew what he was doing by then.' She shifted slightly as he came to sit beside her and raised her glass to his. 'Happy birthday,' she smiled.

'It's not my—'

'Shut up and drink your wine,' she teased.

The rich red liquid was so deep it was almost purple. An explosion of blackcurrant and spice that made his mouth water filled his senses and he clung to the trace of vanilla left on his tongue. It was a light wine, but it packed a delicious punch.

'Wow,' he couldn't help but exclaim.

Lily nodded knowingly. 'It's good, right? He did love that Pinot Noir.'

'Yes, it is and yes, he did.'

For a moment, Henry marvelled in the fact that he was drinking something created by his father. Something that had been bottled and put aside just for him. He tried to ignore the fact that he might have been able to share this with his father, but for some reason, it felt especially *right* that he was sharing it with Lily Atwell.

Before he could change his mind, he prised open the envelope that had come with this bottle of wine and retrieved the slip of paper.

Dear Henry,

Today is your eighteenth. Today you become a man. And no matter the arguments and what you think of me, I am proud of the person you are becoming.

With love,
Your father

'Did he write that after your argument, do you think?' she asked.

'Not necessarily. We were arguing a lot by that point,' Henry mused.

'So, what did you do?'

'When?'

'On your birthday. After you left the estate?' she asked, taking another sip of the wine, unaware of the sudden sharp stab of pain that cut into his heart. And guilt. Because he'd not really given it much thought in the years since, but …

'That was the night I met Claudia for the first time.'

★ ★ ★

Lily forced herself to swallow the wine on her tongue. It suddenly felt as if they were venturing into an area that they had silently agreed not to broach. Not once had they mentioned the accident, the events of the night of the summer ball or really what had happened after.

'How did you meet?' she couldn't help herself from asking.

He shrugged. 'Like any two teenagers from small towns. She was in the pub.'

'The Hope and Anchor?'

'No. John wouldn't have served her. It was the Half Moon, on the way to the old Merrow's Rest property.'

'Ah. Yes, I know it.'

He looked at her skew-eyed.

'What? I have been to a pub before, Henry,' she scolded.

'Really? When was the last time you were in pub?' he demanded, his tongue practically sticking in his cheek.

She had to think. Because it had been an age since she was last in a pub.

'All work and no play,' he teased.

'You're getting off topic.'

'I am. Mum had sent me down here after my A Levels. I was pretty much the youngest in the year, so everyone from school had already gone travelling or stayed up there. But Blake ...' Henry shook his head. 'He'd seemed more interested in the estate and the vineyards than anything else. At least, that's how it had felt then.'

Lily wanted to reach for him. To touch him, to offer him some kind of ... but she didn't. She could see that he was lost in the memories.

'Anyway, I'd gone to the pub with some of the guys from my year at Hawke's High and saw Claudia. I recognized her from the year below, but she knew some guy called Finn who worked there.' He shrugged. 'She was ... stunning. And cocky,' he added, smiling at the memory. 'She took me down a peg or three even though it was my birthday. And I was hooked. All the other girls had looked up to *Henry Hawkesbury* as if I were lord of the manor. But she didn't care. She made me work for every bit of attention she gave me. It was hot and heavy for that summer and then I had to leave for uni.'

Lily knew that there was a lot he wasn't saying, but it wasn't right to push. She smiled her thanks when he refilled their glasses.

'What about you? I imagine your eighteenth was with the rest of the "awesome foursome"?' he said with a corny American accent.

'The what, now?' she demanded.

'You know, you, Victoria, Malie and Zoe.'

'I know you who were talking about, but what was that name?' Henry shrugged. 'It's just what we called you.'

'Who's "we", Henry?'

'The guys at Hawke's.'

Lily knew she must have looked shocked, but Henry only started to laugh which made it worse. 'That's an awful name. Just … *awful*.'

'But it's … *awesome*,' he repeated in the accent.

'That's it. I'm out. Done. You're on your own.'

'No, wait,' Henry said through his laughter. 'Stop. Please don't go.'

'One condition. Never, *ever* use that phrase again.'

Henry sat up straight, pinched his thumb and forefinger together and zipped his lips. 'Promise.'

He nudged her shoulder with his. 'Drink up, you're lagging behind in both wine and storytelling. Your eighteenth, you were with …'

'The girls,' she said, genuinely terrified that she might now forever mentally and utterly accidentally refer to them as the awesome foursome. Light danced in Henry's eyes as if he knew. 'V wasn't yet eighteen, so there was no chance of us getting into the pub, so we stole Mr Michaels' boat and came to the beach.'

'In January?!' Henry demanded, shivering dramatically as if in punctuation.

'Yup,' she replied, choosing not to ask how he'd known or remembered when her birthday was. 'It was bloody freezing. We started a fire and … I felt bad because Blake had given me a bottle of the Reserve as a present, but I'd already "borrowed" a bottle of white from the kitchen.'

'You stole from my father?' Henry exclaimed in mock outrage. 'So you've been a thief for a long time, then?'

'I … I don't know what to say about that. Honestly, I'd planned to pay him back.' But Henry just waved away her assurances. 'Oh God, we got so drunk that Malie nearly fell into the water pushing the boat back off the beach. There wasn't a jetty there at that point.'

'I was going to ask about that. It's quite a hardcore set-up down there with the jetty and the wooden boardwalk across it.'

Lily couldn't help but smile. 'Blake had that put in about six months ago. It's a real pain for Zoe to have to switch between a beach-friendly wheelchair and the one she normally uses, so he found a way to make the place Zoe-friendly, as he liked to put it.'

'I'm really pleased he did that. What does she think of it?'

'She hasn't seen it yet.'

'Then why did he …' He sighed at the look he must have seen on her face. The desperate, hopeful, pleading look she knew she wore. 'What is it?'

'Blake knew that I was … hoping … pretty please with a cherry on top …'

'Out with it.'

'I really wanted … tohaveV'shenpartyonthebeach,' she rushed out in one breath. One word.

'Oh, for the love of all things holy.' He groaned.

'Please, Henry, please? It would be perfect. And we wouldn't make any noise. You won't even know we're there. I promise.'

'You're going to be the death of me, Lily Atwell.'

She squealed, taking his response as a yes, and turned, throwing her arms around his wide shoulders and hugged him hard, all the while bouncing in her seat. All the excitement managed to mask, just for a moment, that she was hugging Henry Hawkesbury. Then she stopped bouncing. And she felt his chest against hers, the firm muscles and the restrained strength of him, the scent that she drew into her body as she inhaled from where her head was nestled into the crook of his shoulder, her lips barely millimetres from his jaw, his skin … The hug became something else as she felt the shock recede from Henry's body, as she felt him almost settle. As if he wanted it as much as she did. Needed it even.

It was too much. She released her hold on his shoulders and drew back, not quite able to meet his eyes, not quite wanting to see whatever she would find there. She reached for her glass but it was empty and heard Henry clearing his throat.

'Thank you,' she said, barely a whisper.

'In for a penny, if for a pound.'

She smiled, or at least she hoped it was a smile. Her lips were suddenly tingling as if she had actually pressed them against his jaw. 'So, which birthday is this?' she asked, angling her glass at the next wine bottle.

'My twenty-first,' Henry ground out, his voice gravelly to his own ear.

***

What had just happened?

He was still reeling from the hug. It had started out easily enough, Lily's natural excitement and exuberance making him smile. But then it had changed, morphed into something more. He'd felt the press of her chest against his, the softness of her skin against his, he'd inhaled the sweet natural scent of her. Herbs and something sweeter, something mouthwateringly citrusy. And he'd not wanted to let go.

Instead of reaching for her again, he grasped the bottle neck and pulled it towards him, staring at the corkscrew as if he didn't know what it was or how to use it. Because he didn't want the cold glass bottle in his hands. No. He wanted Lily Atwell.

'Here,' she said, reaching her hands towards his. 'I'll do that.'

He nudged the envelope belonging to the bottle his way and it forced him to refocus. Refocus on the first communication he would have received from his father *after* he'd been kicked out. He almost didn't want to know.

He prised open the envelope and retrieved the letter, knowing as much as he wanted to hide from it, he was also desperate to know what his father had written.

Dear Henry,

Today is your twenty-first birthday. It's been just over a year since I saw you last. Since we argued. I knew the moment the words came from my mouth that I regretted them. I do understand that you're hurting and I'm sorry for that. I wish I could, as your father, have protected you better. Done better. I hope that I can in the future.

Love,
Your father

He hadn't read this one out loud, half fearful of what Blake might have written, and he respected that Lily hadn't peered or pried, but he passed her the letter to read anyway as he looked out at the sloping vineyards, now dusted in darkness.

His exhale was shaken by the convulsions gripping and releasing his heart in waves. His father's voice, as if speaking the words, echoing in his mind. He ached. For the loss of his father's hope for the future, the regret of his own actions and words that night, the pain that neither had been able to say the words of reconciliation to each other.

'Can I ask why Blake sent you away? What you argued about?' Lily said into the night.

'He never told you?' Henry had assumed that the entire town knew.

'No. I knew that he regretted it, but that he couldn't seem to find a way through it. He'd always insisted that it was his fault, that he'd said things he shouldn't have.'

'Really?' He was surprised that Blake had said as much to Lily. But then again, Henry was still getting used to the fact that his father had felt as much regret over his departure from Hawke's Cove as he did. 'I guess we both said things we shouldn't have.'

Henry knew that if he told Lily he didn't want to talk about it, she would honour that, but strangely he found that he did. He wanted her to know.

'After Claudia ... after the accident, I went off the rails.' He shrugged, knowing it was the barest description of the hurt and self-destruction he'd felt at the time. 'I'm not proud of it. It certainly wasn't my best moment,' he said, looking into his hands as if they held answers he'd not found before now. 'I wasn't sleeping well at the time and began drinking too much. I started missing classes at uni, and eventually they decided it was better for me not to return. Only ... I didn't tell Dad.'

Lily looked at him, patiently, without judgement. That same incredible acceptance on her face, soothing the way for his words. 'He was sending me money each month and I was in no fit state to get a job, so I just ... kept the money. Guess that makes me a thief too,' he said, a small sad smile pulling at the corner of his lips. Lily shook her head in denial but didn't speak. 'I got arrested – well, cautioned – a few times for drunk and disorderly conduct. I was so angry, I was looking to fight anything and everything. My mum found out and reluctantly called Dad. And then he summoned me back to the Cove.

'We had a terrible argument. Real apocalyptic stuff. We both said things we shouldn't have. Though, in hindsight, it was probably the kick up the arse that I needed. He accused me of being selfish. I was outraged. Because I saw him exactly the same way. Selfish and focused only on the estate, not caring about his wife and son, the estate and the town being more important than his family.'

'*The estate has a bond with the town. Without one there would not be the other.*'

'*Who cares, Dad?!*'

'*I do. And you should too. And until you can see that, until you can care about one thing other than yourself, then you're not welcome in this house.*'

The words cut through the thoughts in his mind.

'He cut me off, said I wasn't welcome in the house. So, I went back to Mum's for a bit and then figured I needed to get out of London. Of the UK. I only had a few months until the trust fund from my grandad kicked in. I'd planned to spend the whole thing on booze and whatever, but then I met Ben in Thailand. On my twenty-first birthday,' he concluded wryly.

'Who's Ben?'

'My business partner and best mate. Without him … I doubt I'd even be sitting here.'

She raised her glass. 'To best mates.'

'To *awesome foursomes*,' he snuck in before she could stop him, receiving a small elbow jab to his side for his efforts. 'What about you? Your twenty-first?'

Lily frowned as if having to remember, smiled and then a shadow passed across her features.

'I was in London. With Alistair. We had dinner. I paid.' She shrugged. 'That was it.'

'You paid? Where were the girls?'

'V had to work,' she said, pressing on against the look of

faint disapproval she must have seen in his face, 'no. Really, she couldn't get out of it. Malie and Zo were halfway around the world. We'd talked about all meeting up midway, but we'd only just seen each other at Christmas down here, so ... we'd done my birthday celebrations then.'

'Why did you pay?'

'Alistair had left his wallet at home.' She shrugged again. It was a small thing. He could see her trying, even now, to brush it off. Could see that it still hurt.

'How did you meet?' he couldn't help but ask, curious about the man Lily would have married.

'In London, in V's bar. He was in investment banking. Or said he was. Probably knew I wouldn't delve too deeply. Who would? Who really knows what investment banking is?'

'I do,' he said.

'Yeah, OK. Fine. *You* do. But I didn't.' She cut him a mock evil glare that wouldn't have frightened a kitten. 'He was tall, lanky ginger. But cute. There was something wry about him that I liked. And he just overwhelmed me. Pursued me. With words anyway. Within months we were living together – because apparently it seemed unnecessary to spend money on two places when we were together all the time anyway.

'So I moved out of V's and we moved into a flat together in South London. It made sense at the time, but ... I didn't realize that he barely contributed to bills or things round the house. He was too tired after a long day, his money was wrapped up in personal investments ... Anytime we *did* talk about money, there would always be a pay day on the horizon in the distant future. But ... he was funny. Charming. Perhaps a little *too* charming.

'He was always forgetting things, his wallet, paying bills. He'd say, "What would I do without you?" I felt ... needed.' She paused, clearly thinking back to the way it had been with him. 'And anytime that I'd get frustrated or annoyed, he would turn it back on me. Say that I was distracted by the cooking course, that I didn't have enough time for him. And every time something went wrong, it wasn't his fault. His company restructured and he lost his job – I now doubt that was the case. He was probably fired. But his helplessness gave me someone to look after. To care for. It made me feel necessary in his life. It made me feel ... wanted.

'He proposed almost accidentally. He didn't even have a ring, but at the time I'd thought it was romantic. So we made plans, sent invitations, saved money. I told the girls, my mother. There's a lovely registry office in Peckham.

'And then a month before the wedding, *pouf*. He just disappeared.'

'With your money.'

Lily nodded and there was nothing pretty about the blush that rose on her cheeks. He could tell it was one of shame, embarrassment.

'I'm hardly the person to give relationship advice—'

'Henry Hawkesbury, you *shock* me.'

'But,' he pressed on, 'the guy sounds like a real shit.'

'Yup. That was Alistair.'

He wanted to chase away the darkness in her eyes. He wanted her to smile the way she had before. He wanted so much more for her than this Alistair guy who had stolen her money and left her doubting herself. That much he could see.

'Exactly. It was him, not you, Lily.'

She shrugged and he saw the way his words rolled off her like water, apparently not convinced.

She finished the wine in her glass. 'That was a good one. The wine,' she clarified.

'It was. They're all pretty good.'

He sighed. 'I guess I'm going to have to wait a year until the thirtieth birthday bottle.'

Lily smiled at that. 'Where do you think you'll be?'

Here. With you.

The thought shocked him. The desire for it shocked him.

'In New York, probably,' he said instead. 'Or Singapore with Ben, Mina and their baby. What about you?'

She shrugged. 'The restaurant?' she answered as if anything else would be unimaginable.

'I disagree.'

'Really?'

'Yeah,' he insisted. 'I reckon you'll be in some far-flung exotic location, tasting incredible food. While Alistair will probably be in prison for fraud.'

She laughed at that, finally, and the sound was like honey. Sweet and pouring over him endlessly. When it finally petered out, she looked about as if realizing for the first time that night had fallen.

'I should be getting home.'

'You could, erm … You could stay? It's not as if there aren't any rooms.' He winced at the uncertainty in his own voice, not quite sure whether he wanted her to stay or wanted her as far from him as possible.

When she looked up at him, he could see that she was torn too. Tempted. And that nearly undid him.

'Very kind of you, but I need to be up early in the morning to open the restaurant.'

'I don't really want you cycling home.'

'It's not *that* far.'

'Drunk in charge of a bicycle?'

'I am *not* drunk, Hawkesbury.'

'Still, I'm calling you a cab.'

'It's really not—'

'I'm calling you a cab,' he replied firmly. There was no way he'd let her head home on the bike in the dark after a bottle of wine. He just wasn't made that way.

They waited, side by side, for the cab in front of the estate, the stars like flashing sequins in the velvet night sky. He'd missed it, he realized suddenly. Missed the clarity of the English countryside at night. There was nothing remotely like it anywhere else in the world.

And suddenly he was struck by a sense of homesickness. Not for New York. But for the estate he was about to sell. Was it even possible to miss something before it had gone? And when he looked at Lily, he knew the answer.

'Lily—'

The gravel on the drive crunched beneath tyres as the cab began its journey towards them.

'That's my cue,' she exclaimed a little too brightly.

'Thank you for this evening,' he rushed out before she disappeared. 'Really. I … thank you.'

She looked up at him, her large dark eyes round, a half smile on her lips, half something he didn't want to name, because he felt it too. Hope. Need. Want. Then she blinked and it was gone. She reached up with her finger and thumb and gently directed his head to the side. Leaning up on tiptoes, she pressed her lips to his cheek.

'Good night, Henry Hawkesbury,' she whispered. And then she was gone.

CHAPTER SEVEN

HENRY REREAD THE TEXT he'd sent to Lily two minutes ago,
just as confused as he had been when he'd woken up to the most
awful screeching message on his answerphone at 6 a.m. with so
few details it would take a crack team of investigators to decipher
its meaning.

I'm not accustomed to hysterical women sobbing into my
answering machine and cancelling My Dream Wedding! Who
the hell is Jenny Langford anyway?!!

Henry grabbed a mouthful of much-needed coffee, watching
the dots on the messaging app appear and disappear.

Really, dude? You're not? You surprise me. Not a recent
conquest, then? What happened to Lily? And … your dream
wedding??

What? He checked and realized that he'd sent the message to
Ben. Crap. He was never going to hear the end of that.

Not you. Not my wedding. Not now! Will call later.

He fired off the text again, copy and pasting for time.

HH, thought I brought u up better! Something u want to tell
me? :0 Sadly, no idea who the lady in question is, but if u do find
out, let me know. Curious and curiouser! ;)

He groaned out loud this time and didn't spare a thought to his mother's use of keyboard emojis and sudden lapse in grammar.

Message not meant for you, Mum. No wedding. No lady and certainly not my fault. Will explain later.

Whatever was going on, Henry decided it would be safer all round if he just went to find Lily in person. She'd know what the hell My Dream Wedding was, but he couldn't quite shift the belief that she wasn't going to be pleased. Not one bit.

As he pulled the old Jeep into the parking area by the harbour, he tried to account for the burst of excitement he felt coursing through his veins. It felt at odds with what he was sure would be the delivery of bad news. Lily had so much invested in this wedding. A little too much, even if it was for her best friend.

He stalked towards the bustling restaurant overflowing with the breakfast rush. People passed him with happy smiles and what he presumed were full bellies as he pushed open the glass front door. The smell of freshly pressed coffee and delicious sweet pastries hit him like a wave as he tried to ignore the few stares he received from the locals. And then it all dropped away the moment his eyes landed on Lily.

She looked glorious. His hungry gaze ate up the way she had her head thrown back and was laughing at something her manager, Kate, must have said. The light blue shirt she wore v'd at the neck, outlining the curve of her chest and exposing more of that smooth creamy skin, and she was wearing … shorts. White shorts that lovingly hugged her perfect thighs, exposed the bareness of long legs he'd been wanting to see for what felt like forever. The dark waves of her auburn hair were loose and rippled down her back as she leaned forward to say something to Kate – until she stopped, the words stalled on her tongue as she noticed him staring at her.

For just a moment, he caught the way her eyes flared, in surprise and then joy. It stopped his breath, and short-circuited his brain. They softened slightly, as if there was a secret shared between them, and he felt it. Felt the connection he'd been trying to deny since the night she gave him the key to his father's gifts.

'Who is My Dream Wedding, and how bad is it if they cancel?' he blurted out without thinking, without even saying hello.

In an instant, her features morphed into shock. The whole damn restaurant seemed to stop. The waitress who had been carrying plates towards the back wobbled and dropped them, the sound of the china smashing on the floor louder for the silence that had suddenly descended.

'What?' Lily's voice cut through the silence as a trembling horror fills her gaze.

Oh God, he hadn't thought it would be *this* bad.

Mrs Whittaker appeared at his side, looking far too gleeful, thrusting some change onto the counter and mumbling about being on her way.

'Someone called Jenny Langford called my mobile and said she had to cancel. Family emergency, lots of tears and drama and—'

Lily had turned a horrible shade of pale.

'Are you—' He'd tried to ask if Lily was OK, when Kate bustled from behind the counter.

'Emma, one coffee. Strong. Kev?' she called to the kitchen behind the counter, where a young kid shoved his head over the pass. 'Brandy? Or whisky. Whatever's nearer.'

Kate came round the counter and grabbed hold of Lily's arms, pushing her back into the seat she had half risen from.

'What's going on?' Henry demanded.

'Oh God, oh God, oh God ...' It was as if that was all Lily could say.

The kid from the kitchen rushed through unscrewing the bottle of brandy, just as the waitress passed Kate the coffee cup, which she held out to Kev, and Henry watched half in horror half in fascination as a rather unhealthy dose of brandy was added to the dark rich liquid.

This will send her over the edge, Kate mouthed at him over Lily's head.

'What will?' he tried again, ignoring the fact Kate hadn't actually spoken out loud.

'Lily, it's OK. We're going to fix this. It's going to be fine,' Kate said to Lily, who now had her head in her hands, and had been reduced to a low painful-sounding groan.

'Oh, for God's sake, will someone just tell me what is going on?' Henry's authoritative voice crashed over the entire restaurant.'

'My Dream Wedding are the wedding decorators,' Kate hissed as if trying not to upset Lily further.

'There's such a thing?' he questioned.

She glared at him in response.

'Right, not important. Carry on,' he gestured.

'They're providing all the decorations for the orangery,' Lily groaned from where her head was almost between her legs in a classic panic-attack pose. 'The ... Oh God. The wedding arch!'

As if it was just sinking in, Lily started to emit a worryingly high-pitched moan of panic and no one seemed to know what to do. Kev was looking at the waitress, who was looking at Kate, who was staring, startled, at Lily.

Any thought of just swinging by to inform Lily of the answering-machine message and returning to the estate evaporated. It was clear to him that no one in the restaurant was used to seeing Lily in such a state, and he wasn't surprised. Usually she was always in control, always knew what to do, or what to say.

'Well, it was only a matter of time that—'

'Not now, Mrs Whittaker,' Kate and Henry said at the same time to the woman who had stayed clearly only to take in the drama.

He couldn't bear it. The panicked and the distraught look on Lily's face, now that she had righted herself back up to sitting.

'Kate, I need another coffee, one for me, another brandy for Lily, pen and paper, and Lily's going to need the rest of the day off,' he commanded.

They all jumped to attention, Kate going for the phone, Emma to the coffee machine, and Kev passed Henry a pad of paper and a pen.

He caught Kate's gaze. *Has she eaten?* He mouthed over Lily's head. Kate pulled a face and disappeared into the kitchen. While he waited for her to return, he got his phone out, pulled up the search engine and typed in wedding decorations. An improbable amount of hits came up and he nearly recoiled from the images on the sidebar.

He was beginning to understand the cause for concern.

He squinted at his phone. Were those … *doves*? Surely Victoria hadn't wanted *doves*?

'Henry?' Lily's shaken voice called him back.

'It's OK,' he said with a reassurance he was beginning most definitely to *not* feel. 'It's going to be fine. I just need a list of things that are going to be affected by this.'

'I don't know where to …'

'Begin at the beginning. Whatever comes into your head. You said something about a wedding arch?'

She began to whine again and her hands were fluttering in panic. Like the doves.

God, please not the doves. How did that work anyway? Were they left to fly free or did some poor bastard have to run around trying to catch them? Henry suddenly had an image of himself halfway up a tree with a net trying to capture an elusive bird.

'It's fine – we're going to fix this. I promise. You can trust me,' he said, determined to do whatever it took to make this wedding whatever Lily wanted it to be.

★★★

They had driven off in Henry's Jeep less than half an hour after Henry had revealed the news that had sent Lily into such a panic. She'd been numb at first, startled by her own level of shock at the wedding decorator's cancellation. But then hopeful, when Henry had announced he'd found a place that should be able to help.

But the moment she'd taken one look at the bright pink, yellow and baby blue cheap plastic, she'd squealed again and had been ushered out of the store by Henry before she could burst into tears.

Back in the Jeep, the windows down, she let the swathes of air rushing in and teasing tendrils of her hair about her face cool her.

'Breathe,' Henry commanded. And she did.

'And again,' he prompted when she failed to take another inhalation. 'I don't understand why Victoria didn't hire a wedding planner to deal with all this,' he grumbled.

'She didn't need one. She has me,' she said thankful that his reply wasn't, *And look how that turned out.* He didn't need to, because she was blaming herself enough as it was.

'It's not your fault, Lily,' he said as if he could read her mind.

She puffed out a breath between pursed lips. 'I know.'

'Do you?'

'Yes, Henry. I know that it's not my fault that Jenny Langford went into early labour and is no longer able to fulfil her contract.'

She shifted in the seat of the battered old Jeep as she tried to remember all the things they would need for the wedding.

'You know I'm going to have to see that mood board now, right?' Henry teased.

'Not going to happen,' she replied without missing a beat.

'Oh come on, please? Just a peek?'

'Nope.' Because she really didn't want him to see just how much she had invested in Victoria's wedding. Perhaps too much, she was beginning to realize. But it was Victoria. Her best friend. The person she'd turned to whenever things had got bad, or gone wrong, or … For everything, really.

Henry pulled the Jeep onto the turning towards the next place on his list.

His list. The one that *he* had found when she had been panicking in the restaurant. She couldn't be mad at him for that. It's just that she wasn't used to being the 'rescued'. She was used to being the 'rescuer'.

The Jeep wasn't exactly a purebred white horse, but she felt very much like the damsel in distress right now and was still marvelling that it was Henry coming to her rescue.

He pulled into the car park of a sprawling warehouse with a corrugated roof. Lily cast him a highly dubious look.

'We'll just see what they have. If it's not right, then we'll move on to the next.'

She reached for her bag in the footwell of the car and before she could grab the handle, Henry was there, car door open, hand outstretched. The small touch of chivalry warmed her and she smiled for the first time since his fatal announcement.

'Thank you.'

'Anytime,' he said. 'Come on. I have a good feeling about this place.'

'Mmm.'

'Aim high, Lily Atwell. Aim high.'

He guided her in front of him, through the swish of the electric doors and almost ran into the back of her when she pulled up short.

She took in the sprawling space in front of her. The shelves were stocked full of so many different things: plates, cutlery, knives and forks, glasses, and all manner of tableware which led on to lighting, where tiny fairy lights twinkled and solar-powered pathway lighting glinted between large trails of plastic floristry and hurricane candle lamps. Swathes of white silks and tulle hung from wooden lattices. Finally, she let out a gasp of pleasure.

'This is it! It's perfect,' she cried, ignoring the hushed, 'Thank

God,' that Henry expelled. She picked an aisle and began to walk down it, trying to work out what they were going to need, beginning to feel a little overwhelmed, even as her earlier panic receded.

'Where do we start?' she asked.

Henry snagged a large trolley, and joined her. 'We get one of everything you think you're going to need and then we'll just multiply by, you know,' he shrugged, 'whatever is required.'

'That simple, huh?'

'Pretty much.'

'You do a lot of party planning in your line of work?'

'Nope, I'm just naturally gifted at whatever I turn my hand to.'

'Oh really?' She couldn't help but return the teasing banter that he wielded, knowing it was a kindness, knowing it was to draw her out of her fears and more thankful for it than she could have imagined.

She went straight to the hurricane lamps, which would be so perfect for the orangery. But they were going to need at least twenty. She fingered the price tag and stopped, the bottom dropping out of the momentary pleasure. She bit her lip. There was no way that she had enough money in her account to cover this. She knew that Victoria and Oliver would absolutely pay her back, but …

She felt Henry's hand over hers where she still held the price tag on the lamp.

'I've got this,' he said, as if understanding.

'I can't, Henry. It's—'

'It's part of an event that is being held at the estate. As such, I'll cover it because I'm sure they can use it all for future functions. I can put it on the contents and the sale price will cover it anyway.'

A sudden wave of sadness hit her as she remembered that Henry was selling the estate. That he would be leaving. Somehow, she'd forgotten that. Or chosen to ignore it. Wanting a moment, needing it, she spun on her heel, 180 degrees. 'Oh look,' she exclaimed as she walked blindly straight towards another display.

'Really?' she heard Henry query behind her and followed his slightly horrified gaze. Lily blushed more furiously than she had ever done before in her life as she realized she was standing right in front of a lurid display of … *penis straws.*

Her squeak turned into a coughing fit, drawing the attention of other couples about the shop, the men all seemingly equally embarrassed and the women smiling knowingly.

The bright pink display of hen party paraphernalia rose over three levels, ranging from black sashes bearing white stitching proclaiming 'Best Hens Ever', large helium balloons, glittering heart confetti, flashing plastic ice cubes, and the aforementioned penis straws.

'Didn't realize this was Victoria's style,' Henry said, looking mildly disturbed by the sight.

'No, I suppose not.'

He cocked his head to one side, apparently unable to tear his gaze away from the straws. 'They're surprisingly anatomically—'

'Let's go,' Lily said, grabbing his arm and pulling him away before he could finish the sentence.

★★★

Henry let Lily draw him down another aisle, unable and unwilling to take the smile from his face. She had looked so mortified when she'd seen the straws; he shuddered again at the thought of them, that he'd not been able to help himself. She'd looked adorable. He doubted she realized how expressive her features were. The way her cheeks would flush, the way her eyes became large and round, the way her shoulders flew back when she was preparing for a fight, and the way she ducked beneath her hair when she wanted to hide.

It was rare that Henry ever spent so much time around a woman he was attract— *A woman*, he clarified mentally. *Just a woman.* Other than Mina or his mother, of course. The last time he'd been with a woman romantically had been … He frowned. When had it been?

He'd dated, of course he had. He'd just never let it go beyond a month or two. He never lied, never cheated and never made promises he wouldn't or couldn't keep. It was just easier that way. No one would build expectations of anything more than he was willing to give. Which, on reflection, was very little indeed.

And he knew – he'd known for long enough now – that Lily deserved more than that. More than he was able to give. In just a few short weeks, he'd seen that she deserved it all. The white picket fence, the family, the perfect husband. He was so far from that he couldn't even see it. Because Hawke's Cove would never be his, not like it was for Lily.

He watched her walking along the aisle, knowing when she saw something she liked because her eyes lit up. There was even the occasional gasp if she found something beautiful. She traced her fingers on glass candleholders, down trails of fake ivy and paused when she came to a display of what looked like jam jars with baby's breath nestled inside, plus more of the fake ivy draped on wine barrels and boxes.

He held himself back, because she looked momentarily lost in her own world as she took it all in. He caught the eye of a man who was trailing behind a woman Henry presumed to be his fiancée. The man rolled his eyes at him in rueful sympathy. It was then that Henry realized he and Lily must look like a couple. Like an engaged couple, planning their own wedding. He nodded back, not bothering to try and explain that they weren't and joined Lily by the display.

'It's pretty,' he commented.

'It is. V has baby's breath in her bouquet and these would look beautiful on the tables in the orangery.'

'Are these fake?' Henry asked of the flowers.

'Yes, but I can always get in touch with the woman doing the flowers for the ceremony for more.'

Lily looked hesitant, though, as if she hated the idea of the extra expense. His heart clutched a little. 'You could. But we have so much ivy at the estate. In fact,' he shrugged, 'the wine barrels, the wine boxes and this stuff,' he said, gesturing to the fronds of small white flowers, 'we've got it all already. You could even take some of the blue hydrangea if you wanted?'

She turned and looked at him.

'You're right. Yes, there are things we'd need, the fairy lights, candles—'

'The hurricane lamps,' he inserted.

'They *are* beautiful.'

'They are,' he agreed, ready to say almost anything to make her smile.

'We'd still need to rent chairs for the outside seating, but a lot of the rest of the things could easily come from the estate.'

'I'm not being tight,' Henry said quickly, worried that she might think he was trying to save money.

'No, I know that. I think it's a wonderful idea. It would just take a lot of time and energy, which—'

'Is fine. Lily. I have the time and the energy. And it would be in keeping with your eco-friendly, locally sourced—'

'Are you mocking me?'

He held his hands up in front of him in surrender. 'No,' he said, shaking his head. 'Just embracing your philosophy.'

She looked up at him, a smile on her face, her eyes lit with excitement. 'It would be beautiful,' she claimed as if she could see it, not him, before her. And suddenly he wondered what it would take for her to look at him that way. With awe, excitement, and joy. Right then, she could have asked for the whole damn store and he would have bought it for her. Because in his heart, he knew that he couldn't give her the one thing she would truly want.

She caught something over his shoulder and her eyes widened even more.

'Wedding arch!'

He couldn't help the small smile pulling at the corner of his mouth as he spun the trolley around in the wide aisle and followed her to the back of the warehouse.

Even he was impressed when he saw what Lily had been drawn to. Across the back wall, there was a series of many different arches. Some rectangular in design, some trailed with white silk, frothy cream creations, others bursting with trailing flowers. They might have been artificial for display purposes but they were all exquisite, making it easy to imagine how real ones would look on the wedding day. Some boughs were wistful and whimsical, some so inconceivably abundant he was surprised the arch hadn't fallen over, and one with such an explosion of rich-coloured silk flowers, he could only think of doilies and old ladies.

But Lily was standing in front of a wide, thick wooden circle, cut away about a metre wide at the bottom so that it rested perfectly on the floor, while looking as if it continued into it. The floral display hung on an asymmetric line, on either side, exploding with beautiful white and cream flowers, offset by the rich dark green leaves supporting it with surprising bursts of blue from the hydrangea that Devon was known for. The wood of the circle could be seen between the two hangings, making it sophisticated but rustic. Lily looked as if she'd fallen in love.

Her fingers were pressed against her lips and her eyes were shinning.

'This is it. This is … *perfect*. It's so much better than what My Dream Wedding had planned to provide.'

He came to stand beneath the arch and when he looked down at Lily, he was struck by such a strange sense, as if he had one foot in the present and one in a possible future that he might never have.

She looked up at him in that moment and he felt floored. The ground dropped away, everything dropped away, apart from her. Even the reasons he'd piled up against doing what he wanted most at that moment. To kiss her.

Snap.

He reared back as the sound of a camera shutter cut through the moment.

'Sorry,' he heard a man say, 'but I couldn't help myself.'

Henry turned to find a skinny guy with thick black-rimmed glasses brandishing a camera before him. The guy shrugged and introduced himself as a wedding photographer. Henry didn't know whether to kill the man or thank him.

'I thought you might like a memento. And,' he shrugged hopefully, 'maybe a photographer?'

Lily smiled awkwardly. 'Thank you, but that's been arranged.'

Henry wondered how on earth she could speak, because in that moment, his mind was completely blank.

'Oh well. But if you would like a copy of the photograph, I can email it to you? And then you have my contact details just in case?'

Henry saw the manager of the warehouse and nodded him over so that Lily could tell him what she wanted from the arch, as he gave his email address to the photographer.

While Lily wrangled the manager into submission over the arch and the delivery, Henry struggled to get his feelings under control.

He and another staff member from the store cruised the aisles getting multiples of the items Lily had picked out, before paying and arranging delivery of it all, including the arch, to the estate. Less than forty minutes later they were heading back out into the car park and towards the Jeep, Henry relishing the slap of slightly cooler air against his skin.

He rounded the passenger side of the Jeep and held the door open for Lily, who paused before getting into the car. She placed a hand on his forearm, and he would have sworn that he could feel the heat of her skin through the layers of his coat and jumper.

'I can't thank you enough, Henry.'

★★★

Lily grabbed the interior handle above the seat and hauled herself into the Jeep. Henry had asked her to trust him. And she had. Without reservation, she realized, without question. And he had made it that the wedding would be even more beautiful than she had hoped. It wound around her heart and pulled tight. She hadn't trusted or relied on anyone other than the girls for a very long time.

She glanced at the clock that illuminated the moment Henry turned the key in the engine.

It was so much later than she had thought. 'I should probably be getting back to the restaurant.'

'Nope,' Henry said, shaking his head.

'What? Why not?'

'Because.'

'That's not an answer, Henry,' she growled. 'Really, I need to get back. There's a lot to do before the dinner service.'

'All of which, I'm sure, Vihaan has perfectly under control,' he said with a confidence she suddenly found infuriating.

She watched as he pulled the Jeep back onto the motorway, only they were heading further away from Hawke's Cove, rather than back to it.

'Henry ...' There was trust and then there was control.

'If it helps, you can consider it a kidnapping.'

'It doesn't help. And I wasn't joking. I need to get back.'

'Kate messaged to tell me that everything was under control and that you weren't needed back at the restaurant.'

'My manager texted *you*?' she demanded, knowing that the proprietorial streak of jealousy suddenly rushing through her veins was wholly unwarranted. Kate was a happily married woman, but it wasn't that. It was the thought of decisions being made about her restaurant without her knowledge or permission that struck her hard. 'This is ridiculous.'

'What is ridiculous is the fact that you're not able to take one day off.'

'I can take a day off if I want. I just—'

'When?'

'When what?'

'Was the last day off you had. No restaurant *and* no wedding planning?' he asked.

Lily bit her lip, scanning her mind back through the last few months. When she realized that she couldn't remember, she tried to come up with a plausible answer that wouldn't make her look so … so pathetic.

'That's what I thought. I'm taking you to dinner.'

'You're taking *me* to a restaurant and you think that's a day off for me?' she answered wryly.

'Well, it's not exactly a restaurant, but we do need to eat. And I'm curious to see if it's still there.'

'What's still there?'

★ ★ ★

An hour later, he pulled the Jeep down into the heart of another cove further up the cost than Hawke's and into a car park looking out over the sea.

Once again, he opened her door, Lily knowing enough to wait for his act of chivalry this time, and oddly touched by it.

'My lady,' he said, gesturing her towards an old pub that banked the harbour.

Dusk was beginning to fall, and the lights inside the small building looked inviting. Now that she was technically kidnapped, she supposed it would be churlish to refuse. Especially after everything Henry had done for her today.

They walked into a small low-slung snug and were greeted by the soft smell of ale and firewood, despite the lingering warmth of the summer's day. Background conversations from the pub drifted over her gently and as she sat at the table Henry had pointed to, she heaved a sigh of relief and tiredness.

She looked about the room: the walls, perhaps once white were slightly yellowed with age and what was probably nicotine stains, brass jugs and various seaworthy paraphernalia hung on the walls, little nooks and crannies were wedged with tables and patrons huddled together over their drinks or meals. It was so cosy, she couldn't help but smile. Warm and inviting, the smell of the food was surprisingly good and she realized she hadn't eaten anything since this morning. Suddenly famished, she reached for the plastic-covered menu on the table.

Henry returned from the bar with a glass of sparkling water for himself and a gin and tonic for her. She frowned. 'I'm not sure I should be drinking on an empty stomach.'

'It won't be empty for long. Besides, a G&T won't hurt you.'

'How did you know what to get me?' she asked.

'I ... it reminds me of you.' He shrugged self-consciously. 'Besides, what self-respecting Englishwoman would ever turn down a G&T?'

'Why does it remind me of you?'

'The juniper-and-gin-cured salmon at your restaurant,' he explained as she took an appreciative mouthful and smiled. God, that was good. 'Can I ask about the name?'

'The Sea Rose?' He nodded in return. She took a breath. 'When I came back from London, I was a bit of a mess. I couldn't have stayed there after Alistair, I just wanted to be home. But I'd left before finishing the culinary college and didn't really have a plan. That's when Blake came to me with the idea of the herb garden. The first herb we planted, having cleared the space, was sea rosemary. It had always reminded me of Dad, because the trawler he worked was called the *Sea Rose*.'

'So The Sea Rose,' Henry concluded.

'It was a way of being connected to them both.' She shrugged, the name of her restaurant having taken on such a more powerful meaning than it had when Blake had still been alive. 'Blake was the one who encouraged me to buy the restaurant, when I would have been content just to work in the kitchen at the estate.' She smiled at the memories.

Henry frowned. 'How did you ...'

'Afford it?' Lily guessed, almost seeing his brain trying to work out the financials. 'I wouldn't have been able to in a million years had it not been for Mr Hailsworth. Rich DFLs have been buying up land in Hawke's Cove for years.'

'DFLs?'

'Down From Londons,' she clarified. 'Mr Hailsworth used to run the butcher's and really didn't like the way things were going. In order to keep the property in local hands, he gave me a price that I still can't quite believe,' she said, shaking her head in wonder. 'He only wanted enough to relocate to Australia to be with his family, so I got it for a song, as they say.'

A waitress came over to take their food order and then retreated.

'Blake helped a little, which I have paid back,' she insisted, even as he raised his hands in a gesture of surrender. 'And quite a few people in the town helped. More than I could have imagined. Much of the building and renovations were done for free or with the help of people chipping in, in their spare time. Mrs Whittaker actually paid for the flooring.'

'Really?' Henry said, clearly surprised.

'Really. It shocked me too. So in return, she gets a free meal once a week. Though she does pay for her wine,' Lily added, taking a sip of her drink. 'And I love the fact that it feels as if it's really part of the town.' And she really did. Loved that wherever she looked in her restaurant, she could name the people who helped with that particular part. Each little bit having a story to tell of an act of kindness, generosity and healing. It had gone a huge way to helping the hurt that had been done by Alistair's selfish actions.

'Did you ever track him down?'

'No. I'm pretty sure he went up to Scotland. But … it wasn't a criminal case, because we'd had a joint bank account. And a civil case would have cost more than I ever would have recovered. And besides, I just wanted to put the whole thing behind me. It was embarrassing enough as it was.'

'But if that's what he was relying on—'

'Then he got what he wanted and that's fine. He might have stolen my money, but look at me. I have a successful restaurant and a wonderful home and I'm happy.'

He levelled her with a gaze as if trying to see through her words to the truth. But it *was* the truth. She didn't undervalue what she had achieved. She knew it had taken hard work, and a few sleepless nights at the beginning. But with Blake's help, her mother's, Victoria, Zoe and Malie's constant cheerleading and support, she *was* happy. Just … a little lonely sometimes, that was all.

'What about you?' she asked, shifting the focus of their conversation over to him. 'Apps? How did that happen?'

'Well, it wouldn't have happened without Ben, or my grandfather's trust fund.'

'Your business partner? From Thailand?'

'He's as English as they come, but yes,' Henry said with a soft smile that gentled his features and made him even more handsome in the half light of the pub. 'We met in Thailand. We were both doing "the travelling thing", and got talking in a bar on the beach one night. He was midway through a tech degree, and had taken some time off because he didn't like the constraints of fitting his ideas into the syllabus.

'Ben was resistant to the sheer amount of weight put on the money-making applications and was disheartened by the lack of support for apps that had a more beneficial impact on society. And we shot some ideas around and came up with one that … that suited us both.'

'Suited?' Lily asked, wondering why Henry was being reticent all of a sudden. He sighed, the deep inhalation widening the breadth of his chest beneath the cables of knitwork on his jumper.

'I … I suggested an idea based on connecting students, teens, with a charity that could provide support for people who felt they couldn't reach out. Who felt they couldn't ask for help through the usual channels – parents and teachers,' he clarified.

'People like Claudia,' Lily realized.

Henry nodded. 'If she'd been able to speak to someone, anyone, things might have been different.' He gripped his glass, his knuckles nearly white. She placed a hand around his, until his grip loosened and a small smile raised his lips. 'It was a success. The app won awards, but more importantly, it actually helped. With that we were able to develop more, invest in other projects, and fund the Avery app without investment. Which was brilliant because it meant there was no need for adverts or monetization that would take away from the app's main goal. To help.'

Claudia Avery. He'd even named the app after her. She realized, in that moment, that Henry hadn't walked away never looking back. He hadn't cut his ties to the past at all. Instead, it had driven him to do something that helped others. To try to make sure that people like Claudia, people who struggled, had some kind of support. To try to make sure that what happened to them, didn't happen to others.

'Do Claudia's parents know?' Lily asked.

Henry shook his head. 'I didn't think that they'd welcome any kind of contact from me. And,' he shrugged, 'it would have taken absolutely no digging whatsoever to see that I was linked to it.'

'That's an amazing thing, Henry. Blake would have been so proud of that and what you've achieved.'

He shrugged off her words and Lily saw that he'd been just as devastated and damaged by the accident as Victoria or Zoe. Not physically, no. But he had most definitely been hurt by it.

Their food arrived, and whether through hunger or mutual agreement, they finished nearly the entire meal without another word until Lily laid down her fork, her belly full and let loose an appreciative moan. 'That was good.'

'Mm hm,' Henry agreed, pushing his plate back.

'How did you know it was here?'

'Mum and I used to stop here before dropping me off at the estate after the divorce. It became our thing.' He smiled fondly.

'How is she doing?' Lily asked.

'Good,' he said, nodding. 'She's doing well. Remarried, and the husband's not a *complete* arse, which helps. No step siblings, but ... she's happy. He makes her happy. Speaking of which, tell me about the man who has stolen Victoria Scott's heart.'

★★★

Lily had fallen asleep only twenty minutes into the drive home, leaving Henry to muse about their conversations over dinner. He hadn't planned on telling her about the app he'd named after Claudia, but he'd not been able to shake the thought planted by Ben during his visit. Henry hadn't told her to impress her, or to in some way make up for his involvement in the accident that had devastated so many people. But he'd wanted her to know about *him*. And that way madness lay. He knew it as surely as he knew he had to leave Hawke's Cove. Eventually.

After dropping Lily off at her restaurant – her 'goodnight'

happily sleepy – he pulled into the driveway of the estate and his phone pinged. He glanced at the notification and paused before opening the email from the wedding photographer from the warehouse. He both did and didn't want to see the image, somehow instinctively knowing that it would change things.

He opened the attachment and waited as the picture downloaded.

The air rushed from his chest when he saw it. Lily looking up at him, her eyes bright and shining, her fingers pressed against her lips, half covering the smile of pure pleasure crossing her features. Her thick auburn hair trailed down her back in waves. And him. Looking down at her as if she was the centre of everything. It was the perfect wedding photo. A wedding that could never be.

And he knew in that moment he would never delete that email. That he'd keep the photo of them, in front of the wedding arch, with him for ever.

CHAPTER EIGHT

LILY LAUGHED. 'I STILL can't believe you moved all those empty barrels.'

'You doubt my manly prowess?' he said in mock shock.

'Not at all.' And she didn't. She really didn't.

They were sitting in the restaurant, after the breakfast rush, having hauled out enough empty wine barrels and cases to decorate the orangery.

'I told you we didn't need to buy them.'

'Yes, you did. And yes, you were right,' she replied, giving him his due.

The smug look of satisfaction on Henry's face was a picture, until his gaze settled on something in her hair. Frowning, he reached over and gently pushed back a fallen lock.

'Cobweb,' he explained as he withdrew his hand, her cheeks hot from just the proximity of him.

Kate came over to the table and placed two more coffees in front of them.

'You are a goddess,' Henry exclaimed as he reached for the hot rich brew.

'I don't think I've ever seen anyone put away so much coffee in my life,' Lily remarked.

'I live on the stuff.'

'It's a good thing I have a constant supply, then,' she said without thinking. Because that implied more. Implied something long-term. And when she risked a look up at him, she knew that he'd realized it too. And something almost sorrowful entered his gaze, and she regretted her careless words. Because after the wedding, he would be gone. The sale of the estate had been agreed, subject to searches and terms. She could have bitten off her own tongue then.

In the last week, Lily had given Vihaan and Kev free rein over the restaurant while she focused almost exclusively on the wedding. And she'd been surprised by how much happier she felt. How much easier it was to have Henry help her with all the wedding stuff. The decorations had arrived, and in a few days they'd have the orangery set up and ready for the wedding that was now only a week away.

Casting her mind over all the things that she and Henry had achieved since the Dream Wedding Disaster, as she was now call-ing it, she couldn't work out what she would have done without Henry. Even just having someone to bounce ideas around with had been a godsend, but more than that, he'd made suggestions and even got stuck in. Manly prowess indeed.

The bell over the door chimed and Lily turned to see who it was. Her sudden and shocking high-pitched squeal was met with one equally as impressive.

'V!' Lily cried as she jumped out of her chair, rushed across the restaurant and gathered her best friend in her arms, squeezing her for dear life. 'I didn't think you were coming until later?'

'We managed to get away from London sooner than we'd planned. It's sooo good to see you, Lils!'

Lily gave Victoria an extra squeeze, thanking all the deities for making this happen. Until the moment that she'd seen Victoria walk through the door – looking amazing in what she could only presume to be another one of her stunning dresses – she hadn't realized just how much she'd been hanging onto this moment. She inhaled the soft floral perfume Victoria had been wearing since they were teens.

'Do I get one of those, or is it just for V?' Oliver asked, laughing.

'Of course,' Lily said, finally letting Victoria go and turning to the man who had won her best friend's heart and hand in marriage. 'Hi, Oliver,' she said with a smile, reaching up to give him an equally strong hug. 'I can't believe you guys are here.'

She couldn't wipe the smile from her face if she tried. 'I've missed you so much,' she said, looking into Victoria's warm brown eyes where a gaze of happiness tinged with understanding answered back.

'I'm sorry that I couldn't get here sooner, Lils.'

'It's fine, V. Truly,' she said, shaking her head, knowing that her friend had wanted to be here sooner, had desperately wanted to be there for Blake's funeral. But Lily hadn't lied. It *was* fine. Because Henry had been there, had somehow filled some of that loneliness she'd felt before they'd reached their agreement.

Taking a step back, she eyed Victoria's dress. It slashed across the neck in a vintage-inspired cut, nipping in at the waist and making the most of Victoria's petite assets. 'Niiice,' she couldn't help but remark as Victoria did a half dip, half curtsy.

'Why thank you. One of my latest creations,' she said with a shoulder shrug that did nothing to dim the light of pride in her eyes, until it morphed into confusion the moment Victoria caught sight of the man sitting at the table behind her.

Henry.

By the time she'd turned, Henry had risen from his chair. It was only by the contrast in how he'd been just moments before that she could tell he was slightly uncomfortable. The cocky arrogance displayed jokingly only minutes ago was gone and something restrained had taken over. Something almost nervous.

Lily realized that this was the first time Henry and Victoria would have seen each other since the accident. And the last thing that Victoria had heard her say about him was that he was horrible. Suddenly all Lily wanted was for Victoria to see the Henry that she had seen in the last few weeks. The one who made her laugh, who helped shoulder her burdens, who had teased her out of her single-minded focus to embrace the moment – and the man who had not only allowed them to have the wedding at the estate, but had helped make it better.

To her surprise, Victoria walked straight to him and gave him a hug. Not as long and deep as the one they had shared, but much more than either she or Henry – judging by the look of slight shock in his eyes – had expected.

'Henry. It's good to see you,' Victoria said with warmth.

'You too, Victoria,' replied Henry, still apparently startled by her greeting.

'And this,' she said, turning and reaching an arm out to her fiancé, 'is Oliver Russell.'

Oliver reached an arm across the table and they shook hands.

Lily directed Ollie and Victoria into chairs on one side and sat beside Henry on the other.

'Do you guys want anything? Coffee? Tea? We're a little late for breakfast, but I can rustle you something up, no problem.'

'Oh my God, do you have any of those almond croissants left? I'd literally swim the ocean for one of those things,' Victoria exclaimed.

Kate, who had been hovering by the counter, smiled as Victoria caught her eye. 'Almond croissants and coffee coming right up.'

'You're a star, Kate.'

'You guys can all come more often, you're doing a-maz-ing things for my ego!'

'Yeah, sorry, Victoria. Henry beat you to it and raised the stakes with the declaration that she was a goddess,' Lily teased.

'Oh, he did, did he?' Victoria replied, eyeing Henry up.

Smiling, Henry shrugged. 'But she is. Best coffee in the whole of Devon.'

'You know it's my coffee, right?' Lily interjected, feeling just a smidge left out of the praise.

'But it takes a steady hand to make that string of hearts in the milk,' teased Victoria.

'And who do you think taught her how to do that?' demanded Lily.

'And who would have milk in their coffee anyways?' Henry said, outraged.

'Sacrilegious,' both Henry and Oliver intoned at the same time.

Kate was back in no time with a heap of almond croissants and four coffees. 'Give me a shout if you need anything, or want to sing my praises more.'

Victoria grabbed for the top one, batting away Ollie's hand reaching for the same croissant, and suddenly Lily remembered batting Henry's hand away from the picnic she'd made the day of the wine tour. She risked a glance up at Henry and when she caught his eye, wondered if he was thinking the same thing.

'I'm so glad we ran into you,' Oliver said to Henry. 'We've been wanting to thank you for allowing us to hold the wedding at the estate.'

'I'm glad we could make it happen,' Henry replied, looking again at Lily and including her in the thanks.

'And I wanted to say how sorry I was to hear about Blake. I never met him, but V's told me a lot about him. He sounded like a good man.'

Henry nodded, his eyes on his coffee cup. Lily felt a sharp stab of pain for him.

Taking a deep sigh, he said, 'Thank you. He ... he was.'

Lily let out a breath she hadn't realized she was holding. The way that Henry had acknowledged the reference to Blake was so different to how it had been weeks before. She couldn't help but feel the warmth that spread through her knowing that Henry had found some sort of peace with his father since the night she had shown him the contents of the wine chest in the cellar at the estate.

'How's your father? Lily said that he's been trying a new treatment?' Henry asked Oliver.

'Yeah, he's actually doing pretty well with it,' Oliver replied, clearly relieved. We're trying to get him to cut back on work completely. We're nearly there, but he can't help it every now and then.'

Lily was trying to focus on the conversation between the boys, but she caught Victoria's overly wide-eyed stare, the tilt of her head indicating, *What the hell?* more effectively than if she'd said it out loud. Lily mouthed, *Later,* with that shock of panic that Henry might see the exchange, and refocused on what Oliver was saying.

'But the department store—'

'The one in Chelsea?' Henry queried.

'Yup, it's doing a roaring trade,' Ollie smiled, taking up Victoria's hand in his and rubbing his thumb over the base of her thumb.

'You've got a pretty good reputation,' Henry remarked of Russell and Co's worldwide department stores.

'Thank you. Yours isn't that bad either, Hawkesbury.' Henry seemed to take the praise on the chin. 'Have you ever partnered with anyone in retail? Because I was thinking—'

'No business talk at breakfast,' Victoria cried before finishing the last bite of her croissant. She sighed, happy and seemingly in food heaven, then leaned back to take in the restaurant. 'Oh, Lils!' she exclaimed, scanning the living wall behind the counter. 'It's not just a green blob!'

Lily nearly choked on her coffee in indignation. 'No, V, it's not just a green blob!'

'So you fixed the irrigation?'

'After a bit of trial and error, yes,' Lily conceded.

'The place looks great, Lils. Really great,' she insisted and a streak of pride and pleasure wound through her.

Oliver threw an arm over Victoria's shoulder and pulled her gently back against his side, pressing a kiss onto the crown of her head. She turned suddenly and snatched the kiss from his lips to hers.

Lily's hands tingled. She wanted that. It wasn't jealousy, or envy, just … a longing. That easy companionship and affection. But every time Lily tried to imagine it, the only person she saw in her mind was Henry and she literally had to sit on her hands to stop herself from reaching for him.

She felt a pull from him, magnetic and impossible to deny. It wasn't just the easy affection between Victoria and Ollie that had conjured it. She'd felt it almost from the beginning, and when they'd stood in front of the wedding arch in the warehouse, she'd wanted … she'd wanted … Oh there was no use pretending, she'd desperately wanted him to kiss her.

'Earth to Lils?'

'What?' she said, looking up, realizing that she'd been staring at the table. 'Sorry?'

'I was just saying,' Victoria pressed on, despite the overly watchful frowning gaze she pinned on her, 'that Ollie has to head back first thing tomorrow and … I have to go with him,' she winced.

'V! I thought you were going to be back now until the wedding?' Lily couldn't help but cry.

'I was … but … well …'

'No need to go full drama queen on me. Spit it out,' Lily demanded, not unkindly.

'I have a meeting about the first Victoria Scott bridal collection … *in Paris!*'

'What?' Lily gasped looking at Oliver, who raised his hands. 'Don't look at me, this was *all* V,' he insisted.

'Paris? *Paris?!* Oh my God, V that's amazing,' Lily said, leaping out of her chair, grabbing her friend, jumping up and down and squealing in sheer delight.

'Here we go again,' Ollie groaned affectionately.

'I know, I know, I can't believe it. I'm still trying to pinch myself and I'm genuinely terrified I won't be able to pull it off—' Victoria's words rushed out in one long breath.

'Of course you will,' Lily replied. 'You're amazing, your designs are fabulous, and they'd be lucky to have the opportunity to sell your creations. So lucky.' She held Victoria at arm's length, only to look her in the eyes when she said, 'You've done it, V. It's all happening for you and I am so, so happy for you.'

'She's going to start crying,' Ollie mock whispered to Henry.

'Which one?' Henry returned in an equally obvious stage whisper.

'Good point. Fiver says they both do it?'

'I'm not touching that bet with a bargepole.'

'And I wondered,' Victoria said over the boys, 'if you might be free this afternoon?'

Lily knew she was worried about asking because rarely was she able to drag herself away from the restaurant. And suddenly she was sad. Sad that her best friend was so worried about asking if Lily had time for her. Had she been that lost in her work? Her restaurant – the estate – that her closest friend feared that she might say no?

But in the last few weeks she'd allowed Vihaan free rein in the kitchen so she could prepare for the wedding.

'Of course!' Lily replied, covering the sense of guilt stirring in her chest. 'I'm free right now and for as long as you need me,' she insisted.

'That's amazing, because I was hoping that you might like to try on your bridesmaid's dress?'

'Yes! Yes, yes, yes!' cried Lily and they descended into another round of excited squealing.

'And *that's* my cue to leave,' Oliver said with a smile.

'Mine too,' Henry said, backing away from the table.

'Actually,' Oliver said, halting Henry's departure, 'I was wondering if you might be able to show me around the estate? I haven't seen it yet.'

'Sure,' Henry said. 'While we're at it, we could … Sample the wines,' he concluded at precisely the same time as Lily said, 'Stay off the wines.'

★★★

'*What*,' Victoria said, gently draping the garment bag over the back of a chair in Lily's apartment, 'is going on with you and Henry Hawkesbury?'

'Nothing,' Lily replied, not making eye contact with her closet friend. Or she'd see. She'd see the very thing that Lily had been trying to deny to herself.

'Don't give me that, Lily Atwell.'

'I don't know what you're talking about.'

'You do.'

'Nope. No idea,' Lily replied determinedly, leaving Victoria in hysterics as Lily muttered about not being a river in Egypt.

'A river where?'

'Denial! I am not in denial,' she said, spinning around and collapsing on her bed.

'Protesteth much?'

'Probably,' Lily groaned, throwing her arms over her eyes. 'Oh, V, I don't know,' she said helplessly. 'He's not the boy we remember.'

'No, he's not. He's very much *all man* now,' Victoria teased.

'Hey! You've got your own one, V.'

'I'm engaged, not blind, Lils. So Henry's yours now, is he?'

'No, yes … maybe? I really don't know. He's changed, V. Really changed.' Lily thought of the way he had been when he came to dinner in her restaurant. He'd teased her, challenged her. He'd made her laugh. Made her feel *funny*. Made her feel more free, looser somehow. And, incomprehensibly, more herself than she had felt in years. In the days since the warehouse expedition, they'd rifled through the estate for things that could be used for the wedding, discovered nooks and crannies that neither had known about. And none of it had felt like work. None of it had that sense of pressure or panic she'd felt about the wedding or … she sighed. Life in general really. Sharing that time and those moments with someone had made her realize just how isolated she had become. No, not isolated as such. Just lonely.

'It's crazy. I like him. I do. I really do.'

Victoria looked at her with a massive smile on her face.

'But it's not like that. We haven't even kissed.'

'You don't need to kiss someone to fall for someone. I know that better than anyone,' Victoria replied, her eyes misting over, clearly lost in the memory of her and Ollie.

'And besides, what do I … how would I even go about … what, asking him out?' she said awkwardly, her face rumpled in embarrassment, before she scooped up a pillow and pressed it over her burning cheeks.

'Aw, you have a crush!' Victoria teased.

'I have an awful feeling it's more than a crush,' Lily moaned, her voice muffled through the feathers.

'Ask him to the wedding!' cried Victoria.

'What?' Lily demanding throwing the pillow onto the floor. 'I can't do that.'

'Of course you can. Ollie's cousin cancelled the other day, so it's not like we don't have the space.'

'But ... that's ...'

'Perfect. It'll be great! You'll look stunning in your dress, he'll be all trussed up in a tux or something – he looks like the kind of guy who has a tux lying around – and it'll be sooooo romantic,' Victoria crooned.

'OK. Fine. I'll give you that,' Lily conceded. 'But ... V, I've seen you, and Malie and Zo each find your person in the last few months. And I want that too.' Victoria's eyes shadowed a little with sympathy. 'But Henry, he's not sticking around. He's selling the estate and leaving Hawke's Cove as soon as he can. And ... I want someone who can stay,' she said helplessly, hating the fact that she felt so vulnerable admitting such a thing.

She didn't have to tell Victoria why. She could see that her best friend understood how important that was, after her father, after Alistair, after Blake. All the important men in her life who had gone – two through no fault of their own, and one just because ... But how it happened didn't really matter. *That* it had happened did. And Henry Hawkesbury, hell–bent on getting out of the cove, was the worst person she could ever fall for.

'Lils, did you not ever think about leaving Hawke's Cove?'

'What? No. London was bad enough.'

'But London isn't the only other place in the world.'

Discomfort swirled in Lily's stomach, but she couldn't quite put her finger on why. Since returning from London Lily had really not liked the idea of leaving Hawke's Cove. She felt safe here. 'V, Hawke's Cove is my home. I love it here. The Sea Rose, the Hawkesbury estate. Mum's just up the road now. And Malie's coming back … It's everything I've always wanted.'

'But it won't have Henry,' Victoria said gently.

'Who – despite popular belief – is not,' Lily asserted, rousing herself, 'the centre of the universe. But V, he has been so amazing with the wedding. He's helping out so much, I don't know what I would have done without him.'

'Oh, Lils. You know I would have been happy with a wedding planner,' she replied, frowning, and Lily hated the fact she'd just made her best friend feel guilty.

'I wouldn't have let you do that. And besides, it's been fun.'

'Really? Because … because I was a bit worried, you know. Given Alistair and your—'

'No. Don't do that, V.' Lily sighed, deep and hard. 'I'm not going to lie … It might have been a bit hard at the beginning, but my … That was something altogether completely different. And Henry's been helping out so much. And it's your wedding, V. *Yours*. And it's going to be amazing. So get that bridesmaid's dress out of the bag and let me see it.'

Instead of reaching for the bag, Victoria walked over to Lily, dragged her, laughing, off the bed, and took her in a warm hug. It was just what Lily needed. 'Thank you,' she whispered into the embrace.

'Anytime, Lils. Anytime you need it ever.'

Over Lily's shoulder, Victoria must have seen the picture on the side table as she pulled away and went to it, picking up the photograph of them taken just hours before the accident. She held it in her hands and Lily knew what she was seeing. Each and every one of them – Victoria, Malie, Zoe, herself – beaming at the camera like they had everything they'd ever wanted.

'We look so young,' Victoria half laughed.

'We *were* so young,' Lily grumbled.

'We had no idea, did we?' Victoria said sadly.

'No,' Lily said, thinking of the horror that night would turn into. Of how it would affect them all. And not just them. Henry too. Henry who had made an app so that people like Claudia – people hurting and in pain – could find some support. Some help. He'd taken their tragedy and made something beautiful from it. Just like Victoria, just like Zoe and Malie.

'But we didn't let it define us,' Victoria pressed on. 'And we're still smiling.'

'Yes, we are,' Lily replied, a warmth spreading through her. 'V, you're getting married!' she cried, feeling the sheen of happy tears against her eyelids.

'I am,' Victoria spun, her smile stretching into pure excitement and glee.

'So let me see that dress!' commanded Lily.

'OK, OK,' she replied, returning to the garment bag. 'Listen, obviously I know your measurements but it might need some tweaks, and—'

'Stop stalling. Gimme!' She held out her hand, her fingers opening and closing over her palm with impatience.

Victoria pulled down the zipper and gently drew out the swathe of sage-green-coloured silk.

A gasp fell from Lily's lips as Victoria held it up against her body so that Lily could see the dress.

'It's beautiful!' Lily cried as she took the beautiful skirts in her hands. The cool silk swam over her skin and poured down towards the floor as she ran her hands beneath the gorgeous material.

'You're all in slightly different styles. Yours is a V-neck,' Victoria said, gesturing to the top half of the dress.

'V. Seriously, this is stunning,' Lily sighed, unable to keep the awe from her voice.

'Well, it will be if it fits,' Victoria replied, biting her lip a little as she studied her creation.

'It will. I'm sure of it. OK,' she said, reaching for the fridge in the small kitchenette. 'You open this.' She retrieved a bottle of Hawkesbury Reserve and passed it to Victoria in exchange for the beautiful dress. She couldn't *wait* to try it on. 'I'll be back in a sec.'

'Didn't you just tell the boys that they weren't allowed to drink?'

Lily couldn't help but snort. 'And if you think for one minute that they'll not be, then I'm more than happy to take that back—'

'Nope! It's mine,' Victoria said of the sparkling wine. 'It's my *precious*,' she hissed in an exaggerated voice.

Lily heard the cork pop from the bottle as she slipped off her clothes and stepped into the stunning dress, loving the way that the material felt against her skin. She reached to her side to pull up the zip, securing the beautiful skirts at her waist and then upwards to where the top half pulled together about her chest, the thin spaghetti straps falling into place above the silk cresting between her breasts. She looked down at the skirts and saw a flash of white silk at her thigh. Frowning, she went to spread the skirts.

'No! Wait!' Victoria said, rushing over to the bathroom door and pulling it open for the floor-length mirror. 'Now. Walk towards it.'

'V—'

'Lils, just walk,' Victoria insisted.

She did as commanded and let out a cry of joy as she saw the way the sage green silk skirt parted as she did, to reveal a bolt of white silk panelled into what would have been a thigh-high split. The effect was stunning, but more than that, Lily spun to her friend, realizing what she'd done.

'It's the same white silk that my dress is made of,' Victoria said, with a shoulder shrug as if she hadn't just done the most beautiful thing. 'I wanted us all to have something from—'

Victoria didn't get to finish the words because Lily grabbed her into a hug, cutting off her words.

'It's stunning, V. So, so stunning,' Lily exclaimed, feeling her eyes well up.

'Don't you dare cry. Don't you dare. You'll set me off and then we'll both be sitting here crying into our bubbles,' Victoria ordered. 'And I *don't* cry into bubbles.'

'I call Lost Hours!' Lily demanded, causing Victoria to laugh and grab her phone. 'Wait, where is Zo at the moment? I've got no idea and I'm not sure what the time difference is.'

'Don't worry about Zo.'

'Oh, but it's, like, 6 a.m. in Hawaii! Malie will be—'

'Perfectly fine to answer the phone,' Victoria insisted, pressing buttons on her phone while Lily gazed at herself in the mirror. As she'd expected, the dress fit perfectly. No alterations needed. Her cheeks were flushed and her eyes sparkled as Victoria pushed a glass of bubbles into her hand. Suddenly, more than anything she wanted Henry to see her. Wanted to know what he would think of her dressed like this. Could almost imagine him standing behind her in a tux, looking so devastatingly handsome. She blinked and the image was gone.

'Morning, Malie,' she heard Victoria cry at the screen of her phone.

'This. Had. Better. Be. Good. V,' came the muffled response.

'Are you doing sit-ups?'

'My body is a lean, meaning, fighting machine. Got to keep it in shape.'

'Have you got the phone between your knees?' Lily laughed as she caught sight of Malie's head getting closer, then further from the screen.

'Yup.'

'My abs are aching in sympathy. Can you stop for a minute, you're making me dizzy? And I just want to get hold of Zo.'

The growl Malie emitted from the phone reached Lily's ears and she turned to reach for her own phone. She'd join Victoria on hers for the call, but she wanted to send them the wedding breakfast menu she'd finalized the day before.

'Stop growling and take a look at this while I get Zo in on the call.'

Lily turned to find Victoria pointing the camera on her phone at her and she was surprised the excited squeal from Malie didn't blow the poor phone's speakers.

'Oh my God, oh my God, Lils! You look amazing!'

'Ouch, what the hell?' Zoe's voice came from the phone.

'Look, just look at her,' commanded Malie. 'Oh, you look so beautiful!'

Lily smiled again, coming to perch beside Victoria, who was sitting in the armchair by the small fireplace. No *way* was she sitting in this dress, she didn't want to ruin it. In fact, she should change. But peering at the screen ...

'Zo, are you in a *bathroom*?' she asked, squinting at the phone.

'Er, yeah?' Zoe replied, looking slightly worriedly at Malie and Victoria.

'Why? And ... where *are* you?' Lily asked.

'Undercover assignment,' Malie rushed in.

'What?' Lily replied, half laughing.

'Yeah, what she said,' replied Zo. 'Is that the bridesmaid's dress? Is that what we're wearing, Victoria?' The conversation quickly descended into fits of giggles and laughter, giving Lily no chance to ask any more questions.

Giving up on her line of enquiry, she pressed send on the email that had the wedding breakfast menu and heard the satisfying ping of it arriving on the others' phones.

'What did you just send, Lils?' Zoe asked.

'The wedding breakfast menu.'

'Ohhhhh yeah. OK, spill.'

'You can read it.'

'But not while I'm doing crunches and on the phone to you guys. I can multitask but I'm not omnipotent.'

'Well,' Lily started, a mischievous light in her eyes. 'For the first course, we're starting with recycled mushroom consommé.'

'Oh … wait, what?' Victoria started in shock.

'You knew about that?' all the girls demanded at the same time.

'I think at this point, it's probably best to assume that I know everything,' Lily said, laughing.

'Not everything,' Zoe muttered cryptically.

Lily frowned, but Malie pressed on, 'What are we really having, Lils?'

She passed Victoria her own phone to read off the screen.

'Oh wow!' she cried. 'Gin-cured gravadlax and crab, goats' cheese and squash … what is a compression of game?' she asked Lily over the top of her phone.

'It's delicious. I promise.'

'Lils, this is incredible,' Victoria exclaimed.

'There's a meat, vegetarian and fish option for all courses—'

'And wine pairings—'

'Of course,' Lily replied in mock outrage; anything less would have been unthinkable.

'Ohhhhh, the celeriac cannelloni sounds amazing,' groaned Zoe from inside her bathroom.

'I want the Hawke's honey-roasted nectarines now. Right now,' demanded Malie.

'Well, you'll need to get them while you can,' Lily said, unable to tear her mind away from Henry and the sale of the estate for long. Malie pulled a sympathetic face.

'Is he still planning to sell the estate?'

'Yep,' Lily concluded, tight-lipped.

'Oh honey. I'm so sorry,' Zoe cut in.

'But for now,' Lily said, cutting through the dampener of the conversation, 'we have bridesmaids' dresses and bubbles, and we're celebrating the fact that Victoria is going to get married in seven days. And you guys will be back. And it will all be beautiful!'

***

Lily was still laughing at the squeals of hysteria from her friends three hours later, long after Victoria and Ollie had left to return to London. No matter what the future may hold, the smile was on her face now. And that was what mattered.

Lily was in the restaurant, helping Vihaan with the dinner prep. She didn't have to, but her flat had felt a little smaller and quieter after Victoria had left and she'd not really wanted to be alone. She'd been tempted to call Henry, but to what end? She didn't have anything from the wedding as an excuse and was still struggling with the knowledge that he wasn't sticking around. She'd made herself a promise after Alistair. No settling, no investing, no more time wasted on anything short of 'The One'.

She vaguely heard the restaurant phone ringing from the kitchen, reminding her that she'd left her mobile on charge back up in her room. She drew the knife along the chopping board, shuffling the small cubes of onion into the frying pan and reached for the garlic as Kate appeared at the pass.

'Lily, it's for you. It's Henry,' she said, presenting her with the phone.

Putting the knife down and wiping her hands on the apron, she reached for the phone, noticing that Kate's features had pulled into a grimace. 'What's wrong?'

'No idea, but he's freaking out,' she whispered.

Gingerly Lily pulled the phone to her ear. 'Henry?'

'Oh thank God. I've been trying to reach you for an hour.'

'I've been in the kitchen. What's wrong?'

'The Bacchus. I saw it today, when I took Oliver round the estate. I don't know what to do.'

'Clearly.'

'Lily!'

'Sorry. What's wrong with the Bacchus?' she asked, despite the fact that she was pretty sure that she knew exactly what was wrong with the grapes. She *had* tried to warn him.

'It's ready. For harvest. And I ... Lily, what the hell do I do?'

'Are you sure? It's been a while since—'

'I know what they look like when they're ready, Lily.'

She tried to hold back the smile, fearing that he'd be able to sense it from the other end of the phone.

'Don't smile.'

'I'm not,' she protested weakly.

'Yes, you are. I can hear it. As surely as I can hear the words "I told you so" circling in your head.'

'Well, I did try to—'

'Lily Atwell, you can crow all you like later. Just, *please*, help me fix this. If it's not harvested soon the whole crop will be wasted and as you're all about zero waste ... Please?'

'OK, OK,' she relented. 'How long do you think we have?'

'Realistically, it needs to be done tomorrow.'

'*Henry!*'

'I didn't know, Lily. I've been busy helping out with the wedding.'

She couldn't really fault him there. They'd both been so busy with it in the last few weeks. 'OK, here's what we do. You call John, he's got the phone tree—'

'A phone what?'

'Tree, it's a cascading phone list.'

'But he's in South Africa.'

'Nope, he got back two days ago.'

'Really?'

'Yes, really. He'll take care of the key people and I'll take care of the rest. I promise, Henry. It'll be fine. You just have to trust me.'

Hanging up the phone, she peered into the restaurant to find exactly the person she was looking for.

'Oh Kate, that was Henry,' she said, loudly enough for her voice to travel. Kate was looking at her as if she'd just lost her mind.

'But—'

'He's really stuck. The Bacchus is ready to be harvested,' she pressed on despite the fact that Kate was now looking around to see if she could fathom why her boss had taken on the projection of a Shakespearean actress. 'And he has no one to help him. It's such a shame that the town can't come together to help him out in his hour of need.'

Hour of need? Kate mouthed at Lily as if she'd gone too far.

'I'll have to go up to the estate tomorrow, but I'm really not sure how much one person can help …' she said, dramatically shrugging her shoulders. OK. She knew she'd never win an acting award, but when Mrs Whittaker popped up to pay her wine bill and promptly disappeared with something a little like glee in her eyes, Lily relaxed and sighed.

'What was that about?' Kate demanded.

'It's much better if Mrs Whittaker thinks it's her idea than for me to ask her to reach out and see who can help us tomorrow. And besides, she'll be able to rustle up a small army. In the meantime, can you call the head at Hawke's High? She's used to the harvest season by now and is more than used to calling in the sixth formers from their summer holidays. They get to put it down as work experience, and we get the help. It's win, win. I'm sure they won't mind the short notice.'

'And you'll be …'

'Preparing the food. No army marches on an empty stomach.'

CHAPTER NINE

AT 6.30 A.M. THE following morning, Henry heard a car coming up the drive.

Thank God.

Henry stopped pacing back and forth in the hallway, and launched for the door, pulling it open to find a beaten-up old beige Volvo pulling into a wide arc and shuddering to a rather alarming stop.

'Lily?'

The window wound down in jerks and he could just about make out Lily pumping the handle on the driver's side door.

'Where did you find *this*? It belongs in a museum!'

'It *belongs* to Kate, and for the use of it you will thank her profusely,' Lily said. 'I'm going to pull it round to the back of the kitchen. Can you open up the—'

'What does the kitchen have to do with the harvest?'

'All in good time,' she replied cryptically. And the only reason he relented was because the kitchen was near the coffee machine. And he needed more coffee.

Lily crunched the gears into place and took off round the side of the estate, leaving him half-open-mouthed and very much confused.

Clamping his mouth shut with a snap, he remembered her words from the night before.

I promise, Henry. It'll be fine. You just have to trust me.

Realizing that they had echoed his words to Lily only a few weeks earlier, he shook his head. How had she done that? She had trusted him, and now it was his turn. And ... And he was freaking out. Maybe *he* should have some brandy.

He'd been stupid to send all the staff away. Yes, he'd been thankful of the time and space he'd had, but Lily had been right. It was a working vineyard and although people could be cancelled, nature couldn't, and he really should have known better.

He couldn't count on two hands, let alone one, the number of times his father and he had been pulled into the vineyards for a sudden and early harvest. Though it had never caught his father by surprise. No. Because he'd known the grapes. He'd be out there daily, walking amongst the vines and keeping an eye on them. But Henry himself now? No. He'd not been paying attention. Because he'd been far too focused on a woman he shouldn't want and couldn't have.

Hearing the car door slam in the distance prompted him to act. He stalked through the estate towards the kitchen at the back and went to open the fire exit door to find Lily standing with several reusable wooden boxes of food piled in her arms.

'What is all this?'

'Brunch and dinner.'

'Lily,' he growled, his hold on the situation losing its grip.

'Henry Hawkesbury. Don't panic. I told you to trust me, so do it.'

She didn't have to remind him that she had trusted him. The unspoken words hung in the air between them.

'Fine,' he said, throwing up his hands in the air and leaving words like *coffee* and *infuriating* in his wake.

He turned on the coffee machine and tried to control his breathing as it warmed up, but the three minutes it took to produce the first two cups of rich, dark, aromatic liquid were just about enough time for him to surrender the fight.

He couldn't shake the feeling that he was letting his father down. He might be selling the damn place, but it didn't mean that he intended it to go to rack and ruin in the short time he had left. If this was to be the last harvest ... He shook his head. Why did that thought raise so much ache in his heart? Surely he shouldn't care. Surely he should have been able to walk away, clear-minded and happy-hearted?

He came back into the kitchen to see Lily embracing a tall, thin, shockingly thick-white-haired man he recognized from his youth.

'John,' he nodded, biting back the childish fear of painful disapproval.

'Henry,' John nodded, giving Lily one last squeeze before extricating himself from the embrace and holding out his hand for Henry to shake. Which he took. Thankfully.

'I can't thank you enough. I'm sorry it's such short notice.'

'Grapes is grapes,' John replied and a shiver of a memory from the past of his father saying exactly the same thing the morning of a harvest crashed over him.

'Grapes is grapes,' both Henry and Lily replied at the same time, her eyes wide at the sound of their voices merging.

'I guess I'm lucky that you were back in town. I hope your family is well?'

John cast a look to Lily, who adamantly looked away, before replying. 'Yeah. Guess so. Family is good. But I'd better make sure the boys are not destroying the distillery.'

'Can I get them coffee?' Lily asked.

'Na, they're young. Running on adrenalin and hormones. We'll be done in time for the volunteers. They can break then.'

Henry watched the exchange, suddenly feeling as if this would have happened whether he'd been there or not. Their conversation – John's familiar truncated sentences – spoke of practice, habit perhaps. And the tendril of suspicion that had begun to unfurl bloomed.

John left with a nod out the back of the kitchen and Lily made herself overly busy, unpacking the boxes she'd brought.

'You both knew, didn't you?' he demanded, finally voicing his suspicions.

'What do you mean?'

'That the Bacchus would harvest early.'

Her hands stalled, as if she wasn't sure what to do with the large loaf of bread. And she sighed, finally relenting. 'It's been an odd year weather wise. We suspected, but couldn't have known precisely when.'

'Precisely being two days after John planned his return?'

Lily let out a gentle laugh. 'John's more accurate than the Met Office.'

'Why didn't you tell me?'

She turned to him then, pinned her with her large dark eyes and grimaced. 'I did try.'

'Not very hard.'

'Well, you were kicking me off the estate at the time, and …'

'And I deserved it?'

'No,' she denied.

'Then what? You wanted to see what I'd do? This was a test?'

'No, Henry. It wasn't. Not for you anyway.'

'What do you mean?' he asked, thoroughly confused.

'I mean, that in just a few months, you won't own the estate, and I'll have nothing to do with it anymore. That I have to let it go just as much as you,' she replied sadly. 'But,' she shrugged, 'you asked for my help. And we'll get the harvest in, Henry. We'll make sure it's the best last harvest for everyone.'

★★★

An hour later, Lily wondered whether she'd said too much. She'd certainly not intended to put her feelings onto him and she hadn't missed the look in his eyes when she'd spoken. She'd buttered the sliced home-made bread, and all the bacon and sausages were in the oven – veggie, vegan and gluten-free options in the other ovens – so finally, she wiped her hands on the apron. Henry had left shortly after their exchange and gone to find John, who was sure to have put him to work.

She grabbed one of the many trays covered in cups and walked it out to the tables just outside the distillery barn as the first cars started to fill up the driveway. *And so it begins.*

Henry came to join her at the tables, several buckets in hand and the keys to the ATV.

'So you get to drive this year?' she commented.

'Apparently so. Though John didn't look too convinced.'

'It's like—'

'Riding a bike,' they both finished together, laughing, but it didn't take the shadow of concern from his eyes.

'What is it?' she asked, not liking seeing it there.

'There are so many vines. So many more than before.'

'It's not our first rodeo, Henry. We've done it before and we can do it again,' she gently insisted.

'But why would they?'

'What do you mean?'

'Why would they help *me*?'

In an instant, Lily saw all the hurt and all the damage done by his childhood. The pain of a whole town turning against him in the wake of the accident with Claudia. She might have missed it at the time, so focused on Victoria and Zoe getting better, the inquest and then just recovering herself. But she hadn't missed the way that the locals had stopped and stared at him once he'd returned. Oh, they were slightly more polite in her restaurant, but even so. Though, the more that he'd been around, the more they got used to him. And she hoped that she was right in what she said next.

'They would help because you need it. And yes, because the estate needs it too. Besides,' she said, brushing away a fallen lock of hair with her forearm, 'it's fun.'

'Fun? Are you *crazy*?'

'It is!'

Anything further she might have said was cut off by the sounds of the school coach making its way up the drive.

'What the …'

As the coach pulled up along the far end of the drive, Mrs Mayberry from Hawke's High disembarked, and counted off the thirty sixth formers as they piled out. Quick on their heels were Kate and Vihaan arriving in his little red beetle.

Henry looked at her then, his eyes bright and an expression so intense she wanted to reach for him. He seemed astounded that so many people would turn out for this, for him, that he was overwhelmed. And suddenly she was sad. Sad for him and the chains of the past she could see so clearly still wrapped around him.

'Henry—'

'We're here,' announced a very eager Mrs Whittaker, with a team of around fifteen villagers queuing up behind her.

'Mrs Whittaker,' Henry exclaimed.

'Don't look so shocked, Henry Hawkesbury. When we are needed, we rally,' she said, almost outraged at the implication that they would do anything but. With a sniff, she was off, leading her little team away towards the vines. 'Don't worry, we know our way,' she called imperiously. And Lily had to bite her tongue at the overly familiar insinuation.

Henry took a deep breath – seeming to stifle the growl Lily could imagine was in the back of his throat – and followed Mrs Whittaker and her team into the vines.

She greeted Kate and Vihaan with warm hugs.

'Where would you like us, *chef*? Vihaan asked.

'Can I leave you two to man the coffee and brunch? All the food is set up in the ovens, ready for the break at about eleven thirty. And when that's done, we'll probably need to set up the large tent – John will know where it is – for after the picking. Grab whatever you can use for seating. The chairs arrived for the wedding, so we can use those; if you can put them around the barn tables outside the distillery, that would work. And we'll probably need a good few bottles of wine for after too. There's bread, cheese, pâté, the makings of potato salad, a whole smoked salmon and—'.

'A banquet fit for a king?'

Lily smiled ruefully. 'Pretty much.'

'Consider it done. And where will you be?'

'Making sure that Henry doesn't kill Mrs Whittaker,' she replied with grim determination as she made her own way towards the vines.

★★★

The early morning sun was warm against the long sleeves of Lily's top. She knew that many people had romantic notions about grape picking, but she hadn't lied. It was hard work. Sticky, messy, dirty, hot and so much fun, she couldn't wipe the smile from her face.

Down the rows of vines she could see at least twenty people snipping at the bunches of grapes with their secateurs. Just like she was. Dropping them into the buckets at their feet and moving on to the next when they'd cleared a section. The other half of the group had started at the opposite end of the vineyard, working their way towards the middle.

Henry was manning one of the ATVs and one of John's boys was collecting full buckets and throwing the grapes into the trailer, their progression up and down the vines painfully slow, stopping and starting every few metres. When the trailer was full, Henry would drive the load over to the distillery where people were already managing the sorting process: emptying the load into the vibrating hopper feeding the grapes into the destemmer which would then pour them onto a conveyor that lifted the grapes into the sorting machine.

Snip, snip, drop.

That was all Lily knew for a while, marvelling at the dusty pearly grapes, so natural and pure and in their element. She smiled. Henry had been right. A few days later and they could have lost the whole crop. The gentle hum of quiet conversations between the pickers washed over her as Lily took a moment just to feel the sun on her face, to take in the scent of earth and grapes, the sound of the birds in the sky. Had it really been nearly a year since she'd last done this? When Blake had been the one driving the ATV? Yes, it was hard work, but it never felt like that. Not really. It felt like she was giving something back to the world. Allowing a crop to have ripened, removing the grapes before they spoiled, allowing the vines to direct their energy into growing new fruit.

Which was why she ignored the calls for coffee and bacon rolls. If this was going to be her last harvest, she wanted just a moment alone. Here. With her memories. It was then that she truly understood Henry's need to send away the staff. She hadn't lied when she told him that at the restaurant. She knew what it was like to have her grief on display for others. But this ...

She felt him approach, even before the long shadow he cast fell over her skin.

'Not hungry?'

She smiled, her face still turned to the sun.

'Not yet,' she replied.

▲ ▲ ▲

Henry didn't think he'd ever seen anything more beautiful than Lily's upturned face, eyes closed, basking in the warmth of the sun. It glinted off the natural highlights in her auburn hair, painted a rosy glow on her pink cheeks. The sight of it all hit him like a punch to the chest. And he drank it in. Imagining a hundred more summers like this one, harvesting the grapes, Lily with him, helping him. Loving him.

Dammit.

'Don't go,' she said before he could even get his mind to listen to his wayward body. He wanted to run, but as she opened her eyes, the look of hope in them cut him to the quick. He nodded, incapable of forming words, incapable of refusing her this, when he knew he would refuse her so much more.

'I love it out here.'

'I can see.'

'Can you see why?' she asked, her eyes sombre.

'I can see why you do.'

'But you can't see yourself loving it?'

I can see myself loving you.

'This was his, Lily. Not mine. It was never mine,' he ground out, walking away before he said something, did something that couldn't be taken back. Like promise her he would stay. Like taking her in his arms and kissing her.

★ ★ ★

Over the next few hours, he lost himself in work, in driving the ATV between the vines and delivering the grapes to the distillery.

At least John seemed to appreciate his focus, even if he knew that Lily sent long, lingering glances at his back as he did so.

Why couldn't she see that she deserved better – *more*. More than he could ever give her. He wasn't stupid, had felt the attraction between them, building the more he got to know her, rather than lessening like all of his previous relationships. And he both desperately wanted it and thoroughly resented it. There was no future for them. Not one that didn't involve him staying in Hawke's Cove.

But he pushed those thoughts aside, as he slowly joined in the banter between John and the guys working directly with him. Jokes about previous harvests, about lovers and friends, football teams and pecking orders. It reminded him of being with Ben, but … Henry realized that much of his work really was just him and Ben. Yes, they had staff and they had teams of people working for them, but the one-to-one contact was just that. One to one. He could no longer deny the sense of community that rose up around him.

As did the memories. Images of his father hauling his little eight-year-old self beside him onto the ATV, perched like a little prince on a carriage surveying his kingdom. John – no white hair then – raising a salute as they passed, an affectionate smile on his face.

Then, only a few years later, trying and failing to throw the grapes into the trailer, still nowhere near tall enough to reach up over the edge. Instead, he'd retrieved all the full buckets, bringing them to whoever it was who hauled the grapes over the lip and poured them into the trailer.

When his father had pressed £5 into his hands for all his hard work, he'd stared at the money, thinking he was the richest boy in town. He'd clutched that £5 note for at least three days, until they'd gone into town and he'd blown the entire amount in a sweetshop, his mother complaining that it would ruin his teeth, his father remaining silent, but beaming with pride.

A pride only matched by the sight of the entire village coming together to help with the harvest. He remembered how his father had loved it. Walking the vines, stopping to talk to each and every volunteer, joining in with the picking as well as the driving. He frowned as he remembered his mother hating every minute of it and rarely trying to hide her displeasure. And suddenly he felt sad. Sad that his father had loved something so much and that the two people closest to him, his wife and son, had so clearly not. Until Lily. It dawned on him that he was happy – and so very thankful – that his father had found someone to share the love and passion for the vines with.

'Reckon that'll do, don't you?'

John appeared at his shoulder pointing to where the two opposing lines of pickers had met in the middle of the vines.

'Honestly, John, I'm deferring to you in all matters wine-related,' he said, more than happy to leave it in the expert's capable hands.

'I don't know, you didn't do too badly, Hawkesbury.'

'High praise!' Henry exclaimed with a smile. 'But I'm taking it.'

John slapped him on his back and it really did feel like high praise. 'Right, we'll handle the last of the pick-ups, and if we can get the must into the presser in the next hour or so, we should be able to get it into the vats for the primary fermentation before midnight.'

'Right, I'll bring the last loads over to the distillery,' Henry said, flicking the ATV keys around his fingers, suddenly feeling a bit at a loss in the face of the forty or so volunteers who were now beginning to mill around, satisfied with all their hard work.

'Lily'll see to them,' John added before heading off to the barn.

As he walked towards where the last of John's staff were chucking the final buckets into the trailer, he recognized faces from his past. PC Ellis giving him a brief salute and a knowing smile, Mrs Whittaker issuing a raised eyebrow and an imperious hair toss – not that her perfectly coiffured mass of permed curls moved an inch – Henry was convinced that both of them were seeing little Father Christmases. The beefy owner of the Hope and Anchor with his thick arm thrown around his overly petite wife, both rosy-cheeked and smiling. Even a few of the men from the trawlers were there, but none of them had cast sneery side glances in his direction once since the beginning of the day.

Lily had been right, he realized. He had needed their help, and they had come. Not to inspect the estate, not to peer into his character, or judge or dredge up the past. But they'd come with open arms and hearts, and it humbled him. A group of teens whooped and hollered as they drifted towards the estate and he couldn't help but smile because he'd been like that once – carefree and fun.

The young guy filling the trailer nodded to him and went to retrieve the empty buckets, loading them on the side of the ATV so they could clear the vineyard.

'See you back there,' the guy said and headed off with a loping stride.

For just a moment, Henry stood in the now silent rows of vines that sloped down the hill. Yesterday, when he'd realized that the Bacchus was ready for harvest, he'd felt so helpless, panicked. But more than that, he'd cared. He'd cared that the harvest wouldn't get done, worried about damaging his father's vines. And now? As the sun was beginning to lower in the sky, the heat still there, the land full of the scent of sweetness from accidentally crushed grapes, the warm earth beneath his feet, he wanted to see it, taste it. The wines from today's harvest. He wanted to see how the vines would recover into the next season. Wondered briefly what other grapes his father had wanted to experiment with.

Was that what Lily had seen when he'd caught her basking in the sun earlier? Not the way things were, but what they could be?

Suddenly he wasn't sure he did want to sell the estate. As if she'd cast a spell over him, over the estate, and he was beginning to see less of the past and more of the future. Beyond Victoria's wedding, beyond the remaining three harvests that would be needed before the end of autumn. He wanted to see a Christmas here, the ground covered in snow, the estate decorated in holly, ivy, red ribbons and gold. The rooms full, not just of guests, but families and friends. A new year celebration, and spring.

The sound of laughter and a squeal of delight coming from the estate called him back to the present and back to sanity. His life wasn't here. It was in New York, or Singapore. His business was apps not vines. Maybe he'd been out in the sun too long. He jumped into the ATV and turned the key in the ignition, secretly relishing the bumpy drive through the vines to the distillery now that the pace wasn't slowed by the constant filling of the trailer. All men were boys at heart and even he couldn't deny the joy of driving the ATV.

He got the trailer backed into the wide open doorway of the barn they used for the distillery and jumped off the driving seat, pleasantly surprised by the hum of industry. When he'd been here ten years before, everything had been done by hand. But now sleek machines conveyed the destemmed grapes towards the sorting machine.

'Anything I can do?' he asked John as he came up to stand beside the man overseeing the operation.

'You can keep Mrs Whittaker out of the distillery. That bloody woman ...'

'Consider it done,' Henry promised.

'Aside from that, you just have to do the speech.'

Henry felt the blood drain from his face and his stomach turn. 'Speech?'

★ ★ ★

Lily stood back from putting the last finishing touches on to the cloth-covered table displaying the large picnic-style food she, Vihaan and Kate had put together. Well, mostly Vihaan and Kate, as they had shooed her out of the kitchen every time she got near.

Absentmindedly she scanned the groups of volunteers, some sitting and some standing around the area they'd created under the white tent. Benches and seating had been put out around the grass bank and throws scattered on the floor.

Each of the tables had large coolers with glistening bottles of white wine and rosé, the reds left out on the side by the glasses. Huge jugs of squash had already been nearly decimated by the thirsty teens who were filling the air with sounds of teasing and laughter. She caught sight of Kev staring longingly at Emma, surrounded by a group of her friends and the sight reminded her of Victoria, Malie and Zoe.

And suddenly she wished they were here, wished they could see this. Because this was why she loved Hawke's Cove. The community coming together, the different generations and groups of people all laughing and celebrating a successful harvest. She knew that her friends thought she should have seen more of the world than she had. Done some of the things they had, escaped the confines of their childhood and experienced life out there. But, she thought, shaking her head, she really did have everything she needed right here.

She continued to scan the crowd for something – not quite sure what she was looking for – until she caught sight of Henry making his way towards her. It stole her breath and made her heart soar.

He was looking down, so he couldn't see her staring. He looked so devastatingly handsome, his skin sun-kissed and building to a deep tan, his hair ruffled by hard work and the wind. His khaki T-shirt was no longer pristine, but slightly muddy and stained by grape juice from where he'd clearly wiped his hands on his flanks. The muscles in his strong arms were displayed to perfection, and the eye was drawn to narrow hips where his T was half tucked in at the waist of his jeans. It made her mouth water.

'Here, take this,' Kate commanded, pressing a cool glass, slick with condensation, into her hands.

She frowned at it.

'You just looked like you might need to cool off,' Kate said with a knowing glint in her eye. Before Lily could object, Kate pressed on. 'Just smile and say thank you.'

She did as Kate commanded, before looking back towards Henry in time to see his gaze search her out. For just a second, it was the two of them. She saw the flash of excitement, happiness even, as he saw her, and felt her own answering pleasure rise within her. And it made her yearn, made her want more. Want for this to be something they did together: the harvest, the party after, welcoming and giving.

He seemed startled when the entire group of volunteers registered his presence and began to clap. It morphed into a resounding cheer, and she could have sworn a blush rose to his cheeks. He waved the applause down and came to a halt, seemingly trying to find the right words to say.

'Before we get to the drinking and the amazing food, thanks to Lily,' another burst of applause ensued, 'there are a few key people I'd like to thank. I'd probably better thank John while he's not here, as he'd sooner push me off the estate before accepting thanks for his incredible efforts.' His words were followed by a round of laughter. 'I'd also like to thank Lily Atwell, because without her, I very much doubt that any of this would have actually happened.' He gestured to where she stood behind the table. Lily felt a blush rise to her cheeks as the applause turned in her direction. 'Not to mention the delicious food she and her team have given us today.' A few cheers sputtered through the claps and she wiggled her fingers in a little wave. 'I'd also like to thank Mrs Whittaker, who managed to rally a small army and, of course, the students from Hawke's High.'

Henry paused, waiting for the cheers and sustained applause to die down.

'I'd forgotten,' Henry said, trying again, 'I'd forgotten what it was to see everyone come together for a harvest. I'd forgotten that it wasn't something that you did on your own. Or hired outsiders in to do. I know that I've been away for a while,' he waved off the gentle catcalls and groans from the people, 'and for that I'm sorry. Because what you've done today – how you've come to help me, to help the estate – that's not something my father ever forgot,' he said as a gentle hush fell over the group. 'Nor was it something he ever took for granted.'

Lily felt the rise of goosebumps across her skin, sadness mixed with nostalgia and swirled with a strange happy kind of peace that Henry could not only see as much, but acknowledge.

'And I wanted you to know that. I also want you to know how thankful I am that you are here today. Not just to help, which of course you did,' he insisted as a gentle laughter broke out. 'But also, for a moment, giving me back something of my father.' At that, his gaze finally settled on Lily and pierced her heart with a look as much as his words.

She couldn't have held back the tear that escaped and rolled down her cheek so she hastily swiped at it before anyone could see.

'And that's it! Now is the time to drink – responsibly! – and eat and be merry,' Henry concluded.

It was some time before Lily saw him again, as she'd seen him stop and talk to each and every one of the volunteers, laughing with them and thanking them in person. And she didn't mind one bit. It felt good to see him do the very thing that his father had once done. She had just seen the last of the volunteers off and packed up Kate in her old Volvo – having deposited Lily's bicycle – and Vihaan in his beetle with all the now empty food containers and trays, before patting the little car on the back window and watching them disappear down the drive.

'Was that Kate and Vihaan?' Henry asked, coming to stand beside her.

'Yes, they said to say goodbye. They've still got prep for tomorrow's breakfast before they finish for the day.'

'I'm sorry you had to close the restaurant.'

'It's OK. It makes a nice change, and besides we do – *did* – it every year,' she said, trying to keep the dull ache at the thought of not getting to do another harvest at the estate at bay.

'One more for the road?' he asked, tipping the bottle of rosé in his hand.

'Why not?' she said, smiling as they went to the last of the blankets on the grass bank that looked out over the vineyard. It had been a beautiful day and … and she couldn't deny it. The desire to have Henry all to herself was too much.

He poured her a glass and passed it to her as she came to sit beside him, waiting. Because he seemed to have something he wanted to say.

'Was that OK? What I said,' he asked, refusing to look at her just in case it wasn't.

'Yes, Henry. It was more than OK. It was beautiful.'

He let out a small growl as if it was unmanly to be accused of being beautiful and she laughed.

'I couldn't remember what my father used to say and I wasn't sure …'

'You said what was right for you, and that's what counts. *And* I think you won over Mrs Whittaker.'

She thought he grumbled something about killing her with

kindness and resisted the desperate urge to lay her head on his shoulder. They were sitting so close, it wouldn't have taken much. She felt that same stirring within her. The desire to reach out, to touch, to take some of the strength she thought he might not realize he had. She was exhausted, but it was a happy exhaustion. One born from a hard day of good work.

'Dad used to say something and it always irritated me. But I think I might have misunderstood it,' he said into the setting sun.

'What was it?'

'He used to tell me that the estate had a bond with the town. That without one there wouldn't be the other.'

Lily nodded, smiling at the memory of hearing Blake say as much.

'I used to think that he meant that without the estate there wouldn't be a town. But,' he shrugged, 'I'm beginning to think he meant the opposite. That without the town, there wouldn't be an estate.'

Lily took a sip of her wine, not really believing that Henry wanted an answer or an opinion. Just someone to listen. She looked up at him then. The beautiful rich, almost golden hazel colour of his eyes so deep she could get lost in them. She saw his eyes draw to her lips and the spike of desire burst within her. The desire to kiss him so strong then, his own lips just an inch from hers. The moment stretched into an eternity and just when she thought he might close the distance between them, he turned away—

Taking with him the invitation to Victoria's wedding that had sat ready on her tongue. For all the love and pride she'd seen in his eyes that day, the excitement and satisfaction, he'd still not said anything about staying. About cancelling the sale of the estate. And she couldn't, wouldn't, watch another man she loved walk away from her.

CHAPTER TEN

TWO DAYS AFTER THE harvest, a storm blew in from nowhere. It was as if the sky just couldn't take the heat anymore and cracked open with jagged lines of lightning and claps of thunder so loud they shook the window panes all over the estate. From the living room, Henry stood at the window watching the rain bounce off the driveway below, reminding him of a Mediterranean storm he'd once been caught out in on his travels.

He'd not seen Lily since the harvest. Since he'd watched her head down the drive on that bicycle of hers. Another fork of lightning split the sky and his thoughts simultaneously. He should have kissed her. He was right not to have. Back and forth he went between the two. He tried to tell himself that nothing had changed. But Henry knew he was lying to himself.

The harvest had changed everything. Because this time it felt strangely as if he'd planted his own memories. Not ones heavy with the burden of parental dissatisfaction, or teenage angst. No, these were his own adult memories. An investment in a future that he was about to sell. And those seeds had been plunged deep into his heart and were already unfurling, growing within him, binding him to this place with green ivy-like vines. Seeds he couldn't help but feel that Lily had given him. On purpose. As if she wanted him to be bound to this place like she was. Like his father had been.

He knew it was an irrational thought, just as heated and unfounded as his sudden anger with her. No, it wasn't anger as such, but something a little bit more like resentment. Because in spite of everything he wanted – to get out, to never come back – he was beginning to ... *what?* he asked himself as he ran a hand through a thick head of hair already tufting in places from earlier manhandling. Was he beginning to want something different?

It had been easier when he'd told himself that the town hated him. That they all whispered behind their hands and his back and blamed him just as they should for the accident that devastated the community and cost Claudia her life. But the harvest had made him see that it wasn't how they saw him, or at least *not only* how they saw him. And slowly the reasons for him leaving were beginning to drop away, and the ones making him want to stay were increasing in number.

And Lily ... she was always at the top of that list. Lily who worked too hard for other people, Lily who the whole town seemed to adore, Lily who would drop everything at a moment's notice to help someone else, Lily who was so beautiful, so kind, so unwavering. He felt as if she had cast a spell over him. Making him want things he shouldn't. Making him want to do better, *be* better.

But he just couldn't see it. Couldn't see how he could have what he wanted and her at the same time. Not without irrevocably taking something from her. Whether it be the estate, or her home here in Hawke's Cove. Either one was the price of being with him, and he wasn't enough of a bastard not to know that, nor to ask her to make that choice.

A huge thunderclap drew him to the other side of the living room. He was going to have to draw the interior shutters across the windows if this carried on much longer. And then he nearly laughed at himself. A few weeks ago, he wouldn't have cared if the glass broke, if the estate was damaged. But it was beginning to get under his skin. He was suddenly concerned about the vines weathering the storm. Any damage to the estate, he knew was not down to concern about the sale price, but concern for the building that was vastly coming to mean more to him now than it had ever done before. He was worried about the glass panes in the orangery and what that might mean for Victoria's wedding in just a few days. Was he really ready to hand all this over to someone who might not care about the weird and wonderful people in Hawke's Cove?

He looked out of the window, down to the forest towards the beach below and …

Was that a light? A white beam glinted in between the dark shadowy trees. He must have been imagining it. No, wait. There it was again.

Who the hell would be out there at this time of night in this weather? Suddenly he had a horrible suspicion that there was only one possible answer. But she couldn't be, could she?

Cursing out loud into the silence of the room, he ran down the sweeping staircase, grabbed his coat and keys to the Jeep, fear firing his actions. Rain slashed against him in harsh waves as he flung himself out of the front door and raced towards the car.

Switching on the headlights and the windscreen wipers he

had a sudden flash from the accident ten years before. White-knuckled, he gripped the steering wheel as he guided the Jeep down the track towards the woods that would take him to the beach.

Leaves and broken twigs lashed the old Jeep's windscreen and he revved the engine as he bumped and dipped through the uneven ground of the forest floor. If it was her, he was going to throttle her. He realized at that moment he might be the only person on earth hoping that there were burglars or smugglers on the beach rather than a wholly irresponsible, wedding-crazed, overly soft-hearted, incredibly beautiful, absolutely infuriating Lily Atwell.

As the Jeep crested the bank to the border of the beach, the headlights picked out a scene of utter madness. He knew that Lily had been making hen party preparations down here in the last few days, but ... he was shocked.

He was just able to make out a boat on the jetty, bobbing up and down dangerously on the waves and heard himself growl within the confines of the Jeep. Had she taken that boat out in this weather? The thought filled him with dread. Of all the—

His thoughts were cut off as he saw Lily's shadowy figure outlined in the beam of the headlights, trying to wrestle something that looked suspiciously like a large swathe of fabric from the clutches of a near-gale-force wind. She was standing beside a wooden structure that impossibly looked like a gazebo. How on earth had she got all that on the beach?

Launching himself from the Jeep towards her, Lily finally turned towards him, arms full of soaking wet fabric, surrounded by what seemed to have once been at least fifteen cushions.

'What the hell do you think you're doing?' he demanded, having to shout to make himself heard over the roaring wind. 'What *is* all this stuff?'

'It's for the hen party,' she shouted, the roar of the wind and crashing of the waves competing. 'I brought it over earlier today.' She was shaking her head now, pushing thick ropes of wet hair from her face. 'This wasn't forecast! It wasn't supposed to happen!'

'Did you come here in that?' he demanded, his eyes snagging on the boat rocking dangerously on the water by the jetty.

'It wasn't this bad when I set out.'

'Whose is it?' he shouted over to her.

'Does it matter? Right now?' she called back, clearly irritated. 'Blake bought it for us. So we could get Zoe out here for the hen party,' she said, the mass of material slipping in her hands. 'Can you just—'

Whatever she'd been about to say was lost as a huge gust of wind nearly pushed her and the sodden bundle of material clutched to her chest over into the sand.

'Are you crazy?' he demanded, reaching her and taking the heavy weight from her arms.

'Determined,' she shouted at him.

'It's a fine bloody line, Lily.'

'You can yell at me later. Just … Help? Please?!'

He cast an eye about him. Cushions, hanging lanterns, rugs and throws were scattered halfway along the beach that now looked as if a tsunami had struck. He turned back to Lily. Her clothes were soaked through and sticking to her frame. She wasn't even wearing a coat.

'Get in the car,' he growled, infuriated that she had risked herself for a bloody hen party.

'I can—'

'Get. In. The. Car.'

She stared at him a moment longer, her large dark eyes poking holes in his conscience.

'Please, Lily,' he practically begged.

When she nodded, he followed her back to the Jeep, made sure she was sitting in the passenger seat and was half tempted to strap her into the seatbelt. He closed the passenger door, locking her in, then went round to the back doors, pulling at them and depositing the soaking wet heap of material.

Quickly and efficiently, he grabbed cushions, swathes of material, hanging lanterns and whatever else he could find and thrust them into the back. He eyed the wooden pallet and decided to leave it. He gave the wooden structure a nudge to check how securely it was in place, immediately thankful that its solidity meant he didn't have to worry about it falling down and causing more damage.

As he shoved another armful of fancy material into the Jeep, he saw her cast a longing look towards the gazebo and pallet.

'Don't even think about it. It's staying.'

'But it's the table and—'

'I am *not* putting that in the back.'

'Please!'

'No, Lily. This is literally the definition of madness,' he yelled through to where she sat in the front.

He slammed the Jeep's back doors shut and walked round to the driver's seat, getting a face full of frigid rain that was almost horizontal. He launched himself into the car and slammed the door behind him.

Lily was staring mournfully out the window at the gazebo frame.

'Will it be OK?' she half shouted over the sounds of the driving rain smashing against the frame and window of the Jeep.

'It will survive the night,' he said, having to raise his own voice to be heard.

He looked at her then, shivering beside him, her long hair turned to wet ropes hanging around her face and shoulders. He reached for the air con and turned it up to full, hoping that it would at least take the edge off the cold biting into their skin.

Putting the car into gear, the wheels spun for an excruciating moment before finding purchase and they launched forward onto the path through the forest. Conversation was impossible as the rain continued to drive against the battered old Jeep and Henry expelled a deep breath, not realizing he'd held it locked into his chest until he saw the light over the entrance to the estate.

He got out of the Jeep, silently cursing up a storm in his mind, and when he saw Lily hovering by the boot, he shook his head. 'I'll get it later, Lily. Just get inside,' he commanded, still absolutely brimming with fury that she had risked herself. And for what? A hen party? Some cushions?

Reluctantly she followed him through the front door and he practically pushed her up the stairs to the living room where the fire he'd started earlier that night was now in full swing. She stood in the middle of the room as if unsure what to do now and he cursed. She looked so lost, so miserable. She looked up at him in utter confusion.

'It can't be raining. It just can't be. The hen party—'

'That's what you're worried about? Seriously? You could have got hurt, Lily. Or worse. What the hell were you thinking?' he demanded, unable to rid himself of the shocking fear that had crashed over him when he'd realized she'd been down on the beach in the middle of a thunderstorm.

'I … I didn't want it to be ruined. I … It had to be perfect. And now, it—'

'Will be just fine,' he said, aiming for reassurance and knowing that he just sounded mutinous. 'You know what these coastal storms are like. All rain and bluster and tomorrow blue skies and a heat wave. It will be fine, Lily.' He spoke with a confidence he genuinely didn't feel at that point. But he knew it was what she needed to hear.

He stalked over to the drinks cabinet and poured two large glasses of brandy. He pressed one into her shaking hands, watching her until she took a mouthful before gratefully taking a large swallow of his own.

Lily choked a little but his slipped smoothly down his throat. After a moment, she took another sip and he finally began to relax, now that she was safe, now that the colour was returning to her pale skin and the shivering that had racked her frame lessened just a little.

He grabbed a large throw from the sofa and placed it around her shoulders, ignoring her protests.

'I'm soaking,' she said, trying to shrug it off.

'I don't care. You need to warm up.' And she needed to cover up, because the way that her clothes were clinging to her skin – showing off every curve, every delicious inch of her – was too much. He turned away, gritting his jaw and hating himself for ogling her when she was clearly so distressed. Or insane. He really wasn't sure at this point.

'Look, why don't you head to one of the rooms and take a shower? I'll find you some clothes to change into, but you can't stay like that, or you'll catch a cold. And what would that do for the wedding?'

'I … thank you for helping me but I should really be going,' she said, looking forlornly out the window at the storm raging beyond.

'Not tonight. We've both had a drink, so no driving,' he said, barely looking her in the eye, 'and before you say it, I'm not letting you walk back home in this weather either.'

'I should—'

'Take the damn shower, Lily.'

She looked for a moment as if she might argue, but when her shoulders dropped, he heaved a sigh of relief, thankful that she was finally listening to him. He followed the beige mass of the throw wrapped around her body out of the room and down towards the wing where he was staying. She paused halfway down the hall as if unsure where to go and he suddenly felt guilty. Guilty for being so harsh with her, guilty for shouting and yelling, and guilty even that she'd felt she had to tackle the beach by herself, that she hadn't felt able to call him to ask for help.

Which then, irrationally, morphed back into frustration that she had nearly hurt herself in the process.

'I'm in here,' he said, gesturing to the door on the left. 'Why don't you take the next one down? I'll leave something for you to change into for when you're done in the shower.'

She nodded, eyes still round and wide, and body still shivering. 'You'll feel better,' he promised.

She nodded again and disappeared through the door next to his. Sighing for what felt like the hundredth time in the last hour, he entered his room and went to the chest of drawers containing his clothes.

He tried to keep his mind blank as he rifled through the items, trying to figure out what she'd be comfortable in, rather than the way thoughts of Lily in his clothing made him feel, the sudden urge to see her in one of his shirts, something that had been on his own skin on hers ... He bit back a curse and reached for a pair of grey sweatpants, a white T-shirt and a stone-coloured knit jumper. They'd probably swamp her, but he didn't have anything smaller and at least they'd be dry and warm.

He turned back into the hallway, listening through her door for the sounds of the shower running. The last thing he wanted to do was to burst in on her getting undressed. Well, perhaps not the last, but he did know how inappropriate that would have been.

Satisfied that he'd left enough time for her to get into the bathroom, he knocked, then padded gently into the room, placing the clothes on the bed and retreated as quickly as possible.

He stood for a moment, back out in the hallway, trying to keep his mind on wringing – rather than kissing – Lily's neck. Walking back into the living room, the sound of the rain lashed against the windows and all he could think of was water sluicing down Lily's skin.

Which made him suddenly aware of the soaking wet jeans painfully clinging to his legs, the smell of damp wool rising from his jumper. Thankful for the discomfort cutting through the enticing fog of arousal ignited by thoughts of Lily, he decided to retrieve the hen party paraphernalia from the Jeep before he took his own shower. He was going to get soaked either way, but he might as well only do it once.

As he made his way back and forth between the Jeep and the estate building – bringing all the sequin-covered cushions and wet material, for what use Lily intended he had no idea – he managed to calm down, to level his breathing and the chaotic thoughts of his mind. Yes, he'd been scared that she'd be hurt or worse by the storm. But it went beyond that. It was almost more selfish than that. He just couldn't bear the idea that something would have happened to her, because she'd become a part of his life. He'd become used to the gentle teasing between them, to working together. He'd found himself wanting to know what she thought, wanting to know her hopes, wanting to help make them happen.

★★★

Lily stood beneath the hot spray of the shower and had only just stopped shivering. She pressed her head against the cool stone tile of the beautiful bathroom and leaned. *What had she been thinking?* Henry was right. To go out in that storm *had* been madness.

The storm hadn't been so bad when she'd taken the boat out, but it had just got worse and worse from the moment she'd moored it on the jetty. If Henry hadn't come to her rescue, she didn't know what she would have done.

But the idea of it all going wrong, the idea of the hen party being anything other than what she'd imagined for Victoria …

It would have been perfect. She bit back a sob, and let the almost punishing heat of the water spray after the frigid cold rain turn her skin pink. A wave of sadness almost overwhelmed her. But it wasn't for the hen party this time. It was for herself.

Perhaps it's for the best.

Did you not ever think about leaving Hawke's Cove?

Her hand formed a fist against the tiles and pressed hard. She realized she'd been hiding. Hiding, because without Blake, without the hen party, the wedding – restaurant aside – what did she have? What had she done with her life? Malie, Zoe and Victoria had been out in the world and they'd all found people that they loved and who loved them in return. And within weeks, the wedding would be over, Henry would be gone and she'd ...

She bit back the tears that were threatening to fall.

She wanted. Plain and simple. She wanted more. From her life, from Henry ... The image of him staring at her in the car, the way that he'd searched her features, making sure that she was OK. It had felt ... painful. Because she did want that, did want *him*. She wanted him to be her person. The person that put her first. The first person she could turn to and who would turn to her. She didn't for a minute begrudge her friend's happiness, but in reality – real, real hard reality – although they would *always* be there for each other, they each now had their person. And that was only right.

It couldn't help but make Lily feel lonely. Because she wanted Henry in a way that was beyond attraction. Because having someone to help her with the wedding, to talk questions over with, to get reassurances from ... she'd missed that in her life. And suddenly she could name it. Name her loneliness. Realize that she'd been lonely for a very long time, and that she'd just managed to fool everyone including herself, that she was fine. When in reality, she'd just been treading water, going nowhere.

She pulled the handle on the shower and reached for a towel, wrapping herself up tight as if holding herself together when really she felt as if she might come completely undone.

Stepping through to the bedroom of the suite she saw the sweatpants, T-shirt and jumper that Henry had left out for her. An image of him wearing them flashed into her mind and feeling like a fool, she couldn't help but reach for the jumper, the fine texture of the wool so soft. It was probably cashmere or some other material Victoria would know the name of. As if stroking the material released the scent of Henry, she drew it to her face and rubbed the soft smoothness against her skin, relishing in the faint traces of Henry's aftershave that still clung to the knit.

The rain, the storm, it was like a flood letting, a dam bursting and she was suddenly feeling everything at once. She pulled on the clothes, fastening the jogging bottoms at her waist with the string and having to roll up the ankles so she didn't trip. The T-shirt hung low and wide at the neck as if he'd pulled at it over the years. She thrust her arms through the jumper and pulled it down over her head.

Checking in the mirror, her eyes looked huge, but at least they weren't red from the tears she had cried in the shower. She towel-dried her hair roughly and, although part of her just wanted to collapse on to the bed, bundle herself into the thick inviting duvet, she couldn't put off seeing Henry any longer.

When she entered the living room, she was startled to find the floor dotted with pastel-coloured sequined cushions and the

large white lengths of tulle she'd bought to drape over the gazebo
for the hen party. She nearly laughed because it had transformed
the clean, calming cream living room into a bohemian harem.

There was no sign of Henry, other than the soft blanket placed
in front of the fire and the two glasses of red wine – Ruby, if
she wasn't mistaken. The whole room had a strange sense of
expectation. She passed the two wine glasses placed next to each
other and walked over to the window, the rain lashing against
it in angry bursts. She flinched when lightning cracked the sky
and counted. *One, two, three.*

Boom.

Not that close, but not that far either. Again, anticipation
filled the air. Would the storm turn away from the cove and drift
further afield? Out into the sea even? Lily couldn't help but bite
her lip, momentarily unsure she was still thinking of the storm.

Thunder burst through the night sky making her flinch.

'I didn't know you were scared of storms.'

She wasn't surprised by his voice. She'd felt him enter the
room in a way that the storm hadn't been able to disguise. 'I'm
not,' she denied a little too hotly, because when she turned he'd
raised a wry brow. 'OK, fine. What are *you* scared of?'

'Me? Nothing,' he replied with so much false arrogance she
couldn't help but laugh. When his eyes sparkled in the firelight,
she wondered if that had been his intention.

'And you said you wouldn't lie to me again.' Her voice was
full of mock disappointment and teasing.

'OK,' he said, then reached down to the glass of wine by the
fire and passed it to her. 'Ask me.'

'What?'

'Anything.'

'*Anything?*'

'Yes,' he said, gesturing for her to sit by the fire, as he settled down onto the plush throw he'd placed in front of it, his face a picture of openness and sincerity.

A thousand questions raced through her mind, some deep and personal, some just curious. About him. But all options felt a little too much. His hand was still out between them, waiting for her to join him by the fire. Expectant.

She crossed her feet at her ankles and gently collapsed down onto the throw beside him, causing him to laugh.

'What?'

'You looked like a princess deigning to sit on a cloud.'

'Really?'

'Really,' he insisted. 'Never seen anything like it.'

She slapped his hand away. 'Yoga.'

'You have time for yoga?'

'Not always.'

He snorted a half laugh again, making her smile.

'What's your favourite colour?' she asked.

'I give you carte blanche and that's what you ask?' She watched as Henry's brow arched in the flickering light from the fire.

'Lulling you into a false sense of security.'

He seemed to look at her then, taking in the whole of her … more than just her features, and it claimed a part of her heart she didn't know she had.

'Auburn.'

Lily nodded, suddenly feeling self-conscious, but ridiculously pleased. She wasn't sure he was thinking of the colour of her hair, but that he could be was enough. For now.

'What did you want to be when you were kid?'

'Get the hell out of the Cove,' he replied in the space of a heartbeat.

'That's not a thing,' she chided.

'OK.' He seemed to give it some thought, as if he had to work hard to remember. 'I … A fireman.'

Lily suddenly had an image of Henry as a child, playing with toys and full of innocent concentration and contentment. It felt so real for a moment she was completely lost.

'And you?' he asked.

She paused, just for a moment remembering something *before* wanting to be a chef, but discarded the half-formed memory before it could take hold.

'A chef, clearly.'

'Mmm, not sure about that.'

'What do you mean?'

'You thought of something else first.'

'How do you—'

'Lily Atwell, I hate to break it to you, but your face gives away almost every single thought you have.'

'No it does not,' she said, blushing furiously and hoping beyond all hope that it wasn't true. Otherwise, he'd know … know *everything*.

'My point exactly,' he said, his eyes firmly on cheeks that she realized must have been bright red.

She looked up at his teasing, the sparkle in his eyes, the confident quirk to his lips and just for a moment, they both breathed in, held onto the moment stretching between them, before once again, she felt the wall come down and she, too, took a step back.

'A mum.'

'What?' he asked, frowning.

'I wanted to be a mum. I wanted a husband and children and the white picket fence around a beautiful house overlooking the sea. It's not *cool* to admit that, though, is it?'

'Why not?' he asked, seemingly genuinely intrigued.

Lily sighed. 'Because we're supposed to have it all. The high-flying career, the family, the independence and the dependence all wrapped up into one.'

'Well, according to my very wise – and very wonderful – mother, bras weren't burned to break the glass ceiling but to give women the choice over what they wanted, whether that be a high-flying career or not. So I'd imagine it's more than OK for you to *choose* to be a mother if you want to.'

Oh God. He loved his mum. The feelings building between them were too much. She had to cling to the memory of when he had accused her of trespassing. Of when he had lied to her.

Ask me anything.

She shook the thoughts away from her head, Henry clearly misinterpreting her reaction.

'Or not,' he said, holding his hands up in surrender.

'What do you want to be now?' she asked, trying to shift his hawk-like focus from her.

He frowned, confused by her question. 'I *am* what I want to be now,' he said, only he didn't quite look as certain as she thought he should.

'An app developer?'

'A very rich, very successful app developer, thank you,' he replied, full of that familiar false arrogance of his.

'You don't want more?' she couldn't help but ask.

'Do you?'

Yes. Yes, she did. She wanted him. But instead of responding, she clamped her jaw shut for fear that she might actually speak the words.

★★★

Henry hadn't lied when he'd told her how expressive her face was. He suddenly wished he'd been so very wrong, because he could see the desire shining in her eyes. Could almost feel the beat of her heart against his chest, across the foot of air between them. Would have sworn on the Bible that he could taste her on his tongue. Sweet, citrusy ... like coming home.

Home.

The word echoed in his mind. Perhaps she hadn't noticed that he hadn't answered her question about wanting more. Because until a month ago, he'd not wanted for anything. But in the last few weeks, something had begun to change. It was as if she had cast a spell over him. When she'd confessed that she'd wanted to be a mother, he'd known it, seen it, felt it. Just as much as he had when he'd imagined her pregnant with a child only a few weeks earlier.

White picket fence, house overlooking the sea.

He had those things. Well, not the fence, but still. But could he offer her more? Could he offer her himself? A man so haunted by the past he was determined to sell the very thing he would profess to offer? This time it was his turn to shake his head, cast aside the thoughts filling his mind and heart, before he could be tempted to beg, to plead, to ask … to take.

'So what's stopping you?' he said into the quiet that had descended over the room.

'What do you mean?'

'What's stopping you from having what you want … the family?'

She looked at him as if he were a little mad. 'I have a few things on my plate at the moment.'

'So clear the plate.'

'It's not that simple, Henry.'

He shrugged. 'Pretty sure it is.' He knew he was on the verge of being obnoxious, but something about their conversation had irritated a wound that was now burning and hurting. He swallowed the last mouthful of the wine and reached for the bottle to top them up, strangely angry with himself and knowing it was just the start. It really hadn't taken much, it was like throwing kindling on the embers of a fire stoked when he'd first seen her down on the beach earlier that night.

'It's just not the right time now, that's all.'

'I don't buy that.'

'Says the man who can clearly afford to up and leave his business for months,' she said, the blush now becoming tinged with an anger he almost relished to see. Almost, because in truth he was beginning to hate himself for the way he was talking to her.

'Says the woman who has quite easily and happily taken weeks away from *her* business to arrange her friend's wedding. Even if that wedding will run you in to the ground.'

'Run me into the …? I don't know what you're talking about,' she said, her eyes now picking up a storm that would rival the tempest happening outside.

'What? Someone's got to say it, Lily. You've been running around like a blue-arsed fly, exhausting yourself to the point of madness, where you go out into the middle of a storm, put yourself in considerable danger, all for what? A hen party? What the hell is so important about this wedding that you would put your own health at risk?'

CHAPTER ELEVEN

LILY REARED BACK, SHOCKED by his outburst for which he seemed instantly regretful. He shook his head and passed a hand over his face.

'I know it was silly—'

'Dangerous.'

'OK, fine. Dangerous, but …' Lily suddenly couldn't find the words. Because it had been dangerous. Reckless even.

'But what, Lily? *Why?* Just tell me why so that I can understand.' He looked so pained, she wanted him to understand. Needed him to.

'Victoria's been through so much, Henry. Not being able to have children was so difficult for her and she's finally found someone who cares about her – *her* for the amazing, wonderful person she is.'

'I get that. I really do. They have an epic love—'

'Don't mock me,' she bit.

'I'm not, I've seen it. I'm a believer. Trust me. But the extremes you've gone to … It's not because of her.' And before she could object, he clarified, 'Not *just* because of her.'

His words, his questions were getting too close to the mark.

Too close to what she'd been thinking about in the shower. And suddenly it all swirled up about her and she couldn't keep it in anymore.

'OK, fine. Really? It's because I know how much and how hard you can dream about your wedding. I know how you can spend days, weeks, months, planning every single detail – what kinds of bridesmaids' dresses, your own bridal dress, the family and friends you want to invite to show the whole world that you love and are loved. And I know, Henry,' she said taking a desperate breath, 'I know what it's like to have that taken away from you. To have it not only removed from your life, but for the shame and embarrassment to know that you were played for a fool. Used like a sodding piggy bank. For all that to have been a sham. A pretence. A lie. It destroys you,' she whispered, her voice breaking on the word as memories of that time after Alistair, of the realization that he'd not only left, but used her. The dark, black hole of months she'd experienced after she'd returned to Hawke's Cove. 'It takes away your sense of self and your faith, not just in other people. But yourself. Because it was *me* who believed him, *me* who put my faith in him, *me* who refused to see that he wasn't interested in me. In my hopes and dreams. He wasn't interested in my life and didn't hope to have a future and a family with me. He left. And I had to call everyone and tell them he'd left. I had to cancel the venue, the vendors, I had to call the guests and announce to each and every one of them that I wasn't worthy of a wedding, of love. That I wasn't good enough.

'And I don't care what you say, Henry, but I'm going to make damn sure that V or any of my friends never have to go through that.'

She finally looked up at him to see his eyes wide and shocked, that horrid mixture of sadness and sympathy and helplessness that had been inflicted on her by almost everyone in town after those first few months.

'Jesus, Lily, Oliver would never ...' He stopped and shook his head. 'But that's not the point.'

Henry was really shocked. All this time, he'd seen her as such a driving force, a power to be reckoned with. He'd seen her in all her glory in the kitchen, at the harvest, and not for a second did he imagine the kind of hurt she so clearly still felt beneath the surface. And in that moment, he realized that she didn't see it.

'Do you know what an incredible person you are, and what a complete arse-hat Alistair was?'

Lily choked on her mouthful of brandy again. 'Arse-hat?' She laughed, and Henry was relieved to see it, the gentle tinkle cutting through the tension in the room in a much-needed way. 'Yes, I totally understand what an *arse-hat* Alistair was. But it doesn't take away from the fact that—'

'That you were betrayed by someone you loved. And it made you doubt yourself, when you're the last person in the world who should do so. You've done such incredible things, Lily,' he said, still not able to fathom how she couldn't see it.

'Says the man who has apartments in Singapore, New York, London ...'

'Says the man who doesn't have a home. Who hadn't spoken to his father for over ten years. Who may have a load of money—'

'Which is not to have a stick shaken at it,' she interrupted.

'But it's not about money. It never was,' he said, sighing. 'What you have ... friends, family that love you, a community that genuinely seem lost without you …? 'That's nothing to *shake a stick at.'*

He went to sit beside her on the sofa, because he couldn't stand towering over her when she seemed so vulnerable. This close, he could see the natural rich coppery golden strands in her drying hair. How her skin glowed in the firelight like cream. She was so beautiful, so incredible, and it hurt him that she couldn't see it.

'But Lily, it's not about what you have. This is about who you are. And you're …' he shook his head, 'Incredible.' He nearly smiled as the rosy blush slashed across her cheeks. 'You're such a kind, generous person. You repeatedly go above and beyond. Putting yourself out for your friends and family. And not just them. You've even worn down Mrs Whittaker, which no one could ever have imagined. But it's more than that, Lily,' he said, reaching for her shoulder and giving in to the desire to pull her into his side. 'You've made me see that no matter what had happened, Blake did love me. You made me find a sense of peace within a place that I'd only found childhood hurts and upset. And above all, you do deserve love. You deserve your happy ever after.'

She looked up at him then and he could almost see himself in her eyes, he could almost taste the need, the desire on the air between them. But he couldn't take that next step. He couldn't do that to her, because she did deserve her happy ever after, and he just wasn't the person to give that to her. But he might just be able to help her see.

'But I'm just worried that you won't find it if you're always putting someone else first.'

'What do you mean?' she asked, as if shaking herself back into the conversation.

He sighed, knowing that she wouldn't like what he had to say, but also knowing that she really needed to hear it. 'You're always rushing around doing something, rescuing someone. You rescued me and the harvest the other day. And you tried to rescue the hen party in the middle of a thunderstorm. But why? What do you think will happen if you don't?'

He hated the look of hurt flashing in her eyes. Wanted so much to take it away.

'I don't know.'

'Because you've never not? Or because you genuinely don't know why you have to be the one who fixes everything?' he asked gently.

'That's not fair, Henry.'

'I'm not trying to be fair – or mean. I'm trying to make you see that you're always putting someone else first. You could have told me to call John about the harvest. V could have hired a wedding planner to do all the million and one things that you've taken on, while your chef was on holiday, and you needed to run a full-time working restaurant.'

'But I *could* help,' she insisted. 'It didn't take much to phone a few people and of course I was going to help V with her wedding.'

'That's not ...' Henry was getting frustrated because she genuinely couldn't seem to see what he was getting at. Thinking back to that time after Claudia and the accident, he'd thrown himself into every wayward experience wholeheartedly because he didn't want to stop. Didn't want to think about it all, didn't want to feel it all. And he couldn't help but fear that Lily was doing the same and, even though on the surface it seemed more healthy, it was just as damaging.

'But what happens after the wedding?'

'What do you mean?'

'What will you do?' he probed gently.

'Do? I'll run my restaurant and have my friends,' she said defensively.

* * *

She hated that he was giving words to the fears she'd faced in the shower. Not only that he was saying them, but that he had read her so accurately, knew her to the extent where he was able to pinpoint the very thing she'd been hiding from.

'Don't you want to go anywhere? Somewhere other than Hawke's Cove? Don't you want to experience all the amazing different food places in person? For real? Rather than online?'

The spike of pain cut through her, and suddenly she couldn't keep in all the hurt anymore.

'You make it sound as if my world is small,' she said, pulling out of his arms and getting to her feet. 'And it's not. It *is* full of friendship and family, and community. Hawke's Cove is special. It's a beautiful place full of amazing people. It's a home, it's *my* home and Henry Hawkesbury, if you can't see that then I feel sorry for you!'

With that, Lily stalked from the room, wiping the tears falling once again, and slammed the door of the suite behind her. Because … she couldn't shake the feeling that he was right. She hadn't lied, she'd meant what she said about her world. She loved it. But neither did that make him wrong. There was a world out there and she had hidden from it. Because ... because ... she didn't want to lose anyone else. She'd lost enough.

***

It was taking Lily ages to get to sleep. She tossed and turned and spun in the sheets of the unfamiliar room, the words of their argument going round and round in her head. The fiery burn of anger and self-recrimination heating her to the point where she had to throw off the sheets. She'd seen that Henry had only been trying to help. And somewhere mixed in with all the hurt was the fact that he'd said she was incredible. That he'd painted a picture of her that she'd not really seen in herself.

But if he thought she was so incredible, why didn't he want her? Why didn't he kiss her the way she'd wanted him to? And why was she waiting for him to kiss her?

She growled out loud in the dark room. Her thoughts a confusing, jumbled mess. He'd helped her, saved her even, but then he'd hurt her. Or had she in reality been hurting herself all this time?

Get a grip, Lily.

She had two days before the wedding. The hen party ...

Oh God.

This time she groaned and grabbed a pillow and pressed her face into it. What was she going to do?

By the time she extricated herself from the pillow and the sheets, she realized that it was no longer her making a noise, but something else. It started like a moan of pain, of anguish, and crescendo'd into a shout. First one, then another.

Lily launched out of bed and into the hallway. It was coming from Henry's room and panic hit her thick and fast. She gently knocked on the door, despite the urge to slam her fist against it, but there was no response. When another cry cut through the silence of the estate, she pushed open the door and stepped into the room.

The curtains were open, the moon casting the room in a half light, and she could see Henry on the bed tossing and turning. Not like she had done, but as if he were fighting for his life.

Knowing better than to yank him out of the dream, she closed the distance between her and the bed, gently calling to him to try and bring him out of the nightmare.

'Henry? Henry, it's OK. It's just a dream.'

He thrashed again, his arm flinging out and, having dodged it, she reached for it, wrapping her small hand around his forearm.

'Henry?'

He stilled in an instant, his eyes open and staring at the ceiling for a second before focusing on her. He sat bolt up in the bed, grabbing on to her hand.

'Are you OK?' he demanded.

'Yes.' She nodded, momentarily confused by the intensity of his demand, by the fact that his first thought had been her, not himself. 'I'm fine. Are you?'

He took in a deep breath, and looked about him as if finally taking in his surroundings and realizing where he was.

He nodded slowly and passed a hand over his jaw, working it as if he'd been clenching it the entire time. Leaning up in the bed, she could see that he wasn't wearing a T-shirt. She looked at where his hand was still on her arm, along the tanned skin of his forearm, up to the powerful outline of well-honed muscles on his biceps, across his collar bone to the dusting of dark hair across a chest that made her mouth water and her guilt rise. She shouldn't be checking him out. Not right now. Here he was in pain, and she was … on fire. Then his gaze returned to hers, intent and devastating.

She suddenly felt self-conscious. She'd gone to sleep in just the T-shirt and hadn't thought to put anything else on, she'd been so worried about him. Now she pulled at the length of the T-shirt that reached her mid-thigh, completely unaware that the neckline then pulled low exposing the delicate v between her breasts.

★★★

'Nightmare?' she asked.

'Yeah. I get them when it rains like this. It reminds me …'

'Of the accident? I had them for a few years after too,' she confessed.

'Really?'

'Mm hm,' she said, rubbing her arms, and for the first time Henry could see the faint silvery traces of scars. Frowning, he took hold of her arms and ran his fingers over them, only belatedly questioning whether his touch would be welcome. Seeing the marks on her arms hurt. He'd managed to escape the accident almost untouched. Physically at least. He turned her hands in his, exposing the soft undersides of her forearms and noticing a red burn slashed just above her wrist.

'That was from the kitchen,' she said, twisting her hands back over. 'And that one,' she nodded to the other arm, 'was from the oven. I don't know a chef who doesn't have the same marks.' She smiled sadly and shrugged, her arms still within his hands. 'I ... I don't usually wear short sleeves, but ...' She leaned her head towards her upper arms where the silvery traces spoke of a different hurt, 'I got off easy,' she said quietly. And he realized that she was comparing herself to Victoria, who had lost the possibility of having children, and Zoe in her wheelchair.

He shook his head. So much damage from that night. So much devastation and loss.

'Tell me about the nightmares?' she asked.

Such a simple question, such a hard one to answer. He wanted to say no. He wanted to turn away, but the sincerity in her eyes, the compassion ... Flashes of the nightmare crashed through his mind. Shattered glass, Claudia, smiling, then screaming, his hand slammed against the car's console, the sound of the revving engine and screeching tyres. He swallowed and blanked his mind against the images.

'They're mostly the same,' he said, his voice harsh and throat sore from the way he must have been yelling out in the night, 'but sometimes there are little differences. Sometimes, I'm the one driving, and she's in the passenger seat beside me, in her prom dress, happy, smiling, laughing ...'

'Like the way she was when you first met her?'

'Yes. She was cool and beautiful, occasionally dropping something salty into the conversation, taking me by surprise. She seemed so much older than seventeen, knowing, worldly. But now I think she was just ... sad.'

He was still running his thumb over the slivery scars on her arms but he couldn't stop himself. He needed her warmth, the smoothness of her skin beneath his. It made talking about it easier somehow.

'Sometimes, like tonight, Claudia is full of energy and laughter. Not like she was the night of the accident, when she was ...' He shrugged as if trying to shift the memory but searching for it at the same time. 'Then she was almost angry, determined, focused on something else from the instant I got into the car. But tonight, in the dream she was happy, talking about how excited she was for the dance, but I knew that something terrible was about to happen, I just didn't know what. I tried to tell her, to warn her, but she ignored me, refused to believe me. And all the while that sense, that belief that danger was a hair's breadth away, it just built and built and I couldn't understand why she wouldn't believe me, why I couldn't stop driving the car. It's as if my body wasn't responding to my commands and ...' He trailed off, feeling just as helpless now as in the dream.

'I used to get the same thing.'

'Really?'

Lily nodded. 'For about three years after, I would have nightmares maybe, three, four times a week? They were exhausting and awful and traumatic,' she said and sighed. 'I'd never be driving, though. But sometimes, Dad would be in the car with me. They were the worst, because I got to see him, only to know that I would lose him all over again each time. Though admittedly sometimes there was a cat.'

'A cat?' Henry asked, half laughing.

'A *massive* cat. It would just be attacking me and I was constantly trying to fight off the cat without hurting it. But V would swerve because of the fight, and the car would fall off the side of the road and just keep falling and falling and falling.'

He might have laughed about the cat, but he knew that it wasn't funny. Not really. She'd felt that same sense of building horror, one that never seemed to reach its climax. But perhaps that was because they already had experienced it. Maybe it was their minds protecting them from the memories of the real trauma they had shared.

'When did they stop?' he asked, hoping that Lily might somehow hold the magical key.

'I don't know,' she said, shifting beside him on the bed, unaware that the hem of the T-shirt had ridden up just a little. 'Maybe three years after? I think it happened as I realized that V and Zo were out there, living their lives. That Malie was doing amazing things on the surfing circuit. They had managed to move on and with that came a kind of peace. There was nothing holding them back anymore.'

Henry's thoughts stopped.

He knew what had been holding him back all these years, he'd just never really wanted to admit it. To say it out loud. Because that would mean that ... it would mean that they would all see, all know. But for the first time in ten years, Henry thought that Lily might be the first person who would understand. She'd known Claudia, been involved in the accident. Perhaps he could trust her.

Of course he could trust her. But he'd never told anyone and that secret had been a heavy burden. Because he'd always wondered – believed – that the entire accident had really been his fault.

He swept aside the covers on the opposite side of the bed to where Lily was sitting, switching on the small light on the table. If he was going to do this, he didn't want it to be in the shadows, he wanted to see Lily. See her reaction. And for her to finally, really, see him.

'I … I don't really know where to start.'

She frowned, clearly not quite sure what he had to say, but then her expression smoothed into that beautiful openness he'd come to expect from her. 'At the beginning, seems to be where most people start,' she said, with a gentle smile.

Despite her calm assurance he couldn't help but pace the room. He'd never told anyone this, not even Ben. And all this time, it had been tearing him up.

'That summer was really hard for me. I'd been at university for a year and it had been like a breath of fresh air. Finally being away from both my parents. Blake, who was almost completely absent and Mum, who was so desperate to make up for the disastrous early years she'd give me almost anything I wanted, not realizing how damaging and cloying that was. But being at university? Getting a taste of what life was like by myself … it was intoxicating. There I was, with mates from uni, doing silly things, getting drunk … meeting girls.'

He cast a look at Lily. 'I didn't cheat on her,' he said, needing her to know that. Needing her to understand.

'Henry, we were young. You were eighteen. Even if you had—'

'But I didn't,' he stressed.

'I believe you,' she said simply, not realizing how much those three little words meant to him and desperately hoping that she'd still feel that way after he'd told her what had happened that night.

'I think it might have been easier if I had. But I fear what I did was worse. I knew that I didn't want to be with her, but I just didn't have the courage to just tell her. I kept on hoping that it would just peter out. That she'd get bored of waiting for me. But when she sensed that I was pulling away, she became more insistent, more needy,' he said, thinking of the texts and the phone calls. He remembered being in his dorm room, drinking with his friends or   on the few occasions he did try to study – having to get up and answer his phone to a hysterical Claudia, crying one time, or giggling hysterically another. 'I knew that she was having a hard time with her parents, hated being at school, hated being in the Cove, all of which I could totally relate to, but ... I just wrote it off. I kept telling her that she'd be out of there soon, just like I was. She just had to wait. But then I'd go for a few weeks without hearing from her and each time, it felt like a relief. Like, that might have been the time she'd got the message, and I'd not have to actually say it.

'I was *such* a coward,' he threw out into the room. 'All around me, I just saw parties and people and it felt like the beginning of something. Of my life. I was so selfish, I resented Claudia and the way she tied me to the Cove, to my father, to everything I wanted to run away from.

'So when she asked me to take her to the summer ball, I thought ... this is it. I'd take her to the prom and then break things off with her. Like that makes any sense,' he said, hating the way he'd been back then. The sheer selfishness of it all. Running a hand through his hair, he turned to look at Lily, fearing disgust or disappointment. But there she was, still open, still compassionate.

'When she offered to drive, I was thankful. Not because I wanted to drink, but because I thought that at least it would mean I wouldn't have to drive her home after any kind of awkward confrontation,' he said, desperately wanting to pull at his hair. Anger at himself and frustration scoured deeply into his chest. 'So when she picked me up, I think I was so focused on trying to figure out what to say that I just didn't realize. I couldn't see that she wasn't sober. I just thought she was excited about the party.

'I'd had no idea things had got so bad that she'd started taking drugs, let alone drinking. If I hadn't been so damn focused on myself, I would have realized sooner. I would have made her stop the car.

'But I didn't.' He ran another hand over his face. 'A friend from uni called while we were in the car. A picture of her flashed up on the screen and Claudia saw it. Demanded to know whether I was seeing her. It ... was awful. She was screaming and crying and I told her it wasn't like that. Tried to make her see. I asked her to pull over, but she just increased the speed. We came up so fast behind you – behind Victoria's car – and I was yelling at her to slow down, but she didn't and when she tried to overtake you ...' He didn't need to say the rest. Lily knew. They all knew. But the pain in his chest, it was tearing him apart.

Lily finally came up from the bed to stand in front of him, taking his hands in the warmth of hers, the smoothness of her skin once again somehow lessening the biting hold of the past.

'It wasn't your fault that Claudia was high and drunk. The rain was torrential and it quite possibly would have happened anyway. Maybe not to us, but to someone else,' Lily said.

'But I should have known. I should have been able to tell that she wasn't sober,' he insisted to himself as much as to Lily. After all, it was exactly what Claudia's parents had shouted to him at the inquest.

Why didn't you stop her?! Why didn't you do something?!

The sounds of their voices loud in his ears, despite the intervening years. He'd never forgotten it, or them.

'Do you know how many times I've thought the same thing?' Lily asked him. 'That I – that we – should have known that something was wrong with Claudia? She was in our year, in some of our classes. And no one – not her friends, not teachers, not the school – said anything. *Did* anything. She was in such pain, emotionally, and no one knew.' She shrugged helplessly. 'Claudia was the popular girl, a little naughty, but ... In hindsight, we'd all realized that in the months before the prom, she'd been acting a little differently. But we just ignored it. We could have told the teachers, could have gone to someone, told someone ... But we didn't. If we had, you might never have been in the car. Claudia might never have felt the need to take drugs or get drunk that night.'

'You can't blame yourself,' he insisted.

'Yet you get to blame *yourself*?' she asked.

'I should have done something.'

'You did. You stayed with her.'

'What?'

'I ...' She hesitated. 'You stayed, in the car with her. You wouldn't let the paramedics touch you until they'd got Claudia out. I saw it.'

Shocked, he searched her eyes, for something, he didn't know what.

'It gave me strength,' she said sadly. 'The strength to stay with V, Zo and Malie. For a while, in our car, I was the only person conscious. And although part of me wanted out, wanted so desperately to run, to flee, I saw how much you fought to stay with Claudia. And it made me hold on. I grabbed V's hand from the front and Malie beside me. But over Zo's shoulder I could see you. You held her and didn't stop talking to her until they practically dragged you from the car. The entire time, I saw.'

Goosebumps pebbled his skin, and a cold shiver cut through his body. She closed the distance between them – bare inches between his chest and hers – and her hands came up to frame his face, bringing his gaze to hers.

'It wasn't your fault, Henry. Claudia was a deeply unhappy person and it took a lot of people to ignore that. What you did with the app? Your first one? It helps make the world a safer place for people that are struggling. You did that. But you need to forgive yourself. There is no one who can do that for you.'

He knew that what Lily was saying was right. That he did need to forgive himself. But she was also wrong. There were two people who could still help him move forward. Who could help him really put this behind him.

Why didn't you stop her?! Why didn't you do something?!

He shivered and Lily went to remove her hands as if she'd thought he was trying to shuck them off. In a second, he'd placed his hands over hers, keeping them there, desperate for the warmth, comfort and reassurance they offered. He bowed his head, too ashamed to meet her eyes.

★ ★ ★

Lily saw the top of Henry's bowed head and hurt for him. Hurt for all the guilt that he'd been carrying for years. She wished she could take it away, but knew that only he could do that for himself. And knew that as much as the accident had shaped Malie, Zoe and Victoria's lives, it had also shaped him into the man that stood before her today. The man who had, from something devastating, created something so powerful. The app that she'd checked out online the night he'd told her about it, had been astounding. The reviews and accolades it had received had been full of thanks and praise. A resource for struggling teens, and parents who had named it as lifesaving for their children. But more than that, he was a man who felt things deeply. She could see it in his actions and words. And he deserved to move on. They all did.

She felt his sigh against her skin, the slow, deep exhale gentle and warming. And suddenly she was painfully aware of where they touched, of their closeness, of the scent of him wrapping around her, sandalwood and smoke and something still fresh and clean from his shower earlier. It drew her in, and their breaths became an exchange of give and take and the tension in the air between them morphed from grief and loss into hope and desire.

'You should go,' he said quietly without raising his head, his eyes still closed, perhaps purposefully so.

She knew she could. *Should* walk away from this, from him. But she didn't want to. For the first time in so, so long, she wanted to stay. To be selfish and take what she wanted. What she'd wanted for weeks now.

'I'd like to stay.'

He shook his head still in her hands, and all she wanted to do was cradle it, hold him to her even as he would leave.

'You don't know what you're saying.'

'I do,' she insisted gently. And she did. She felt the rightness of it settle over her skin, sink into her heart, and she knew that she wanted this more than she'd ever wanted anything before.

'You know that I can't stay here.'

'I know that. And I know what I want.'

'I can't give you what you deserve,' he said, finally raising his head and piercing her with his rich golden-flecked gaze.

'It's not about what we deserve, Henry. I'm not hiding anymore,' she said, locking her eyes with his, hoping that he'd see the truth of it, of her. 'You were right. I'm tired of being safe. And boring—'

'God, Lily, you're not boring, you're … incredible.'

He trailed off, his eyes drawn to her lips and suddenly his mouth was on hers, his hands at her back, bringing her body flush with his as if he wanted to hold her to him and never let go. It was the most incredible feeling she'd ever felt. So thrilled and pleasurable that she was almost dizzy with it. It felt like coming home.

His hand came up to the nape of her neck, warming the skin with the heat of his palm, and gently angling her to deepen the kiss. And with it came need, and desire. She wouldn't be passive in this. She would claim him as much as he would claim her. Her hands flew to his waist, one arm circling around him to draw them even closer together, the other tracing up his flanks to the biceps of his arm that she'd been so intent on earlier. His skin, smooth beneath hers, hot and enthralling.

The groan that left his throat covered her body, causing her to shiver with need. Knowing that he felt as she did, wanted what she wanted, was empowering, encouraging, firing her desire like nothing ever had before.

Their kiss deepened and became urgent until his lips left hers and he pressed open-mouthed kisses along her neck and collarbone, causing her head to fall back and simply accept the way he worshipped her.

The sigh of her own pleasure filled the air between them and she nearly cried when his lips left her skin. Drawing back in the embrace that still held them together, he pierced her with a gaze so intent.

'Lily, I want this, I want *you*, so much. But I can't promise—'

'I don't want promises,' she said sincerely. 'I don't want pretty words that can turn into lies. I want you. Here, now. Please don't turn me away,' she almost begged.

'I would *never* turn you away, Lily. Ever. Please know that.'

'Then please know that I want this. I want you. And,' she said, half on a laugh, sure of herself and of him from the need flaring in his eyes, 'please don't make me ask again.'

His dark eyes, flecked with gold shone in that moment, just before he bent his head and pressed his lips against hers in a kiss that Lily would remember for the rest of her life.

He swept her up in his arms and the little squeal she made turned into a peal of laughter as he placed her on the bed gently. She couldn't help but smile as he chased her up the mattress, a smile that almost stopped as she felt the entire length of him cover her as he framed her face with his hands.

'You are the most beautiful person I've ever met, Lily Atwell.'

And suddenly she felt it, beautiful, right down to her very toes.

'Only, there's one thing in the way. My horrible T-shirt.'

* * *

Laughter turned to kisses, which turned to cries of pleasure as they fell into each other's arms. A heady mix of sensation and passion that continued long into the night, cutting free chains that bound hearts, allowing them to soar above a sea of joy.

It was the most incredible night Henry had ever experienced. Never could he have imagined anything more perfect, or the way that it had made him feel. He knew, instantly, that one night would never be enough. One day, week or month. He wanted them all. But he couldn't tell her that. Not yet. There was something he needed to do first.

CHAPTER TWELVE

LILY STIRRED AS SUNLIGHT from the uncurtained windows fell in shafts across the room. It had gently heated the sheets that she ran her hand over, and she stopped. Before even opening her eyes she knew that she was alone, sensed that Henry was gone.

She gave herself a moment to sink into the feeling, the way her body still hummed pleasurably after their night together. Over and over again they had reached for one another, losing themselves in touches, kisses, caresses. Still without opening her eyes, she drew her hand to her mouth, and ran her fingers gently over her lips where Henry had poured passion into her. And her heart felt both settled and completely energized. She marvelled at the heights of pleasure he had taken her to, almost shaking her head at the impossibility of feelings she never could have imagined.

Now she understood what Malie always joked about. It had never been that way with Alistair, but even that sad thought couldn't dim the joy vibrating beneath her skin.

Lily sat upright in the bed, holding the sheets around her, not that she had anyone to fear exposing her modesty to. Then, she remembered. It was the day of the hen party and the restaurant run-through for the wedding breakfast. She cast a glance at the clock and squealed. *Nine thirty?!*

Thanking whatever god was out there for the beautiful blue skies and brilliant sunshine she saw through the windows, she ran to the door of Henry's room, dragging the sheet with her, peering out into the hallway to make sure the coast was clear – even though she knew it was highly unlikely that anyone would be traipsing around the estate – and did a two-metre dance back to the room where her hopefully-now-dry clothes would be. There was nothing about a walk of shame in her steps, because shame was the *last* thing she was feeling at that moment.

Lily threw off the bed sheet and jumped into the shower. The hot spray of water pounded against her skin and she couldn't believe that only hours before she'd stood beneath the same hot water and … everything had changed. Hadn't it? She bit her lip. Maybe it hadn't. Henry had said he'd not be able to make her any promises, and she'd meant it when she'd said she didn't need them.

She closed her eyes against the slight ache in her chest. If he didn't want anything further than what they'd shared last night, she'd have to be OK with that. She'd made her peace with it before she'd asked him not to turn her away. Because, in truth, even if it was only for one night, it had been incredible. Even now, she still felt the worship in his touch, the consideration, the care and the … no. Anything more had been solely on her part. She couldn't – wouldn't – make the same mistake again and misinterpret someone else's feelings. The only ones she could be responsible for were her own. Last night she had honoured them. And nothing and no one would make her regret that.

But still. A girl could hope, right?

She got out of the shower, drying quickly and thrusting on the jeans and T-shirt that had dried overnight. Her shoes must still be by the fire, with the rest of the hen party things in the living room.

But when she got to the room she stopped. Her shoes were there, yes, right where she left them, but the cushions, the silks ... they were gone. Frowning, she peered around the room, trying to see if they had been tucked away somewhere. As if you *could* tuck away eight large teal sequined sitting cushions and approximately five square metres of tulle and silk. She groaned out loud at the thought of the damage to the silk.

Maybe Henry had taken them downstairs?

She left the east wing and made her way down the central staircase into the grand hallway and turned, bumping straight into Anabelle, the estate's head chef.

'Lily!' she cried, taking her into a warm, strong hug.

'Annabelle,' Lily replied, when Annabelle released her, blushing and hoping that she hadn't been seen coming down from the guest suites. *No shame. No shame*, she told herself sternly. 'What are you doing here?'

'Are you OK?' the small, wiry woman asked, her head to one side as if that would somehow magically help divine what was going on with Lily.

'Yes, of course.'

'Then you're ready?'

'Ready?'

'Lily?'

'Mmm?' Lily was thoroughly confused, still half keeping an eye out for Henry, and wondering ... Oh!

'Ah, now you remember.'

'Of course I do! I'm sorry. I … I haven't had any coffee yet this morning.'

'So eager to get up here and crack on with the wedding breakfast run-through.'

'And the cakes.'

'Yes! Now, I wanted to talk to you about that. Are you sure about the wedding cake plans, I mean it does seem quite—'

'Coffee first? Please?' Lily asked, comically pulling on her old friend's elbow and dragging her to the counter where the machine was, thankfully, already on. She wondered if that had been Henry.

'I don't suppose, I mean … Have you seen Henry this morning?'

'Ahh,' said Annabelle knowingly.

'Don't *ahh* me. Coffee should be the first thing to scold me this early in the morning,' Lily replied, refusing to meet her gaze, while the older woman chuckled.

'Early?' Annabelle teased.

'Henry?' she almost pleaded.

'Was here this morning, up and about before I got here. With very explicit instructions for you.' The word 'explicit' exploded in Lily's mind and she had to force the sudden spike in her pulse back down. Utterly oblivious to the effect of her words, Annabelle pressed on. 'You are not allowed to go down to the beach until you're with the girls at six tonight.'

'What?'

'You are officially banned from the beach until tonight. He said, and I quote, *It's taken care of.* Including the boat. He said that it's back at the harbour.'

'Oh,' Lily said, more to herself and not really liking the thought that she'd been shut out of the hen party preparations. What if he got it wrong, what if the decorations weren't placed the way she'd intended? What if—

'Now,' Annabelle said, pressing a small espresso cup into her hands, 'we have thirty sponges to talk about. Thirty? Really?'

'Well, technically they're layers, so it's really only ten cakes …'

★★★

By the time Lily got back to her flat above the restaurant, she was beaming. The trial run of each of the dishes for the wedding breakfast had been almost perfect. Just a few touches to the seasoning and the plating, but Annabelle and her team had brought her menu to life with as much care and attention as if she'd been the one cooking it herself.

Despite her grumbling, Annabelle had been happy with the thirty sponges, all of which would be iced and decorated first thing in the morning. It was Lily's favourite bit of the menu. Lime and blackberry sponge with buttercream icing and decorated with a half-moon of blackberries and edible flowers and micro herbs. Even Annabelle had been impressed.

She flung off her clothes and popped into the shower to quickly wash away the heat and mess from the kitchen, and put on the dress that Victoria had made her years before. The one she'd worn for the VIP tour at the estate, knowing how much her best friend would love seeing her in it.

She checked her watch and yelped. She felt as if she were playing catch up the entire day and it made her laugh. She really was never usually like this. Always on time, if not early. Always ready and prepared. But last night with Henry had allowed a different part of herself to come alive. One that was a little reckless, a little more free and … she liked it. Really liked it.

She realized that usually she'd be terrified of not knowing what would greet them on the beach for the hen party, but this way she got to join in with the excitement, the surprise. Lily felt as if she were getting as much of a treat as the girls and she was thrilled! Which reminded her …

She left through the back door and walked around to the front of the restaurant to where the sign in the doorway declared 'Closed for a private event'. She realized that she hadn't actually been in her kitchen for a couple of days now. And strangely she hadn't missed it. She truly trusted Kate and Vihaan with her business, and was beginning to quite enjoy having some free time. For a second, she began to imagine what she could do if she gave herself more time. Perhaps do some of the travelling that Henry had suggested. Only it hadn't just been Henry, but also her mother and even Victoria. Had they all been trying to tell her the same thing? That she needed to put herself out there a bit more?

She was just about to check her watch when she saw a familiar black SUV approach the restaurant. Through the window she could just make out Zoe and frowned. Could there really be two black SUVs with people in the front passenger seats that looked like her?

'That's a nice way to greet me after all these months,' groused Zoe when the window glided down.

'No, it's not that, sorry, it's just that I could have sworn—'

'Never mind that, V's getting married,' Zoe squealed excitedly.

'Here we go again,' grumbled Finn Doherty happily from the driver's seat. He jumped out of the car, leaving the engine running and the hazard lights on, and came round to pull back the large side-panel door to retrieve Zoe's wheelchair. In the meantime, Zoe opened her door and swung herself around in the seat, ready for Finn to help her into the chair. Lily batted him away for a moment and took her friend in a warm embrace.

'It's so good to see you,' she said.

'I've missed you!' Zoe replied, pulling back in her arms a little. 'Are you OK?'

'Why does everyone keep asking me that?' Lily laughed.

'Because you – I don't know. Look different?'

'I don't know what you're talking about,' Lily evaded, blushing deeply.

'Oh yes you do,' Zoe said, her green eyes sparkling with mischief. 'Oh my God, did you—'

'Hi, Finn,' Lily said overly brightly, cutting through whatever revealing insight Zoe had been about to announce to the world.

'Hi, Lily,' Finn exclaimed with reciprocal brightness, clearly knowing something was going on from the way his eyes swivelled between Lily and his fiancée.

'Oh no you don't, you can't get away that—'

'Lils! Zo!'

The cry from Malie was so loud and Lily spun just in time to catch the hug her friend threw around her shoulders. Her glorious curls swamped her as she felt her whole body yanked up and down by Malie's exuberance. Lily couldn't help but laugh.

'Where's Todd?' Zoe asked, peering over Malie's shoulder.

'Oh, he's on a top-secret stag-related mission,' Malie replied.

'Stripper?' Zoe asked, grinning.

'He wouldn't dare,' Malie replied, the growl in her voice making the girls laugh. 'So where's the bride then? Trust V to be late for her own hen—'

'Hey, I'm not late! How dare you!' Victoria called from the other side of the SUV having snuck up from the harbour.

The squeals reached an almost ear-piercing level and Finn thrust his hands over his ears as if to block out the sound. Victoria and Malie were jumping up and down, Lily was laughing and Zoe was manoeuvring herself into her wheelchair.

'You set?' Finn asked Zoe, with a love shining in his eyes that was clear to see.

'Sure am,' Zoe replied, smiling as he leaned in for a kiss that would have made Mrs Whittaker call PC Ellis and probably have them arrested for public indecency – it definitely made Lily a little jealous that she'd not been able to see Henry that morning.

'Good. Have fun, ladies!' he called, before jumping back into the SUV and pulling away.

'We're all here,' Lily exclaimed, fisting her hands so she didn't grab them all into a massive hug.

'You're wearing it!' Victoria cried with delight.

'Of course I am, it's a beautiful dress made by a very talented, soon to be utterly famous and completely sold out designer!' Lily replied, giving the girls a little twirl and loving the way the fabric swirled around her legs.

'Show-off,' Zoe replied with a smile so wide it made Lily's heart soar.

'Jealous?' Malie joked.

'Utterly,' Zoe replied without malice and suffered a smacking great kiss on her cheek from Malie.

'Right. So what's the plan? You've kept us in the dark long enough, Lily Atwell,' Victoria said.

'And not just about the hen do,' Zoe replied under her breath, her emerald eyes still twinkling.

'What's that?' Malie asked.

'Nothing,' Lily replied, brightly enough for everyone to know it was most *definitely* something.

'Oh come on, Lils, what gives?'

'I'm not saying a word until I have a glass of Hawkesbury Reserve in my hands.'

'Ohhh, you tease.'

'Yes.' Lily smiled at the slightly bemused faces of her friends. 'I am,' she replied confidently. 'Come on.'

'Where are we going? Aren't we having it at the restaurant?'

'Nope,' Lily said, shaking her head and leading them all down the street towards the harbour.

'What's got into her?' she heard Malie ask Victoria.

'My money's on Henry Hawkesbury,' Zoe answered.

Lily choked, Malie screamed, Victoria laughed and Zoe smiled.

'Really?' demanded Malie. 'Seriously?!'

'Sparkling Reserve, Malie. Sparkling Reserve,' Lily said, smiling and feeling a well of something incredibly like glee rising within her. Her friends were all home, and Henry was … well. She didn't really know what he – or they – were, but right now, Lily felt as if she could conquer the world. And it was a feeling she could most definitely get used to.

As they reached the harbour, Zoe began to slow. 'Lils, I'm not sure—'

'It'll be fine, Zo, honestly.'

'Well, unless you guys know where I can chain up the wheelchair and are prepared to carry me for the rest of the evening … because there's no way Mr Michaels' old rowboat will fit all of us *and* my wheels.'

As they reached the row of boats moored up at the harbour's jetty, Zoe was beginning to look a little less than excited. And Victoria was looking at Lily as if she were a little mad.

'Where's the trust?' she asked as she pulled up to the sleek white boat that, as promised, Henry had brought back to the harbour last night.

Ignoring the confused faces of her friends, she hopped over the side of the boat, opened the small gate-like door in the side, retrieved the ramp and placed it between the jetty and the boat.

'Mr Michaels upgraded?' Malie asked, clearly flabbergasted.

'Not Mr Michaels. Blake,' Lily said, her smile tinged with a softness. 'This is … our boat. For us. To use whenever we want.'

'What?!' cried Victoria, promptly being shoved out of the way by Zoe, who couldn't wait to get on board.

'You're kidding me?' demanded Malie.

'It's incredible,' Zoe squealed, wheeling across the wide access ramp onto the back end of the boat that had enough space for all the girls *and* for her to be able to spin in a circle. 'He did this? Blake? For us?'

Lily nodded, a tear gathering in the corner of her eye and hoping beyond all hope that wherever Blake was, he could see this – the joy and happiness he'd given to her friends. To her. Zoe clutched a hand to her chest, unable to form any more words.

'And it doesn't stop there. Just wait until we get to the beach,' Lily promised.

'There's more?'

'There's always more,' cried Victoria taking Lily into a brief but strong hug.

'Henry Hawkesbury more, or—'

'La, la, la, la, la,' Lily replied with her fingers stuck comically in her ears. 'Malie? Care to do the honours?'

'Hell yeah,' she exclaimed, lovingly caressing the wheel and pressing the button to start the engine with a reverence reserved for greatness. 'Hear that, girls?' she yelled over the revving engine. 'That's the sound of this hen party getting *started*.'

***

The snazzy new boat took less than a quarter of the time it used to take to get to the beach in the old rowing boat. Lily relished the feel of the wind in her hair, the cool sea salt spray as they surfed the waves. The look of delight on her friends' faces was something that she would remember for the rest of her life. She sent up a prayer of thanks to Blake for all the wondrous things he'd done for each of them, not only for the hen party and wedding, but over the years. Because in a way, he had given them something precious, something that they never really imagined they'd have again.

Malie whooped when she saw the large jetty sprawling out from the beach into the bay, slowing and then gently reversing the engines so that Lily could jump out and moor them at the end.

'Is that …' Zoe trailed off, looking at the concrete walkway that led from the jetty across the beach towards the gazebo and the base of the road that Henry had driven to the night before.

'Yes,' Lily replied absently, knowing that her friend was thinking of the pathway that would make her chair able to handle the soft sand on the beach. But Lily wasn't seeing that. She was seeing what Henry had done for her. For them.

The gazebo was draped beautifully in the silks and tulle gently swaying in the wind. The lanterns, some hanging from the wooden gazebo frame, some dotted around the area that he'd created around the wooden pallets, glowed gently in the setting sun's light. Battery-powered fairy lights had been bundled into jam jars in a way that echoed the decorations they'd placed in the orangery for the wedding.

The large sequined cushions were dotted around the pallet tables on large reed matting to protect them from the sand. Several ice buckets brimming full of bottles of Hawkesbury Reserve were positioned strategically so that no matter where anyone sat they were within arm's reach of them.

It looked magical. It *was* magical.

'Oh my …' Victoria trailed off. 'Lily, it's beautiful.'

Henry had managed to not only recreate but add to her idea to bring all her friends back to the beach they'd loved so much as kids. Shaking off the goosebumps that had risen to her skin, Lily tried to fight the tears of joy simmering in her eyes.

'I … It wasn't me,' she said, shrugging. 'Well, not *all* me anyway.'

'Don't tell me this was—'

'Henry Hawkesbury,' all the girls cried in unison.

'Oh my God, what did you *do* to the poor man?' demanded Zoe as Malie opened the boat's side gate and placed the ramp down.

'My money's on orgasms. Lots of them,' Malie joked.

Lily laughed and said nothing as they all trooped down the jetty with exclamations and squeals of delight, the cool boxes she'd packed earlier with food swinging in her hands as Victoria bumped her shoulder against Lily's.

'This is *incredible*, Lils, really It's just so beautiful.'

Lily couldn't help but agree, amazed by all the details that Henry had put into place. As they drew nearer to the wooden pallets covered in a thick heavy white cloth, she saw place settings fit for a banquet. She'd told Henry about the food she'd planned, how she vowed not to produce the simple plates and cutlery from the bottom of the coolers. He'd really thought of everything.

Then she spied the small white boxes with ribbon gently twirling in the wind, placed in the centre of each of the four plates. Frowning, she reached for the one with the tag proclaiming her name.

'Oh.' Zoe sighed as if disappointed.

'What?' Lily asked, casting a glance to her place setting, making sure that she, too, had a box.

'There are no penis straws,' she moaned, with a mock pout.

Lily slapped her on the arm, but couldn't help but remember Henry, head tipped quizzically to the side, remarking on anatomical correctness, and she bit back a laugh.

'What's this?' Malie asked, helping Zoe navigate from the concrete path over to the cushions.

'Beats me,' Lily replied, confused. '*With love and thanks from O Xx*,' she read out loud.

Victoria looked on smiling as her friends opened their presents, and more squeals of delight rang out across the secluded beach.

'No way,' Malie demanded.

'Is that a——'

'Green sapphire?' Lily interrupted Zoe in shock.

Lily gently fingered the beautiful golden necklace chain, on which hung a perfect little green sapphire twinkling in the setting sun.

She dropped onto one of the cushions, staring at the necklace.

'Here,' Malie said to Lily, passing her a cream envelope. 'It's addressed to you.'

She prised open the thick cartridge paper and retrieved the sleeve of paper, just about managing to hide her disappointment when she saw the signed name at the bottom. Not Henry's, but Oliver's.

'*Dear Lily,*' she read out loud for the girls. '*We can't thank you enough for all you have done for us and the wedding, including this amazing hen party. That V has such amazing friends as you, Malie and Zoe, was blessing enough, but the bond you all share is something that not only V, but I, too, have gained incredible joy from. I want each of you to wear these at our wedding. They'll match V's beautiful bridesmaids' dresses perfectly, but will also unite you together in a way that has already been cemented through the years, with silk and sapphires. And hopefully when you wear these in the future it will remind you of the greatest gift each of you has given us on our wedding day. Your friendship, your love, and your support.*'

'I'm going to cry. I'm going to cry.' Malie rushed out, flapping her hands at her eyes as if to dry the tears before they could be shed.

Lily felt exactly the same way, and reached a hand to clutch Victoria's in hers.

'Todd's going to lose his mind. Ollie's just set a massive precedent,' Malie groaned.

'I'm asking for diamonds when it's your turn to be my bridesmaids,' Zoe laughed.

'Dibs on blue sapphires,' Malie called.

Lily stayed silent, fixing the smile on her face so as not to betray her thoughts. She daren't even hope for a wedding in her near future, even as the image of Henry standing beside her in front of the wedding arch crashed through her mind.

'OK, hand them over,' she demanded.

'Whaaat? Noooo!' cried Malie, 'It's mine. All mine!'

'I just don't want you to lose them before the wedding,' she explained.

'I'm not letting it out of my sight,' hissed Zoe.

'Give,' she said, her hand reaching for the beautiful presents. Reluctantly they each handed over their necklaces for her safekeeping, while Victoria reached for the first bottle of Hawkesbury Reserve. The pop echoed around the beach and all the girls descended into fits of uncontrollable giggles.

'Could you ever have imagined it? All the way back then, when we were here, catching mackerel—'

'We don't have mackerel for dinner, do we?' Zoe interrupted desperately, trying to hide the panic in her voice.

'Of course we do, Zo. In fact, it's a mackerel-themed—'

Malie's hysterical giggle cut through the menu Lily was about to make up on the spot, and Zoe's eyes went from wide-eyed horror to fury quicker in milliseconds.

'You knew?' she demanded in a threatening whisper. 'All this time and you knew?' Lily laughed as her friend's voice rose an octave.

'I would say, had a good idea rather than knew,' Lily replied nonchalantly. '*No mackerel*,' she mock whispered to Zoe.

'Good. I can't stand the bloody things.'

Victoria reached over and poured a glass of sparkling wine for each of them as Malie dug around in the coolers.

'Ten years ago we were here talking of all the things we would do with our lives. The people we would meet, the places we would go. And we did it! Look! We're all here.'

'And you're getting married,' Zoe, Malie and Lily chimed in.

'OK, seriously, I know I'm getting married, you don't have to remind me *all the time*. But yes ...' She broke off laughing. 'Oh my God, I'm getting married!'

'You know, if we just had some vodka, we could do shots every time someone says—'

'To you and Ollie,' Zoe said heavily, interrupting Malie and raising her glass in a toast.

'To V and Ollie!'

A silence settled over the four of them as they each took their sips of the Reserve and just looked at each other, relishing the bonds of friendship that drew them together.

'OK, now I want to hear about the orgasms,' Malie insisted, and Lily nearly choked.

'Hope you didn't do that last night,' Zoe threw out.

'Zo!' Lily cried.

'I'm just really happy for you,' Victoria said, grabbing Lily's hands. 'You deserve it, Lils.'

'I ... Look, I don't know what's going to happen. Henry might still sell the estate and fly back off to Singapore or New York.'

'Oh my God, you could go to New York?!' Malie cried.

'Not so fast,' Lily said, laughing until it petered out. Because in truth, she really didn't know whether Henry, or even *she* wanted that. 'Hawke's Cove is my home.'

'And it won't stop being your home, just because you spend a bit of time elsewhere, Lils,' Zoe replied, taking the hand that Victoria wasn't holding.

'Says the woman who is living in Sydney and flying all around the globe at a moment's notice,' Lily said gently.

Malie and Victoria went suddenly quiet, causing Lily to frown at the group.

'What?' Zoe's eyes became as wide as saucers, and she cast a panicked look to Malie, who looked at Victoria. 'Seriously, guys, what's going on?'

'Nothing,' all three girls replied at once.

'Don't give me that,' she insisted. 'What is it?'

Malie gestured to Zoe, her hand waving before her.

'Well,' Zoe paused, 'I'd wanted to wait until after the wedding, but I've got some news.'

'OK, enough with the dramatic pauses. Get to the point already,' Lily cried impatiently.

'I'm ...' She broke off, a huge smile brightening her beautiful features. 'I'm coming home. Actually, I'm kind of already home.'

'It *was* you!' Lily cried as Zoe's words settled about her. 'Oh my God, you're home! And Malie is home now, and V's only in London!' The words rushed out of her as Lily realized that finally, after all these years, her friends were back. Her heart soared and she felt tears press against the backs of her eyes.

'Don't start,' Malie warned. 'Don't, because you'll set me off and I'll ruin my mascara.'

'Why didn't you tell me?' Lily turned to Zoe.

'Oh, hun, we knew you had so much on your plate with the restaurant and the wedding, we didn't want you to get sucked into our drama as well.'

'Drama?'

'Finn bought the old Merrow's Rest property and we've been doing it up.'

'Has my mum been helping? She had paint brushes and rollers—'

'She's been a godsend.'

'You made my mum keep a secret from me?!' Lily demanded, her voice reaching impossible pitches which made Victoria wince.

'She wanted to. And she agreed that if you'd known …'

'I would have taken that on too?' Lily interjected sadly. For the first time, she'd realized that her friends had been half managing her in recent months. Or at least, felt that they'd had to. Perhaps Henry and her mother were right. She'd taken on too much to cover the need, the yearning for something else. In an instant she remembered her thoughts in the shower the night before. That she wanted more and it was beginning to get harder to ignore. It was sounding like a battle cry within her head and heart.

Zoe nodded. 'But I'm soooo pleased you know now. Mostly because I've been dying to bring Finn to the restaurant! Seriously, V hasn't stopped talking about almond croissants for at least a week and now they're all I can think about.'

'Well, I don't have almond croissants, but I do have something else,' Lily replied, digging into the cool boxes and retrieving the food that she'd prepared.

Boxes full of little canapes and smoked salmon, dips and crisps – because, who didn't love a crisp! – and potato salads, mackerel pâté for old times' sake, and more and more things that she could barely remember making in the chaos of the afternoon, while promising to give her thoughts a bit more time. She had some decisions to make, she realized, but now was not the time to do it.

At each new plate of food the girls oohed and aahed.

'I can't wait for the wedding breakfast,' Malie said. 'Obviously the ceremony is important, V, but Lily, the menu was incredible. Have you thought of doing more catering for weddings?'

'Is that you angling?' Zoe cut in with a smile.

'The only weddings I'll cater for are yours,' Lily insisted, laughing.

'Well, we'll just have to return the favour,' Malie said absently, not noticing the look of horror across Lily's features until Victoria descended into giggles.

'I. Am. Not. Letting. You. Near. My. Wedding. Food.'

'Oh, so there's going to *be* a wedding? That Hawkesbury better be ready.'

'Lily and Henry, sitting in a tree, K-I-S-S-I-N—'

'Will you just stop,' Lily said through the laughter. 'When did you get so childish?'

'When was I ever not?!'

★★★

The evening drifted on with much laughter, love, gossip and giggles, and when the stars were shining and the bottles empty, a very sensible, if slightly inebriated Victoria suggested that they should head back. Malie had heroically volunteered to remain sober enough to drive them back in the boat and was helping Victoria into her coat.

As Lily began to pack up the cool boxes and bring them towards the boat, Zoe stopped.

'Where do you think you're going?' she demanded.

'To the boat?' Lily replied.

'Na ah. Put those boxes down. Malie? A little help here?'

'Yeah?'

'She's trying to get back in the boat.'

'Oh no, that won't do. Rookie error,' replied Malie.

'What on earth are you guys talking about?'

'They're talking about the fact that yes, the boat might be this way, but *Henry*, is *that* way,' Victoria interjected, pointing up at the path cutting through the forest to the estate.

'I can't just turn up—'

'Of course you can. You can do anything that you want to do, my love,' Victoria insisted. 'In the meantime, we're going *home*,' she replied, the smile on her face showing just how much she knew Lily would love to hear that.

Lily drew all the girls into a massive hug. They were closer than sisters and she was so happy to have them back. But at that moment, all she could think about was Henry. Seeing him. Thanking him for the amazing things he did for the hen party … Kissing him … Losing herself in his arms again. A thrill shot through her and she turned to leave.

'Love you guys,' she called over her shoulder. The responding shouts – *You go get your man,* and catcalls from Malie about orgasms – followed her as she raced up the pathway, giddy excitement driving her forward.

She crested the hill slightly out of breath and jogged up the gravel drive, thankful to see a few lights on. She checked her watch; it wasn't too late, surely. She knocked on the door and was about to speak when Annabelle opened the door.

'Oh, hi, Annabelle.'

'Lily? Everything OK?'

'Yes, absolutely,' she replied, trying to shake off a bit of the surprise. She'd expected Henry to answer the door. 'Is Henry here? I … wanted to thank him for the hen party.'

'No, hun. I'm sorry. He left a few hours ago.'

'Left?' The word nicked her heart. 'Did he say when he'd be back?'

Annabelle shook her head. 'I'm sorry, my love, he had a packed bag with him and …'

'Oh,' Lily replied, suddenly completely lost. All the giddy happy excitement soured and made her nauseous. And lost. Completely lost.

'Do you want John to give you a lift back to town?' Annabelle asked. 'I'm sure he wouldn't mind.'

'No, it's OK, I'll walk,' Lily whispered.

'Are you sure? It looks like it might rain.'

'No, but thank you, Annabelle.'

Lily didn't see Annabelle's worried look as she turned away from the closing door. She barely saw the gravel driveway as she walked back down the path towards the road that would lead her home.

As the heavens opened and rain split the air, falling to the ground and covering her in a light fine haze, Lily gave no thought to the wedding or the weather, or the way that once again her clothing was soaking wet and clinging to her body.

As she reached the fork in the road, all she could hear was the pulse thudding in her ear to the beat of *can't promise, can't promise, can't promise.*

And as she finally crested the hill back towards her apartment, she told herself that it was rain, not tears, falling against her cheeks.

CHAPTER THIRTEEN

WHEN LILY WOKE ON the morning of the wedding, she was confused. Couldn't quite account for the ache that she felt, the tear that had escaped and run down her cheek during the night. And then she remembered.

Henry.

He had gone. The burst of hurt cut through her shakily inhaled breath and she turned in her duvet and pressed her face into a pillow to stifle the low moan rising in her chest.

It hurt. More than she had tried to prepare herself for the night before. How had he come to mean so much to her in such a short space of time?

Stupid. Stupid. Stupid.

It blared through her mind in time with the buzz of the alarm she had set for 6.30. But then she stopped as surely as she stopped the screech of the alarm.

No. She wasn't stupid, she determined, refusing to be unkind to herself. She had known what she was doing the night they shared such incredible passion. Such heartfelt honesty. And she wouldn't take it back for all the hurt she felt in that moment, or would probably continue to feel for quite some time. Henry had been right. She'd been hiding for too long now and she wouldn't do it anymore. Giving herself to Henry had honoured her feelings for him. She had been truthful with herself, and he in turn had been truthful with her.

I can't promise ...

She knew how painful it was for him to be back in Hawke's Cove. She'd seen the raw grief in his eyes not only that night, but before. How painful it was for him to be back at the estate that represented so much hurt and loss and how much strength it had taken for him to stay here as long as he had.

But she couldn't deny that while he'd accused her of hiding, he'd been running. Running ever since the accident, trying to outpace the demons that still drove him to this day. She couldn't – wouldn't – ask him to face them. Only he could do that. And all she could hope was that she had met his hurt with comfort and acceptance. Hope that she had given him some sense of relief from that – even if it came at a personal cost to herself – because he deserved that much at least.

With a sigh she pushed up from the bed and threw off the covers. No matter what she felt, it was Victoria's wedding today. And although suddenly it didn't seem as all-consuming as it had in the last few months, it was going to be beautiful and wonderful and Lily would never let her own feelings ruin this day for her best friend. So with one last sweep of her cheek, Lily got into the shower and washed off the sadness, ready to face the day fresh and new.

And she wouldn't be alone, she firmly told herself. She would have the best friends anyone could ever ask for. And with that thought, hope and love bloomed.

★★★

By the time she had cycled up to the Hawkesbury estate and round to the back entrance, she could see that the property was already humming with life. She locked up her bicycle and made her way into the kitchen, smiling the moment she caught the scent of the food being prepared by the busy kitchen.

'And just what do you think you're doing in here?' Annabelle demanded.

Lily held up her hands in surrender. 'Just grabbing breakfast for the girls.'

'A breakfast that we are more than capable of managing and the staff is more than capable of delivering to the suite.'

Lily bit her tongue at the question rising in her chest. As if sensing the direction of her thoughts, Annabelle stilled and sadly shook her head. Henry hadn't returned.

'Is the '

'That had better not be a question about the wedding menu!' Annabelle cut in.

'I just—' Lily tried again and nearly jumped when Annabelle slammed her hand down on the clean metal benches.

'Chefs, are we prepped for today?' she called out to the small army behind her.

'Yes, chef,' they all immediately shouted.

'Are the cakes iced and decorated?'

'Yes, chef.'

'Is there going to be a single thing wrong with any dish we present today?'

'No, chef.'

Lily couldn't help but smile.

'Good,' Annabelle said, satisfied. 'Now, you, Lily, are banned from the kitchen.'

'But—'

'Banned! Do I make myself clear?'

'Yes, chef,' Lily dutifully replied, not missing the twinkle in Annabelle's eyes removing any possible sting to her words.

Lily made her way up the staircase that had been decorated with wreaths of ivy and baby's breath, a long, beautiful length of silk winding around the banister. Her eyes widened in wonder. Uniformed staff paced through the building with purpose and industry, and it began to feel real. Victoria was getting married and Lily's heart began to fill with happiness.

She knocked gently on the door to the suite that had been assigned to the bridal party. Oliver and the groomsmen had spent the night in a nearby hotel and would arrive about half an hour before the ceremony. Victoria had stayed the night at home with her parents, as had Malie, and, picking Zoe up from Marrow's Rest this morning, they had come here so they could all get ready together. Checking her watch – Lily realized the photographer would be arriving soon.

The door swept open and she found herself yanked over the threshold into … chaos.

Malie was lying on the large sofa of the living area, eyes wide with something horribly like panic, and Zoe's mouth was pulled into a visual representation of the word 'eek'. Clothes were thrown around the room, bed covers in a mess, steam from a recently used shower was wafting into the room. Victoria looked as if she were about to tear her hair out.

'What—'

'I'm going to kill her,' Victoria shouted. 'Kill her!'

'Who?' Lily demanded, looking at Malie and Zoe, who were looking at Lily as if she needed to fix whatever was going on before Victoria was arrested and hauled away for murder.

'My cousin! She told her daughter she could be a flower girl.'

'What?'

'It was the only way she could get her in the car apparently. She's a little—'

'Child,' Lily interjected before Victoria could say anything further. 'Really? Is that it?'

'*That it?* It's a nightmare. Now her son is throwing a fit because his sister gets to be part of the wedding and it will mess up the seating, my parents will have to move, which will mean that Ollie's parents will have to move and Ollie's bloody best man wants to not only bring his dog but give a speech that will be as dull as—'

Lily's laughter cut through Victoria's words like a knife. It wasn't just a giggle, it was a full belly laugh that she couldn't quit. Lily had to bend to relieve the strain as she tried to control the spasms wracking her chest. Sucking in desperate breaths between her laughs it felt … good. Good, as if she were letting go. Letting go of the hurt, of the panic, of the exhaustion that had led up to today.

'Are you OK?' Victoria asked, clearly very concerned about her.

'I'm fine,' she managed as the laughter began to subside. 'I'm more than fine, V, and so will you be.'

'But—'

'But your cousin's daughter can hold your bouquet, which is flowers, which makes her the flower girl.'

'But you were supposed to—'

'I'll be holding my own, as will Malie and Zo, so there's no reason why she can't be in charge of your bouquet, with strict instructions not to damage it. We'll move chairs from the back row on either side of the aisle and place them up at the front, so that your cousin and her daughter can sit on your side, and her husband and son can sit on Ollie's. We'll give him a little boutonniere so he'll feel like a member of the wedding party too, and it will keep the brother and sister far enough apart for them not to argue. And the dog? Well, he'll be fine. We're outside anyway.'

'I told you she'd fix it,' Zoe said.

Lily wiped at the stray happy tear that had escaped. 'V, this is a teeny tiny thing that is very easy to fix and in no way detracts from you, or Ollie, or your vows, or the love you are declaring today in front of friends and family who love you.'

'Oh, Lils,' Victoria cried, rushing over to give her a massive hug.

Lily closed her eyes the moment Victoria's arms reached around her and held on. For Victoria, for herself, for that moment and for future moments. This was why she stayed in the cove. To be here, with her friends, to be loved and to love.

'You're getting married,' she whispered to Victoria.

'Shot!' Malie called from the sofa, dodging a slap from Zoe.

'We don't have any vodka,' Victoria replied, her voice slightly muffled from the embrace.

'But we do have Reserve. So, bucks fizz anyone?' Malie said, swinging the bottle in her hands.

'Yes please!' Zoe, Victoria and Lily all replied at once before descending into laughter.

While Malie set about pouring the drinks, Lily answered the knock on the door and retrieved the tray Annabelle had promised to send up to the suite.

'Are those—'

'Oh my God, *finally*,' Victoria exclaimed, almost pushing Lily out of the way in order to get to the almond croissants on the tray.

'Lily, if you don't get me one of those before V eats them *all*, I'll be the one done for murder,' Zoe insisted.

Lily raised the tray away from Victoria's grabbing hands and placed it on a small table in the middle of the room. She passed Zoe the biggest pastry she could find, slapping Malie's fingers aside as she did so.

'Are you not having one?' Malie asked.

'I'm diving into the coffee first.'

Zoe frowned. 'I don't remember you being such a coffee fiend.'

'A habit I must have picked up,' Lily said, trying desperately not to think of Henry.

'Any word from him?'

Lily shook her head. The girls knew that he'd left the night of the hen party and had since oscillated between promising to commit actual bodily harm, threatening to come to her flat and drown her in alcohol, romcoms or anything else that might work, and the worst … the sympathetic glances sent her way. But today wasn't the day for any of that.

'So what's the plan?' Lily asked between mouthfuls of the delicious coffee that still reminded her of Henry while Victoria ducked back into the bathroom.

'You mean … you don't have one?' Zoe asked. 'Seriously, are you OK?'

Lily smiled. 'I am. I'm just … trying out something new. A little more carefree.'

'Shouldn't you wait until after today to do that? We need you, Lils, and your not-so-secret-superpower.'

Lily laughed. 'Which is?'

'I don't know, you're kind of like a fixer, you know?'

'Yeah,' Lily replied, trying to hide the ache in her tone.

A fixer.

She reached into her bag for the beautiful necklaces Ollie had gifted them at the hen party. 'Don't forget these,' she said, holding the boxes out to the girls.

You genuinely don't know why you have to be the one who fixes everything?

Henry's words rushed into her mind before she could stop them.

We need you, Lils.

Is that why she did it? Because only then did she feel needed? Loved?

And suddenly she realized that she had felt it. The night she had shared with Henry. Cherished, worshipped and … *loved.*

'Come to Mama,' Malie said, reaching for the little box that had the label with her name on it.

Shaking herself from her thoughts, Lily crossed the room to where the three garment bags containing the bridesmaids' dresses hung near the window. Through the white cover she could see glimpses of the beautiful dress she had tried on … was it only a week ago? It felt like an age. The harvest, the night of the storm. All the things she had shared with Henry …

She loved him.

The realization nearly drew a gasp from her.

She couldn't, could she? She'd only really got to know him in these last few weeks. Surely it would take longer than that? But she answered her own question. She *knew* him. He might not be here, right in front of her, right now. But she did know him. His fears, his secrets, his hopes … And she accepted each and every one of them because they made him the person he was. The person who had made something good from a terrible tragedy. The person who – almost against his own will – brought the town together for a harvest he hadn't needed to worry about. Not really. Not if he truly intended to sell the estate. The person who had made her laugh, and yes, made her cry. But the person who had pushed her to see to her own truths. Her beauty, her power, which he had drawn from her during the night they shared, but also her hurts, and her own secrets. The ones she'd kept from herself. Without that, without him, she might not have ever seen. Seen that she had been hiding. He'd shown her her own strength. And even though he wasn't here today, beside her, that strength meant that she could stand on her own feet, owning herself and finally making plans for a future.

Malie and Zoe's giggles drew her back to the present.

'Right. Who dresses first?'

'You,' they both replied.

★ ★ ★

An hour later, Lily, Malie and Zoe were in front of the large mirror hanging above the fireplace, in their bridesmaids' dresses staring at their reflections.

The sage green silks of the material suited each of them perfectly, as did the green sapphires twinkling from their necklaces.

'Oh,' a voice from behind them came. 'You all look so beautiful!'

They each turned to find Victoria standing before them in her wedding dress. Lily gasped, Malie squealed, and Zoe practically sobbed.

The ivory silk of the dress practically glowed. The strapless bustier bodice was embellished with crystals that caught the shafts of summer sun pouring in through the windows. There was a sheer lace overlay that fell across the stunning silhouette of Victoria's waist and down towards a floor-length skirt and train that flowed out behind her like a pool of silk. It was dramatic, but simple, sophisticated and breathtaking. It was perfect.

'I'm going to cry,' Zoe exclaimed.

'I'm going to dump Todd and propose to you myself,' Malie whispered in awe.

But Lily was speechless. Her best friend looked simply stunning and in that moment, she genuinely couldn't have been happier. As if they all felt exactly the same thing at exactly the same time, they came together in a hug, not for a minute caring about crushing the beautiful silks of their dresses, or the running of mascara.

They were all so caught up in the moment, no one heard the knock on the door, the gentle swish as it opened, and no one saw the look of pure pleasure on the photographer's face as she raised her camera and caught the moment the four girls were utterly lost in each other in front of the fireplace of the bridal suite.

Click.

'Oh,' Malie cried, a little shocked.

'I'm so sorry,' the photographer exclaimed, 'I just couldn't resist. You all looked so beautiful.' She checked the screen on the back of her camera and barely contained a cry of excitement. 'Perfect,' she said more to herself than the girls. Then she apologized and introduced herself. Soon after that, another knock on the door came and within seconds the room descended into chaos again with the arrival of Victoria's mother, Ellen, and her soon-to-be mother-in-law, Stella.

Tissues and Reserve were passed around as freely as the gushing compliments on the dresses and the beauty of the bride and her friends. The photographer, only slightly miffed at having missed the 'prep' shots as she called them – to a wryly raised eyebrow from Zoe – snapped at least a thousand images of the room of women that spanned two generations and before they knew it, it was time to make their way to the ceremony.

David, Victoria's father, was pacing outside the room and when Victoria emerged, his cheeks took a red tinge and eyes a watery shine.

'Don't,' commanded Ellen sternly. 'I know how you get.'

'I …' He raised his hands in surrender, as if incapable of further speech.

'Oh, you're going to be terrible when it comes to the speech,' she scolded.

The photographer sneaked past and jogged down the stairs, determined to get another perfect picture.

Victoria looped her arm through her father's and kissed him gently on the cheek to a blush deeper than any Lily had managed to achieve thus far. Stella busied herself by leading Zoe and Malie to the lift to take them down to the ground floor, while Ellen fanned the train of the bridal dress out behind her daughter.

Lily was halfway down the stairs when David whispered something to Victoria that made her laugh. She turned to see the entire group looking back at the perfect sight of the bride looking at her father, her eyes sparkling with the sheen of unshed tears of joy.

By the time they all regrouped at the bottom of the stairs, the photographer already had at least five new stunning shots for her website, the bride and groom would have pictures they would cherish for the rest of their lives, and the bridesmaids had memories that they would never forget.

Distracted by the perfect moment, it took a while for Lily to notice the slightly worried conversation between Malie and Zoe that soon included Victoria.

'What's wrong?' she asked.

'Nothing,' Victoria replied, although clearly it was something. Zoe was still frowning, and Malie looked torn.

'It's really not anything, but V thought it would be nice to have Todd and Finn walk with us down the aisle, and we thought that maybe …'

'Henry might be here to walk me down too,' Lily concluded a little sadly. 'It's OK,' she insisted, 'just because he's not here, doesn't mean that has to change.'

'If Lils is walking down the aisle on her own, so am I. And before you say anything,' Zoe rushed on, 'I am perfectly capable of wheeling myself down that aisle.' She was adamant.

'But you don't have to,' insisted Lily.

'You're right, I don't have to. But I *want* to.'

Lily felt her heart pressing against her ribs and tears beginning to well in her eyes. She reached out and placed a hand on Zoe's arm. Zoe had taken Malie's hand in hers, while Malie had her arm around Victoria's shoulders. Victoria entwined her fingers with Malie's own.

They stayed like that for a moment, connected, until Ellen cleared her throat impatiently. They turned to find a look of pure indulgence from Stella and saw David repeatedly dabbing his eyes. Zoe and Malie fired off texts to their partners, giving them an update on the procession, then tucked their phones back into their bags and left them by the doors.

'Is he going to be OK?' Zoe asked Victoria in a hushed voice, referring to the bride's father.

'Probably not, no,' she said with more love than sincerity. 'Come on, Dad, we can't be late.'

The photographer scurried out of the hallway to get herself in place to take the best shot of the bride arriving.

'What does it look like?' Malie whispered to Lily.

'You haven't seen it?' Lily asked, shocked.

'We went straight up to the suite, so didn't have time.'

'Oh,' said Lily, secretly pleased. 'Then you tell me.'

She led the party from the hall's back doorway and out towards the bank of grass that looked out over to where the vineyards dropped away to reveal the bay and the sea beyond.

Zoe gasped, Malie gently cursed, and Victoria stopped in her tracks. Even Stella squealed a little at the beautiful sight before her.

The white chairs – where guests were now seated – linked by streams of white silk and tied with bows, had been placed each side of the wicker runner creating the aisle leading towards the stunning thick wooden hoop of the wedding arch. Bows of rich green ivy and fresh baby's breath, the purest white trailing roses, sprigs of scented lavender and blue hydrangea hung in bunches at a diagonal to frame the celebrant standing at the centre of it. Through the arch could be seen the distant horizon where the sky met the sea in an almost endless vista of shades of blue. To the left, Ollie stood talking to his best man, until he caught sight of the bridal party at the foot of the aisle and stopped. The shock on his face as his eyes landed on Victoria drew the gazes of the guests and they all turned, each seeming to look upon the other with awe.

As the girls arranged themselves, Zoe in front, Malie just behind, Lily turned to Victoria, who had begun to tremble slightly.

'I'm not sure why I'm nervous,' she whispered to Lily, who shook her head and smiled.

'It's not nerves, V. It's joy. It's love,' she whispered back and her best friend's eyes grew wide with wonder, nodding at Lily's words and smiling in return.

'Loves you, Lils,' Victoria whispered, catching Lily's hand before she could turn back to the aisle.

'Loves you too, V. But he loves you more. That's OK. I can handle it,' Lily replied, softly joking. Feeling a sense of rightness settle about her as she recognized the first gentle sounds of the orchestral version of 'O Mio Babbino Caro', the piece Victoria had chosen for her walk up the aisle, she took a deep breath.

With the posy on her lap where the stunning sage silk skirts parted to reveal the bolt of ivory silk, and hands on the wheels of her chair, Zoe began the procession down the aisle, slowly followed by Malie.

When it was Lily's turn, she cast a look at Oliver, who was trying to surreptitiously wipe a tear from his eye and failing. The look on his face was full of wonder, his eyes focused on his bride just behind Lily as if he had never believed he'd actually be here with family and friends to declare his love for Victoria.

At the front row of the chairs on Ollie's side, she could see Stella beside Eric, Ollie's father, looking full of health and happiness, and Lily was thankful for the experimental treatment that had done wonders for him. Beside them she could see Victoria's cousin's husband and the little boy who was proudly showing off his boutonniere but all eyes were on the bride. Behind, sat Ollie's cousin Andrew, who she'd heard so much about over the Christmas period, looking much less angry and stressed than she'd imagined him to be.

On the other side at the front row, Ellen took her seat beside the chair designated for her husband, and next to them were Victoria's cousin and her daughter, whose face was a mask of concentration and pent-up energy as she had yet to take ownership of Victoria's flowers. Lily just hoped that would be enough to make the little girl happy.

In the rows of chairs behind, Lily recognized Victoria's brother, Charles, and saw her own mother, her eyes shining with love and understanding which Lily forced herself to acknowledge, then she moved on. Hani and Helena Pukui, Malie's parents, sat beside her – his large Hawaiian frame almost exaggerated by the petite blonde form of his wife. Selena and Noel Tayler beamed pure joy as they watched Zoe, then Malie and Lily herself come down the aisle.

She passed Jasmine, Nisha and Taylor, Victoria's students from the class she taught, sat beside Sarah and Paul from her work in the pub, with their partners, all beaming and full of happiness for Victoria and Ollie. And then came a few faces from the town, and even Mrs Whittaker looked happy for possibly the first time ever. The thought had Lily stifling a laugh.

She reached the top of the aisle to stand beside Malie and Zoe and turned in time to see Victoria take her final steps towards the arch, her eyes bright and fixed firmly on Ollie, even when the photographer snapped about seventy pictures of them together at the top of the aisle, then ran round the back to take some more.

Lily quickly and discreetly fanned out the back of the dress and the train, and slid back in line with the girls, Malie giving her a gentle nudge on the shoulder, and Zoe leaning her head slightly towards Malie, whispering in a contented sigh, 'They're getting married.'

To which, Lily and Malie replied 'Shot,' in a whisper, causing all three to smile their secret smile.

'We are gathered here today …'

As the gentle words of the celebrant began, Lily tried to keep her eyes locked on the happy couple, but couldn't help occasionally running her gaze over the guests. At first she didn't realize what she was looking for. But then, when unsuccessful, she realized it was Henry.

The feeling in her chest wasn't hurt but a yearning. She didn't *need* him here, but she *wanted* him here. Not for Victoria, which was horribly selfish, but for herself. She wanted to share this moment of love with someone who loved her in that same way. And as much as she hoped that he did – had felt it in his touch that night they shared together – she also knew how much hurt was holding him back. And that was something that only he could overcome.

She was called back to the ceremony the moment the celebrant asked, 'Do you support this union and affirm that these two should be married today?'

A resounding bark came from the best man's dog and a gentle laughter rippled through the guests.

'Well, that's a good thing,' Will Carter, Ollie's best man, said, rubbing his golden Labrador's head proudly.

Victoria shot Lily a look of near murderous venom, causing Lily to bite back a laugh, Malie nearly to choke and Zoe to elbow Malie.

The celebrant cleared her throat, calling the guests' attention back to her. 'Do you, Oliver Russell, take Victoria Scott ...'

Words of love flowed between the bride and groom, touching everyone with a poignancy and joy in witnessing and recognizing such a beautiful union. Even Will's dog remained quiet right until the celebrant declared them husband and wife, upon which his barks joined in the happy cheers of nearly eighty friends and family and not even Victoria minded. Much.

★ ★ ★

Canapes and glasses full of sparkling Reserve were brought out and while the guests milled about the grass bank, the tables were discreetly removed and the photographer began to arrange her shots. Lily watched Malie with Todd and Zoe with Finn, while Oliver and Victoria were positioned for more kisses and more photos in front of the beautiful wedding arch she had stood before with Henry. Had she loved him even then? she wondered.

Somewhere in the middle of the arguments, his help with the wedding and the insane mad dash she'd made to try and save the hen party, it had snuck beneath her skin. And standing there, slightly off to the side, watching all the joyous moments being shared between her friends and their partners, she realized that the hardest thing, the saddest thing, was not that she stood here by herself, but that she hadn't told him. It didn't matter if he didn't or couldn't return her feelings. What suddenly mattered most was that he should know he was loved. Because that, Lily realized, was what bonded the girls, was what had kept them together over the years and continents. The knowledge that they were loved. The telling and sharing of that love. The owning and acceptance of that love.

Which was why she still stood there, by herself, but not alone. Because she was surrounded by people who were glorying in their feelings and sharing those feelings with everyone. Looking back with Alistair, yes, he might have been incredibly selfish and – well, let's face it – a nasty piece of work. But even then, had she hidden him from the others? Had she kept him separate from her life, her work and her friends? It was quite possibly in part down to the fact that, in reality, she had known that he wasn't the right person for her. Had known that she didn't really want him by her side, representing a part of herself. But Malie and Todd, Victoria and Ollie, Zoe and Finn, they let each other shine. They were reflections of the other, like a shard of glass, refracting the light of their love and each other, for the world to see.

And inexplicably she wanted everyone to see the Henry that she saw. And she wanted to be seen the way that he saw her.

Incredible.

That's what he'd said of her. And she wanted to reach for that, *be* that.

No, Lily told herself. She didn't have to reach for it. It was already there, waiting for her to see it for herself. And in that moment, she didn't see the grass bank leading to the vineyards sweeping down the hill. She saw the times she had shared with him. Laughing over coffee, holding the large pot of pasta as he told her he knew that she could hold it all day, leaning slightly against him as they had celebrated his twenty-first birthday several years after the fact, the way he had growled at her to get in the car during the storm on the beach, the moment they'd shared inside the Jeep, the rain pouring against the windscreen just looking at each other, soaking wet and out of breath, the way he'd struggled to tell her that he worried about her, that he thought she was hiding, not because it would hurt, but because it would open her eyes and give her the courage to be better, do more, reach further … *aim higher*, just as she'd once told him to. Then the way he had kissed her, held her, as she'd fallen apart in his arms the night they'd shared together.

'Lils!' Malie's voice cut through her thoughts, and Lily looked up to find her closest friends, smiles on their faces and light in their eyes, beckoning her over.

'Coming,' she said, as she bid one last look at the horizon, hoping that wherever Henry was, he was OK. He was … happy.

★ ★ ★

The sighs and oohs of the guests as they first entered the orangery were great, but the look on Victoria's face made the whole thing worthwhile. Lily couldn't help but smile herself at how beautiful it looked.

The walls and roof above, comprised of glass panels sunk into thick iron leadwork, were stunning enough, but decorated with bows of ivy and baby's breath and white trailing roses carried over from the ceremony and into the orangery made it feel as if this was a magical garden, rich and alive. Ten tables made from reclaimed scaffolding board added a rustic beauty to the scene. The hurricane lamps Henry had bought – bright with glorious white candles glowing beside jam jars with even more baby's breath – made Lily smile. She would always think of him when she saw them. She knew that now.

The seating plan was resting on the large aged wine barrels and a hand-painted sign welcomed each of the guests to the wedding breakfast.

The conversation swelled as people took their places and uniformed waiting staff poured wine and Reserve when they were seated. Lily followed Victoria and Ollie and their parents up to the table that ran along the tops of four long others. She quickly checked the numbers and located where she might direct the wedding cakes to be placed at the end of the meal.

'Stop working,' Victoria mock growled, taking Lily by the crook of her arm, making her smile.

'Can't help it.'

'Seriously, have you thought about wedding planning?'

'What, if my restaurant doesn't work out?' Lily demanded in horror.

'No,' Victoria said, laughing. 'As well as. Kate and Vihaan,' she nodded to where they sat amongst the guests, 'seem to have it pretty much under control. And you're so good at it. Just look at this, it's breathtaking.' Awe was shining from her voice.

'It really is, Lily,' Ollie chimed in. 'We can't thank you enough,' he said, slinging an arm around her shoulder and pulling her into his side.

Lily beamed under the praise and tried to ignore her usual inclination to shrug off the compliment. Instead, she let it sit, let the *suggestion* sit. Because as much as it had been stressful at times, she'd really enjoyed this. Enjoyed putting together something she knew would be perfect for the bride and groom. Realized how much pleasure she got from the joy and happiness felt by the guests who were busy on their phones snapping photos of the table decorations and the orangery and taking selfies. It was almost the same feeling as when she had first cooked dinner for her mum.

Everyone took their seats and Stella and Victoria's mother bonded over how appalling it was that people were drinking their sparkling wine before the speeches.

'You'd better start, dear,' Ellen said finally, turning to her husband who was even more watery-eyed than before – if that was possible.

David nodded, patting the piece of paper from his shirt pocket before retrieving it. He cleared his throat, but the sound barely reached Lily and she was only on the other side of Victoria, Ollie and his parents. Even that distance didn't diminish the look of slight panic Victoria cast her from where she sat.

Stella took the reins and tapped her wine glass with her knife, but even then it took a few moments for the guests to quieten down.

Victoria's dad pushed his chair back, scraping it against the stone flooring, which made his wife wince a little. Lily began to worry in earnest as the older man had to wipe his eyes before he could even open the page. A gentle, supportive laugh broke out amongst the guests, appreciating how overwhelmed he clearly felt at his only daughter's wedding.

'I ...' David cleared his throat again, and adjusted his glasses, peering at the piece of paper now held as far away from him as he could get it.

'Did you bring the wrong glasses, dear?' Victoria's mother prompted, causing her daughter to roll her eyes.

'No. No. It's fine. Ehm. I ... We today ...' *Sniff.*

Lily cast a look at Malie and Zoe, who were staring at her as if to say, *Do something!*

Will piped up from the other end of the table. 'I could—'

'No!' both Ollie and Victoria cried at the same time.

'Do you ...' Ollie began to offer David some kind of assistance, but in response he just waved the paper, looking incredibly uncomfortable and on the verge of irritable. Lily saw Victoria's hands clench a little, then she rose from her seat, quietly stepped behind the table and over to where David was standing.

'Mr Scott,' she whispered. 'Would you like me—'

'Yes,' he hissed with such vehemence she nearly laughed. 'God, yes.'

Smiling, she took the paper he thrust at her with the speech he had prepared, but as she returned to her place at the table realized that she couldn't read a word of the slanted scrawl. She looked out at the expectant faces of the eighty or so guests in front of her. Victoria's face almost defined the word 'imploring', Ollie's was more of a plea; she tried to ignore the miffed expression on the face of the best man and couldn't be sure but was half convinced the golden lab was quietly growling.

Ignoring it all, she blanked her mind, calling instead for the calm and overwhelming love she had felt only moments before. She took a deep breath …

CHAPTER FOURTEEN

'AS MOST – IF not *all* – of you know, I have known V for nearly all my life,' Lily began. 'V, Malie, Zo and I … not even continents could divide the four of us. *And* as most – if not all – of you know, we've had some rough times. Times that shaped our futures in ways that were unimaginable, difficult, hard … but through it all, we've been there for each other. Through the years, months, hours, and some that were lost,' she said, breaking off as Victoria and the girls laughed a little, 'we've stayed together, fierce in our love and support of each other.

'So it's safe to say that Malie, Zo and I were going to have high standards for the man who would steal V's heart.' A gentle laughter rippled through the guests. 'Oliver is a man who sees V as the wonderful, amazing, talented and beautiful person that she is. He sees her like we do and loves her all the more for it. So yeah,' she said shrugging, 'he'll do.'

The guests laughed again, some cried 'Hear! Hear!' and a few whistlers cut through before they quietened down again. She found her mum sitting near to Zoe and Malie, her eyes bright, and felt the love and pride shining there for her as much as for Victoria and Ollie. She thought of all the ways she'd wanted – *needed* – her best friend's wedding to be perfect. But she now realized her mum was right. That was not what was most important.

'I was told a few weeks ago, by a very clever woman,' she said, nodding to her mother, 'that a wedding can be beautiful, it can be perfect, it can also be disastrous and funny and ridiculous. Because what's really important isn't the flower arrangements, or the wedding breakfast – although—' Lily broke off, 'it bloody well will be!' much to the laughter and appreciation of the guests. 'It's not the photographs or the music ... All that really matters, is V and Oliver. Two people who are so very special. Not just because they're amazing but because the love that they share is ... palpable. You can feel it because they choose to share it with each and every one of us.'

As she looked out at the guests, her eyes snagged on the sight of Henry filling the doorway to the orangery, dressed in a dark suit and tie, looking so devastatingly glorious her heart soared.

He'd come back.

She stifled the gasp in her chest, taking a moment to collect herself and called forth the things she wanted to say.

'Three little words,' she said, not taking her eyes off him. Wanting him, needing him to feel her words as much as hear them. 'They're said millions of times a day, all over the world, in hundreds of different languages. Their meaning is shown a thousand different ways, in a touch, a hug, a kiss. They're said in private, in thought, in secret ... whispered, said out loud, screamed from the rooftops and written in the sky. They're said to those both underserving and deserving. They're said between friends,' she said, looking out at Zoe and Malie, and then back to Victoria. 'They're said between family and lovers.' She looked at Ollie, Todd and Finn, who had become part of her family too.

'But the greatest crime of all, would be not to say them at all. Today V and Oliver declared their love in front of you. They shared their love with you. And we are all greater for it. Because love isn't something to hide from. It's something to be given freely and willingly. It's given with trust, and with a leap of faith.'

She turned her gaze back to Henry, seeing his eyes sparkle, feeling the power of the connection between them, seeing the rise and fall of his chest as he took a deep breath, as if understanding what it was she was trying to say.

'Life is short. We know that,' she said sadly, thinking of Blake, of her father, even of Claudia. 'So find your person, turn to them. Look at them, so that they know you see them – the entirety of them – so that they fully understand, believe and accept it when you say ... I love you.'

The half sob that rose in Lily's chest was drowned out by eighty voices gently cresting over each other, filling the orangery with words of love. Goosebumps swept over her skin in waves as people laughed and cried and shared the greatest gift a person could give. The room erupted into a thunderous round of applause and Victoria dragged Ollie by his tie into a passionate kiss, Malie wiped her eyes, not even caring about her mascara, her hand sneaking around Todd's neck and pulling him to her, and Zoe leaned into the crook of Finn's arm. But Lily had eyes for nobody other than Henry. And instead of taking her seat, she made her way past the tables and guests who were already lost in each other and felt the beat of her heart, only for him.

★ ★ ★

Up until that moment – the moment he finally laid eyes on Lily – Henry had felt utterly exhausted. Physically, emotionally, mentally even. But as he'd heard her voice ring out, clear and true, calling for the guests to declare their love for each other, to claim it and to own it, it had cut through all the tiredness caused by the last forty-eight hours.

When she'd said, *I love you*, looking straight at him, deep into his eyes and heart, he'd wanted to beat his chest and shout his love for her, as she had said, from the rooftop. He'd wanted, needed her to know how he'd felt from even before the night they'd shared together. But there were things he needed her to know before he could.

Henry couldn't take his eyes from her as she wound through the tables, a bolt of white silk stretching from the floor-length skirt to her thigh with each step she took, the effect both stunning and sensual at the same time. He instantly regretted being away for her for a second. He'd hated the idea of her being alone for the wedding, and had desperately tried to make it back on time, but the traffic had been wall to wall and with each and every second he'd felt as if he were losing her. Until now.

She was simply the most beautiful thing he'd ever seen and he never, *ever* wanted to be without her again. It took both seconds and hours for her to reach where he stood in the doorway to the orangery and for a moment they just stood and stared at each other.

He was speechless. He'd had so much to say. So much. But in that moment, all he could do was fill his eyes and heart with the sight of her. She seemed as overcome as he, and he searched her gaze for some sign that he hadn't completely ruined everything, still not quite believing that this incredible woman might just feel the same way as him. A shuddering sigh wracked his chest as a strange sense of peace and urgency filled him simultaneously.

'Ah … Can I … can *we* go somewhere to talk?' he stumbled.

She nodded, even as they had to shift out of the way of servers bringing out the first course of the wedding breakfast. She turned to walk past him but guilt stirred in his chest.

'Wait,' he called to her. 'The food, your menu—'

'That's OK.'

'But—'

'Not what's important right now, Hawkesbury.'

She couldn't see, but a huge grin split his features. She'd called him Hawkesbury. That couldn't be a bad sign, could it? Though the grin turned into a frown the moment he realized that for the first time since he'd come back to Hawke's Cove, Lily Atwell didn't care about the wedding. Oh God. Had he already hurt her that much? Had he hurt her *too* much?

He followed her out into the hallway that split the main building and the orangery and back out into the open air towards the benches in front of the distillery. Where they had – was it only weeks ago? – shared wine and talked about their birthdays.

She stood looking out across the estate, her arms wrapped around herself. He had a flash of how those arms had wrapped around him during that night they'd shared. *Mind out of the gutter, Hawkesbury*, he ordered himself. Only it wasn't the gutter. It had been the most magical night of his life. Something he had been sure he'd not deserved. Something he still not might deserve. But he had to tell her. Had to explain.

He shucked off his suit jacket and laid it over the old wooden bench, terrified of damaging the dress that made her look like a wood nymph. Her rich chestnut-coloured hair had been spun into ropes and pinned up into something that probably had a fancy name and looked sophisticated but was still Lily. In the last few weeks he'd become used to seeing her hair down. The way it had fanned out across the pillow and his sheets that night, the way it had framed her beautiful face. The sage green dress flowed around her like silks, caught on the gentle breeze and hinting at, then concealing, her glorious figure.

When she turned to him, he saw the green sapphire Ollie had told him about the day he'd brought him up here to see the vineyard.

'I'm so pleased you got them,' he said, noticing the way it sparkled in the sun. 'Ollie had asked me to make sure they got to the hen party as a surprise for you all.'

Her eyes, watchful and wary – as if suddenly she wasn't sure what he wanted, what he was going to say – cleared for a moment.

'Henry, what you did for the hen party … I can't thank you enough.'

Good God, he'd walked out on her the morning after they had shared an incredible night together without a word, without an explanation and she was thanking him?

'Lily—'

'No. Wait. I want to say this. No matter what happened, before or after, that was truly a beautiful thing you did for us and I … Thank you.'

'You.'

'What?' she asked.

'I did it for *you*.' He wanted her to know that. Needed her to.

He gestured for her to sit on his jacket laid on the bench.

She frowned and started to object.

'Lily, sit on the bloody bench,' he growled. Because if she were sitting, it would be harder for her to run away. And even though, technically he'd done that to her, he had, in his own way, been running *towards* her. Felt as if he'd been doing it even before his return to Hawke's Cove.

She plonked herself down on the bench so primly, he had to stifle a smile. Even now – even when he wanted to tear his heart out and rip the words from his chest – she could still make him smile.

'I … well, first I need to apologize.'

'There's no—'

'Lily Atwell, you had your turn. Now it's mine.' The gruff resolute tone of his voice seemed only to bring a sparkle of something even more wood-nymph-like to his mind. Something almost teasing and he had to look away, or he'd lose all train of thought and gather her into his arms to kiss her. And never stop.

'I should never have left without telling you where I was going, or speaking to you first. Only, I hadn't meant to be away so long. I'm sorry if even for one minute I made you think that I had left you.' He turned back, realizing only a little too late that he'd given this startling monologue to the sea rather than her. He searched her eyes, and said again, 'I'm sorry. Truly and deeply.'

She inhaled and sighed deep. 'OK.'

He followed her breathing as if it were his own. Then ran a hand through his hair, half tempted to pull on it, but trying not to lose all semblance of control.

'The night we spent together, I need you to know. It was

everything to me. It was the most incredible night of my life, and I ...' He broke off as a blush rose to her cheeks and he almost couldn't continue. 'But that night, you said that I was the only person who could forgive myself. You weren't wrong,' he said, reaching for her hand and hoping that she wouldn't pull away, 'but you weren't quite right either.'

At her raised eyebrow, he couldn't help but smile, the indignation quite clear to see. 'It does happen you know,' he gently teased.

'Rarely. Carry on,' she replied as regal as any queen. And just the small echo of a smile gave him the courage to press ahead.

'I realized that to properly put the past to rest, I needed to see Claudia's parents.'

The lips that had quirked ever so slightly in a smile, formed an 'o' as a puff of air fell from her lungs. Eyes wide, glittering and searching, scanned his own, running over his body as if to check for signs of hurt or pain.

'And I'm sorry that it became more important to me than to let you know where I was going. That was unforgivable.'

'Oh, Henry,' she said, and he held up his hand to stop her. He needed to get this out. To explain.

'They live up near Northumberland now. Did you know that?'

She shook her head, biting her lip a little as if wanting to speak but not to interrupt.

'It's a fair old drive, even without the traffic, which is why I left that morning. I'd promised myself I'd be back in time for the wedding, but ... Not the point,' he said more to himself than to Lily. 'I've never been able to forget the last words they said to me, at the inquest. That I should have been able to do something – to stop her.'

Lily's eyes began to fill with tears, and he knew they were for him. That this incredible woman hurt for him.

'And … And I couldn't stand the fact that while I'd accused you of hiding, I realized I'd been running. This whole time. From that. From them. So,' he said, taking a jagged breath, 'I went to see them.'

In his mind, he saw the way that Mr Avery had opened the door, standing in front of his wife as if to protect her. From him. The hurt and fear in his eyes had nearly made Henry turn back, in fact he would have done, had Mrs Avery not pushed past her husband and reached for him, hurt, with tears but also hope in her gaze.

He'd stiffened in her awkward half embrace, but as Mrs Avery's tears had soaked into his shirt, he'd welcomed them, welcomed the sharing of a grief so unspeakable for them and for him.

'It was … hard. Difficult and, yes. It hurt. I hadn't intended to stay so long, but Mrs Avery had made tea and …'

'You always make time for tea,' Lily concluded.

Henry smiled. 'That's what she said. Mr Avery was, for the most part, quiet. Which was good, in a way. It gave me the space to finally say how sorry I was. Not … to accept responsibility, but …'

The look on Mrs Avery's face when he'd done so had been utterly unexpected. She had burst into more tears, looked to her husband, who looked to his shoes.

'They wouldn't hear it. They … they said that they were the ones who should have been apologizing to me.'

He still couldn't believe it now. He could see it, a shadow echo in front of him of how Mrs Avery had said they were so sorry for shouting what they did at him. So sorry for the way they treated him after the accident. Grief-stricken, hurt and lost, they had lashed out. And even as Henry had explained that he understood, they had been unwavering.

'How did that make you feel?' Lily gently asked, bringing him back to the present.

'Shocked? Sad? I'd had no idea they'd felt that way, and I still hate to think that they've been holding on to that for so long.'

And the moment the words were out of his mouth, he realized that he'd been holding on to just as much for just as long. It had been so strange to sit there on the cream-and-pink sofa, holding a tiny porcelain cup with long-since-cold tea as Claudia's parents had clutched each other, as if needing support, as they explained how hard it had been for them following her death. How lost and awful they'd felt and how sorry they were for taking it out on him.

'I hadn't planned to, but I showed them the app. Claudia's app. And they were so … pleased. Happy that something that could help others had come from such a tragedy. They had felt so helpless that they hadn't realized how … difficult it had been for her. How far she had descended into drink and drugs. They asked after you, and the girls,' he said, looking up into her glorious brown eyes. 'They wanted me to say how pleased they were that you were all doing so well. And how sorry they were that they never reached out to you all.'

Lily waved the statement away, and he knew that they had not once placed blame with Claudia's parents. Only perhaps themselves, in the same way he had.

'I can't even begin to imagine how hard it must have been for them.'

Henry nodded his agreement.

'They also asked about me, about what I'd been doing with my life. What I hoped to still do …' He trailed off, finally coming round to the real heart of what he'd wanted to tell her. Share with her. What he hoped might just be their future.

'I told them about you.'

'Me?' Lily looked up, confusion in her eyes.

'Yes. About your restaurant, about the changes to Hawke's Cove. About the work you did with my father to help bring the estate kicking and screaming into the twenty-first century.'

She tried to dismiss the compliment. 'I don't know about that.'

'Don't think I haven't realized just how much you've done at the estate. And not just for the wedding or in the herb garden … Or for my father. I told them that they could come and stay here whenever they wanted, as my guests.'

They'd looked unsure at the time, but he'd asked them to sit with the idea. For when – if – they ever wanted to come back and see some familiar faces.

The confusion was again in Lily's eyes, and he didn't miss a bit of the hurt that shone true either.

'You can't make that promise, Henry.'

'Yes, I can,' he assured her. Not out of stubborn determination, or contrariness. But then he remembered that he hadn't told her everything.

'Henry—'

'I can, because I've also been in touch with the estate agents.'

She went still as a statue, sitting in the soft glow of the setting sun. Her eyes, wide and luminous, her rosebud lips slightly parted as if expectant, hopeful even. He'd remember that image of her for the rest of his life. He knew it as well as he knew his own name.

'I've told them to cancel the sale. To give my sincere apologies to Mr Jameson, but to explain that I'm no longer in a position to leave.'

'Henry—'

'Lily,' he warned, not in the least bit done with what he needed to say yet. She twisted her lips in the most adorable way and pressed the back of her hand against them as if literally stifling the words – the questions – he was sure was on them.

He ran his hand through his hair again, noticing how her eyes flicked to the top of his head, the lips behind her hand curved up slightly, and realized he'd probably made a complete mess of the wayward thick waves, but couldn't care less.

'I have spent far too many years running from Hawke's Cove and yet it was always here,' he said, shaking his head, struggling to find the right words. 'What I mean is that … I don't want you to think that …' He clenched his jaw, to stop himself from growling in frustration. What was it about this that had him so tongue-tied?

He felt Lily's hand slip into his just before he could run it through his hair again.

'Take a breath. Start at the beginning,' she said gently and with the patience of a goddess. Even he was driving himself half mad at this point.

'I love you,' he said finally.

'That's the beginning?'

'*That's* your reaction?' he demanded, even though the smile that lit her face was something that stole the breath from his lungs and the beat from his heart. This time he bit his own lip to stop himself from laughing before sternly telling himself off. This wasn't a laughing matter. This was serious. This felt, or at least had felt before he'd laid eyes on her, like life and death. Bloody hell. How had he got into this mess?

'I'm not not selling the estate because I love you.'

'Double negative much?'

'Why aren't you taking this seriously, Lily?' he groaned. 'I'm trying to tell you that I want to spend the rest of my life with you, and that I don't want to pressure you into thinking you have to say yes, because I know how much the estate means to you, and I want you to know that me not selling the estate isn't dependent *on* you saying yes, and that *if* you say yes, then I want to know it's because you love me as much as I love you, only that's not possible because—'

'Yes to what?'

'What do you mean, yes to what?' he demanded, truly and completely exasperated.

'You haven't asked me anything yet.'

How had he turned into a complete mess overnight? If this was what love did to a person, he wasn't sure he wanted it at all. Only he did. He really did. Especially when he saw the look in Lily's eyes, the smile on her mouth, the way she bit her top lip, making her look both ridiculously happy and ridiculously eager, just as he felt in that moment.

Without a moment's thought, he got on one knee and knelt before her.

'Lily Atwell, you have given me so much. When I thought I had lost my father, you returned him to me. When I thought I had only hurt in my past, you showed me that there had been joy, and laughter and even love. When I thought I had no place here,' he said, drawing a jagged breath, 'you showed me I had a home. A community. You've reminded me of who I am, you've eased my greatest fear and shown me how to overcome it. The things you have achieved make me want to *aim higher*,' he said, remembering that first dinner they shared.

'You have shown me what true friendship is, what love and acceptance is. I love you. I felt it before I knew it. Needed it before I wanted it. Thought that you were my past before I realized you were my future. So I have one more thing to ask you to give. Would you do me the greatest honour and give me your hand in marriage – be my wife, my love, and my home?'

'Yes, oh yes,' Lily cried, reaching for him, until suddenly she pulled back, a frown across her eyes. 'Only ...' Henry felt his heart lurch in his chest

★ ★ ★

'Only,' Lily said again, struggling to find the words that would explain the tearing in her heart, 'are you sure you don't want to sell the estate? It's just that ... I was hoping to do some travelling of my own ...' She noticed Henry still at her words, but pushed on. She had to. Because the yearning – the need in her to see the world, just like the girls had, just like *he* had – was almost overwhelming. 'I think you were right. I don't regret any of the choices I've made, I don't regret any of the things I've achieved, but I've realized that I *do* want to go out and explore more of the world. To see the sun rise over Cairo and sun set in Papua

New Guinea. I want to visit Positano and learn how to make *sfogliatelle*, and Ghana for the chicken and peanut stew, Indonesia for *nasi goreng* and the Philippines for beef pares.' The words were rushing from her mouth but they came from her heart and she couldn't hold them back.

'I want to go to every single place that Zo has ever written about and see it for myself. I want to learn to surf where Malie taught in Hawaii and I want to visit every shop that sells V's clothes. And I want all that,' she said, running out of breath, 'because you showed me that I *could*. You showed me that I can leave home because my family and friends and community will always be here waiting for me when I come back. But also because ...' Lily took a deep breath, hands twisting in front of her, 'because I was hoping that you might be there with me. And it's something I really want to do. And I'd hate to think that you'd chosen not to sell the estate and—'

Henry stopped her words with a kiss, which *almost* infuriated her, but his words that followed soothed her heart a moment later.

'What if we could have them both?' he asked. 'What if we could keep the estate while we travelled the world?

'Do you think we could?' she asked, half terrified that this man had just offered her her heart's desire.

'I would do anything for you, Lily,' he said, and the love shining in his eyes filled her heart so deeply she thought she might burst. The wave of love almost rocked her foundations, but like the tide, gentled back and forth, settling a feeling of rightness about her shoulders and her heart. She reached for him then and their kiss was one that she would cherish for the rest of their lives.

Her hands framed his gorgeous face, fingers threaded through already dishevelled hair and she pressed against him, wanting no more barriers between them, not even air.

Any further thought was cut through by a chorus of chaotic screams, cheers and squeals and she closed her eyes against the smile forming against Henry's lips as she knew those voices as well as her own heartbeat.

She turned in his firm arms, as if he didn't want to let her go either, to see Zoe, Malie and Victoria, arms wrapped around each other, still screaming and crying and celebrating for her. They rushed towards the bench and surrounded her and Henry, arms and smiles and hugs and kisses all mingling together.

'I'm sorry, Victoria, I hadn't meant to propose today, your wedding should be perfect and I didn't want to take away—'

'Oh pssht. It *is* perfect. *This* makes it perfect, Henry Hawkesbury,' Victoria interrupted.

Over Zoe's shoulder, Lily could see Ollie, Todd and Finn leaning back against the house casting what looked to be sympathetic glances at Henry, who was smack bang in the middle of the happiest bridal party ever known.

'Oh God, your dress,' Lily cried, fearing the grass and mud that was dangerously close to being trampled underfoot.

'Forget the dress, what about my—'

'*Mascara*,' Lily, Zoe and Victoria all cried in unison.

'Forget the mascara, what about the wedding cake?' Victoria demanded. 'You can't miss the *pièce de résistance*! Come *on*,' she said, grabbing Lily with one hand and Henry with the other and dragging them out of the melee and back towards the house.

'We'll be there in a minute,' Henry said, reaching for Lily by the waist, anchoring her to him as if he was half afraid Victoria would whisk her away.

'Go,' Lily insisted, relishing the feel of Henry's arms around her, leaning back against him finally believing that he'd always be there, supporting her, loving her.

'OK, but I swear to God, if that dog gets anywhere near the—'

'Come *on*,' Malie said, drawing her away before passing her back to Ollie and reaching for Todd just as Finn hauled Zo towards him for a kiss. Within moments they had disappeared back into the orangery. Lily took a deep breath, turning back to Henry, who was gazing at her as if she were the most incredible thing and that he couldn't even begin to figure her out.

'What is it?' she asked.

'Well, I was hoping to hear you say that you loved me, but if it's too much—'

She silenced his teasing with a kiss. The most perfect kiss yet. With her lips pressed against his, she said, 'I love you. I love you. I love you,' knowing that she would say as much each and every day for the rest of her life.

'Well, that's a good thing, because I wanted to give you this.'

Henry reached into his pocket and retrieved a small red leather box.

'A true proposal needs a ring,' he said, offering her the box to open.

Lily's hands shook as she lifted away the tiny clasp and opened the lid to reveal the most beautiful ring she'd ever seen. Her eyes flitted between the ring and Henry, wondering if this would all disappear.

'Is this real?' she asked in wonder.

'Well, it's not cubic zirconia, if that's what you're asking.'

'No, you silly bugger, this moment,' she said, playfully swatting him on the arm.

The ring was perfect. Three pearls nestled in a gold band, the central and largest of the pearls was bracketed by diamonds laid on top of each other either side of the beautiful pearl.

'It was my grandmother's. Blake's mother,' he clarified. 'On the way back from the Averys' I went to see my mother and told her all about you. It was everything I could do to stop her from getting in the car with me to come here,' he said, smiling at the memory. 'My father had refused to take it back and insisted on her saving it for his future daughter-in-law.'

Goosebumps crested over her skin as she gently touched the ring with her finger.

'I can't help but think that it would have made him the happiest man to see you wear this ring.'

Lily felt the tears press against the back of her eyelids and hastily blinked before one could escape. 'Do you think he can see us?' she whispered hopefully.

Henry sighed. 'I have no idea, but I'd like to think so,' he said, pressing a kiss to the top of her head. They stayed like that until the desire to try on the ring became too much.

She pulled out of his embrace and gave him the box, smiling. He gently eased the ring from his case and Lily didn't even mind that his hands trembled a little as he took her finger.

'I promise never to leave you again,' he said, looking her square in the eye. 'To love you with every single beat of my heart. To spend every single day from now on reminding you how wonderful and amazing you are, and thanking my lucky stars that you said yes. Hawke's Cove is where we will live, but Lily, *you* are my home, my sanctuary, my safe haven.'

He was about to slide the ring onto her finger when she stopped him. For a second, she saw the moment of concern, almost fear, flash in his eyes. And she thought she knew why, which was why she halted his progress.

'Henry, Blake and Hawke's Cove, V, Malie and Zo all gave me a safe space to land when I was hurt. It was more than I could have asked for and everything I thought I wanted. But from the moment I met you, you challenged me. Drove me mad sometimes,' she said with a smile, remembering just half a dozen of the times she had wanted to murder him. 'But you showed me what I couldn't see from the others. That I had been hiding. From the world, from myself even. But you also showed me how strong I was and how deserving – and for some reason that was hard for me. You broke through walls I didn't even know I had, dug me out of holes I didn't realize I was in. And I love you for that. I love you for showing me the woman you see me to be, when I couldn't see it for myself. I will spend every day loving you – the incredible man *I* see in *you*. You've shown me I don't have to do it all by myself. That it's better, easier and infinitely more enjoyable to do it with … not just someone, but with you. Hawke's Cove is where my family and friends are – now at least – but you are my true home.'

The love shining in his eyes was a wonder. No more doubt, no fear, no concern. But pure belief in each other's love … it was a power she never knew had existed.

'Now, are you just going to let that sit there at the tip of my finger?' she asked, nodding to the ring.

As his fingers pushed down the gold band, his lips claimed hers and she had never felt more complete, more excited and more hopeful for a future she could now see, with Henry.

Pulling back from the kiss, she stared at where the ring fit perfectly on her finger as if it had always meant to be there.

'We should probably get back to the wedding. Victoria will have my head,' grumbled Henry.

'The wedding can wait,' she moaned, pulling him into another glorious kiss.

'Lily Atwell, I think I've ruined you,' he said, as she felt the smile of his lips against hers.

He turned her into the crook of his arms and led her, reluctantly, back to the orangery just in time to see Victoria and Ollie about to cut the cake. Victoria locked eyes with Lily and smiled the happiest smile, full of love and laughter. The entire venue rose up in a joyous scream as together, their hands around the same knife, Ollie and Victoria cut their cake.

With Henry's arm holding her to his side, they stood in the doorway, and Lily took in the beautiful sight. Every single person was smiling or laughing, chatting away, forkfuls of cake making people groan in delight, and then she caught her mother's eye, hopeful and eager. Lily brought her hand up and wiggled her fingers so that her mother could see the beautiful ring and laughed when her mother clasped her hands to her heart, and tears glistened in her eyes.

Love you, her mother mouthed and nodded to Henry, who had caught the exchange.

'Love you too,' Lily whispered across the distance, knowing that only Henry would have caught the words.

She sighed and leaned her head against Henry's shoulder. 'I think that this could be the beginning of a beautiful happy-ever-after.'

'Many beautiful happy ever afters,' Henry replied, pressing a kiss to his wife-to-be's forehead. 'Many.'

That night, they ate, drank, danced, laughed and loved long into the night and all the four girls agreed that it was the *most* perfect, *most* beautiful, *most* wonderful night of their lives.

'Until *my* wedding,' claimed Malie.

'Until *my* wedding,' cried Zoe.

'Until *my* wedding,' whispered Lily with eyes only for Henry Hawkesbury, the love of her life.

EPILOGUE

Ten years later ...

THE SOUND OF CHILDREN'S laughter echoed all the way along the private beach at the Hawkesbury estate making Lily smile. It reminded her of all the summers that had passed not only since Henry's return, but before, when she, Victoria, Malie and Zoe – each of whom were here with their families – were just a little older than their own children were. It made her happy and hopeful for all the summers that were to come as she entwined her fingers with Henry's, his hand never far from reach. Just as he'd promised all those years ago.

'Thank you for doing this,' he said, gazing into her eyes.

'Thank you for thinking of it. It's a beautiful thing to do and a wonderful way to honour her memory. We'll take lots of pictures for Claudia's family. I'm sorry they couldn't be here,' she said, resting her head on her husband's arm.

'They're with Caroline – Claudia's sister. They're where they should be. As are we,' he said, looking out at the four families gathered on the beach.

The others had gone ahead, giving Lily and Henry a little space on a day that was difficult for all of them, but that had become something beautiful as they came together to commemorate that night twenty years ago. Coming out from the tree line and onto the beach, Lily followed her husband's gaze to see Todd and Ollie playing football with Koa and Kalani, Malie's two irrepressible boys, and Victoria's adopted daughter Isobel who was turning into more of a tomboy than Malie had ever been.

Instinctively scanning the beach, Lily found her son Jamie and daughter Rose, playing with Louis, the beautiful little boy Victoria and Ollie adopted a few years after Isobel. Her heart easing unconsciously just at the sight of them, Lily felt complete in a way that she could never have imagined.

'I think you should stick to surfing,' Malie called to her husband from the sprawling picnic blanket beneath a gazebo structure that Henry had made permanent in the year following Victoria and Oliver's wedding.

Todd pulled up short, stopping the game, a look of such indignation on his features that everyone, even the children, couldn't help but laugh. 'Wash your mouth out right this minute, Mrs Masters!' he said as he dribbled the ball between his sons, before Isobel came from the left and ran straight into him. Scooping her up in his arms, he fell dramatically to the ground where all the children piled in and Ollie creased up, bent almost double with laughter. Lily's heart warmed to see Victoria capturing the entire event on her camera.

Lily led Henry towards the canopied gazebo where Zoe was sitting with Malie, who was nursing her gorgeous eight-month-old baby girl.

'You never would have thought Todd would been so happy

to take a back seat from the business,' Malie said to Zoe as Lily crossed her feet at her ankles and gently collapsed down onto the throw.

'I love the way you do that,' Zoe said, looking up with a beatific smile across her features.

'Yoga,' replied Henry, leaving only Lily able to recognize the wicked heat in his tone.

Smiling conspiratorially, Lily turned her attention back to Malie. 'But Todd's happy at Fun for All, right? I mean, the help he's been able to give to so many now that the company is international is just incredible.'

'Well, it's only something he's been able to do because of the help from Henry, Ollie and Finn.'

'He would have got there eventually, I have no doubt. But for the Avery app, it was a no brainer. Together we can do so much to help create a safe space and support where it's needed most,' Henry said sincerely and Lily knew that Malie understood how important that was to Henry.

'Gimme, gimme, gimme,' Zoe said, hands outstretched and fingers wriggling towards Malie's little girl, who she snuggled close to her the moment the precious bundle came into her arms. Zoe and Finn had made the decision not to have children, knowing that their lives were complete as they were and full of the love that they showered on every single child in the group.

'I meant to ask,' Lily said, looking to Malie, 'how is your new instructor working out?'

'Really well. Actually, we've just been put forward for a Centre of Excellence award.'

'Malie! That's amazing,' Lily cried, Zoe giving a gentle 'Whoop! Whoop!', conscious of the little girl in her arms.

'Thank you. We've been waiting so long to hear, but Mum and Dad are over the moon. I think they're even more excited about the award than I am.'

'Obviously. *You* know that the rating and the award was due at least two years ago,' Victoria teased as she came in from where she'd been taking photos of the football match. Lily and Zoe smiled, knowing how right she was. Malie's family's surfing business had thrived in the last few years, not only with the help of her parents, but also the teachers who came from all over the world to train in the use of their specialist equipment.

'True. True,' Malie conceded.

'This definitely deserves a toast,' Victoria said, passing around the glasses that they'd brought from the house.

'When will you hear?' asked Zoe.

Malie accepted her non-alcoholic punch with mock sufferance. It was clear to everyone that she loved it. 'A month, I think?'

'Excellent. The revisions on my latest book should be finished by then, so we can have a celebratory dinner at Merrow's Rest.'

Zoe and Finn had slowly restored Merrow's Rest which had been the scene for many a beautiful evening spent with the entire gang, and when she wasn't being a fabulous host, or travelling the world with Finn as he added to his luxury property portfolio, she was furiously writing, adding yet another heart-pounding romance to her hugely successful, incredibly sought-after bestselling book list.

'Yes! Please!' cried Victoria, who loved coming down from London with Oliver, Isobel and Louis. Although they had a beautiful holiday home in Hawke's Cove, they were regular visitors to Merrow's Rest and the Hawkesbury estate. After the roaring success that was Russell & Co's London store, Oliver had been able to take the big step back from the family business that he'd always wanted to do and focus, instead, on his charity for under-privileged children, The Russell Trust.

Lily laughed at Victoria's response. 'Will Nisha let you away from VSD for long enough?'

'I'm sure she will allow me the time away,' Victoria replied drolly. 'Actually, she and Jasmine are both working on a pay-it-forward programme that has them utterly thrilled.'

'Pay-it-forward?' asked Zoe.

'For the scholarships?' Lily asked, and Victoria nodded with such pride in her eyes it was clear it came straight from her heart. To absolutely no one's surprise, Victoria Scott Designs had been a roaring success and was not only very much in demand, but it had also allowed Victoria to employ Nisha and Jasmine after gifting them with scholarships to attend university.

'I love that idea,' Malie said, going a little teary-eyed with sentimentality.

'Malie?' Zoe asked, clearly surprised at the deeply emotional reaction.

'Oh, don't mind me,' she said, flapping at her eyes.

'Hormones,' all the girls replied at the same time, descending into a round of laughter that was rooted in love and friendship.

'Mummy, Mummy, Mummy.' Lily's heart flared at the sound of her son's voice and she turned just in time to catch Jamie as he ran into her arms.

'Hey, sweet pea. You OK?' she asked, affectionately running

her fingers through the mop of thick dark curling waves on his head, even as he tried to veer away from the maternal touch.

'Muuuuum,' he groaned, casting a look to the older children, checking no one was watching, before leaning back into her touch. 'Can we light the lanterns yet? Can we? Pleeeeeease.'

'Not yet, my love. In about half an hour, when the sun is setting, they'll look much better, I promise.'

Jamie pouted but finally shrugged a shoulder and told her that it was OK, he could wait.

'Where's your sister?' Henry asked from where he'd been talking to Finn just beyond the edge of the gazebo.

'Rose is with Louis, looking for crab shells,' he yelled over his shoulder as he ran off to join the football.

'I'm just going to go and—'

'Check up on them?' Lily teased. Her husband had become besotted with both their children even before he'd set eyes on them, fussing more like a mother hen than anyone she'd ever known. 'They're fine. Safe, happy and free. Leave them to it,' she said, reaching up to pull him into a kiss.

He gave her a smile that melted her heart. And then went off to find his daughter anyway and Lily didn't bother to stop her eyes from rolling in loving exasperation.

'Please tell me you brought the stuffed vine leaves,' Zoe begged, her voice slightly hushed, trying not to wake Malie's daughter, now fast asleep in her arms.

'Ohhh, they are gooooood,' Malie groaned orgasmically.

'Better than the almond croissants?' Victoria asked, as if such a thing were impossible.

'Nearly. We found this amazing place in Piraeus, just south of

Athens, and the chef taught me how to make them,' Lily replied, thinking fondly of their last holiday.

'And the squid,' Zoe replied, lost in the same food dream.

Over the years, Henry had made good on his promise to her that they would travel as much as her heart desired. Somehow her husband had discovered the most incredible locations, always rooted in some dish, or some cuisine he knew that Lily would either like or be curious about. They'd driven – crazily – down the Amalfi coast and flown over the Pyrenees. She'd cooked in Hong Kong, Sweden and New Zealand and she'd loved every single minute of it. But they'd always come home to Hawke's Cove.

'Yeah, yeah, yeah,' Malie interrupted. 'You know, for someone who wanted us all back in Hawke's Cove for nearly ten years, you sure do get out and about.'

'Where are you headed to next?' Zoe asked.

Lily looked towards Henry. 'Actually, I think we're going to Tahiti.'

'I have some incredible places to tell you about.'

'Good! I want them all,' cried Lily laughing.

Henry had also taken a bit of a step back from the company he'd founded with Ben. She and Mina had hit it off instantly and Ben, Mina and their three children were hoping to join them in Tahiti. Ben hadn't minded at all that Henry had split his time between the app, the estate and their travels.

A month after Victoria's wedding, the estate had re-opened for guests, and now included a highly sought-after wedding package offered under Lily's guiding hand and two more grape varieties under Henry and John's.

It had taken three years for Henry to get Lily to walk down the aisle towards the same stunning wedding arch they had once stood beneath side by side. And although he'd grumbled, he'd appreciated that Lily hadn't wanted to take away first from Malie's wedding and then from Zoe's. Unless he'd been willing to compromise and for them to have a three-couple wedding. Which he hadn't. And Lily had secretly been happy with that.

Setting out the food drew everyone to the large blankets positioned around several wooden pallets, the offspring's food taking up as much of the adults' focus as their own. Laughter, the occasional screams from the children, one nappy change and an hour later, when Jamie asked – for the hundredth time – if they could light the lanterns, Henry checked the sky and finally agreed.

Lily had laid fourteen lanterns out along the sand ready to be lit, under the very careful supervision of the adults.

'Trust you to find eco-friendly biodegradable paper lanterns,' Malie gently teased, receiving an equally gentle shoulder nudge from Lily.

'Why is there an extra one?' Rose asked.

'That one is for Claudia, who we're remembering today.'

'Was she the girl that died?' Jamie asked, as accidentally blunt as any child who had not yet been touched by grief could be.

'She was,' Henry replied. 'So today, we're lighting a lantern for her so that wherever she is, she knows that there will always be a light shining in Hawke's Cove, just for her.'

'Is there one for Grandpa too?' Rose asked.

Henry paused, but Lily smiled. 'Of course, sweet pea. Do you want to get it? It's in my bag on the throw.'

Their daughter scampered off to retrieve the one that she had kept aside, in case Henry had wanted to light one for his father too. He didn't need to say it, she could see the thanks shining in her husband's eyes, knew that it was right from the touch of his lips to hers, and the love that settled in her heart.

In pairs, each flame from each lantern was lit, then the long line of them – stretching across the sand – was soon released into the sky and watched by thirteen pairs of eyes and lifted by the hope and love in thirteen hearts as the lanterns drifted higher and higher into the night sky, prayers of thanks and love on everyone's lips, to the sound of waves crashing against the shore.

Not long after, the husbands dragged reluctant – but sleepy and satisfied – children back to the estate where they were staying that night, leaving Lily, Victoria, Zoe and Malie at the beach.

'I'm glad we did that,' said Victoria as she stared up at where the lanterns were merging with the stars, drifting over Hawke's Cove and beyond.

'Me too,' Zoe said.

'Me three,' Malie smiled.

'Me four,' Lily added softly.

Victoria shook her head.

'What?' Lily asked cocking her head to one side.

'It's just that … well. Look at us. Ten years on and living our *best* lives.'

'Long may it continue,' said Zoe raising her glass, Malie leaning her head on Zoe's shoulder, and humming her agreement. Victoria and Lily clinked their glasses to Zoe's and each took a sip.

For a moment they were lost in their own thoughts, each unknowingly almost exactly the same. Thinking on how much life had thrown at them, how they'd survived it and how their friendship was stronger than ever. How the bonds of love had expanded to include friends, lovers and children. The joy they shared as their children played and dreamed – as they had done all those years ago on this very same beach – had lit their eyes as much as their hearts.

'So when are you off to Tahiti?' Zoe asked Lily.

'About three weeks? We'll have to figure out the time difference for a Lost Hours call.'

Malie snorted. 'I still can't believe you have three whole hours you can't remember.'

Zoe pulled a face and shrugged.

'Wait … what's that look for?' Malie demanded.

'No idea what you're talking about,' Zoe replied, not meeting anyone's gaze.

'Zoe!' Victoria cried. 'I don't *believe* it.'

'What?' she responded innocently.

'No way,' Lily said. 'No, no, no.'

'Oh, come *on*,' cried Malie. 'Seriously? All this time and you actually *remember* what happened in Ibiza?'

'So you've just *pretended* not to know what happened when you went missing in the foam party? The very event that *created* the Lost Hours! And you knew? This whole time?' Lily demanded.

'Ahh …' Zoe hedged and all the girls descended into a fit of giggles that would have done their teenage selves proud.

'You can't leave us hanging,' Victoria demanded. 'Spill. Now!'

'OK, OK,' Zoe said, raising her hands in surrender and groaning out loud. 'I'm not sure you're ready for it, though.'

'Of course we are,' Malie replied indignantly.

'Out with it,' ordered Lily, unable to take the smile from her face.

Zoe looked at each of the girls in turn. 'OK, so what happened was …'

Acknowledgements

All acknowledgements are special and important, but none as significant as the ones I am penning now. I never thought I would publish a novel, never mind four with such astounding unexpected success. The stories of my four girls have touched so many, and significantly changed my life too. I've found a passion that I hope will stay with me forever. Whilst *Meet Me at the Wedding* is the final hurrah for this series it certainly isn't the end of my love affair with Mills & Boon romantic fiction.

To my readers, my editor Becky Slorach, Lisa Milton and everyone at Mills & Boon, including Kirsty Capes, Tom Keane, Stephanie Heathcote and Sian Baldwin, I will attempt to thank you in this small way and I hope this book does all of our efforts justice. You believed in me and my vision, I'm so proud of our ever expanding and passionate literature family! Long may this continue.

To the immensely talented Pippa Roscoe aka my writing partner in crime…words fail me! I will forever be in debt to you and your brilliance. To illustrator extraordinaire Lucy Truman, thank you for the wonderful illustration - what a way to finish the series.

I'd also like to thank Andrea Villanueva de Milne, navigating both work and life with you by my side is joyous. Thank you for being spectacularly diligent and the kindest person I know. Quick shout out to my dog Monty, alas still unable to read but not thanking him for his unwavering snuggles while writing would have been a total oversight on my behalf.

Lastly, to all of you out there who believe in the beauty and story of love – don't ever stop, it is life's greatest gift.

Toff x

If you loved *Meet me at the Wedding* read on for an extract of where it all began, in Victoria's story *Meet me in London*

Out now by Georgia Toffolo

CHAPTER ONE

OLIVER RUSSELL COULD WRANGLE a wayward balance sheet back into the black, take failing stores apart and breathe new life into them, make difficult calls on staffing and personnel issues, make his shareholders happy and very, *very* rich. But he had never managed to curb his mother's meddling in his private life.

Some things were just impossible.

Earth to Oliver. This is your mother asking about your Christmas Day plans. Will I need to set an extra place at the dinner table? Hint, hint. Your mother xx

Sitting on a stool at the bar in the upmarket wine bar The Landing, Oliver groaned as he interpreted the 'hint' as yet another badly veiled attempt to discover his relationship status. *Great one, Mum. Way to put pressure on a guy.*

Could this week get any worse? He threw his mobile phone onto the sticky, beer-stained counter, gripped the tumbler in front of him and took a sip of a much needed fifteen-year-old Scotch. As the honey-coloured syrup oozed down his throat and hit his stomach with a warming buzz he silently counted all the ways things had gone wrong in such a short space of time.

First mistake; allowing his mother to believe he was finally settling down when in reality his love life could only be described as… non-existent. And now having to think up all the ways he could appease his parents over the holidays without going quietly insane.

Whereas other families had jolly traditions of games and church on Christmas Day, his parents' idea of fun was to corner him in the lounge, pin him down with laser stares and interrogate him for signs of commitment, a potential wife and progeny. A grandchild, or preferably many grandchildren, to spoil and give meaning to their later years, someone to carry on the family name and also an heir to entrust the business to. As an only child Oliver was expected to do so, as his father had done before him.

Trouble was, after his last romantic failure, settling down was not on Oliver's bucket list. At least, not for a very long time.

Second mistake: in the spirit of keeping the family business afloat he'd agreed to clean up the mess his cousin was making of the new build. Ollie should have let him fall on his sword, but that would have meant his parents suffering too and there was no way he was going to allow that. So, here he was in a rowdy bar in Chelsea at ridiculous o'clock at night – or was it early morning? – having only just finished work, with the prospect of another seventeen-hour day tomorrow and the next day, and the next…

He took another sip of whisky but almost choked as someone bumped into his hip, jolted his arm and sloshed the Scotch, rich but burning, down his throat.

'Hey, gorgeous.' A woman old enough to be his mother – and even though deep down he loved his mum, Lord knew he didn't need two of them – appeared at his shoulder and beamed at him. Her eyes were wine-glazed and the lipstick smudged over her mouth almost up to her nostrils made her look like a startled fish. 'I've got mistletoe, you know what that means, right?'

'That it's time I left?' Scraping his stool back he stood, steadying the woman as she swayed, and then handed her into the waiting arms of her friends who were all dressed as… well, he wasn't entirely sure, but there were glitter wings and feathery haloes involved, so he imagined they were supposed to be Christmas angels. In November?

As if knowing all about his work stress and family dilemmas even the music in the bar seemed to mock him. Too loud and too cheery and all about being home and in love at Christmas. He shuddered. *No thanks.*

Which brought him to his third mistake: choosing the bar from hell to drown his sorrows in. It wasn't even December and yet here they all were screeching Christmas carols at the top of their tone-deaf voices. Christmas was everywhere. In the glittery tinsel that hung in loopy garlands across the ceiling and the fake tree in the corner. The soundtrack to the evening. The clothes people were wearing. Christmas was hurtling fast towards him and he was running out of time. He had so much to do to fix his first mistake before the doors of the new Russell & Co department store opened, way behind schedule, but in time for the busiest, and therefore most lucrative time of the year.

He just needed some kind of miracle to make it happen.

On the counter his phone vibrated. He picked up and grimaced at another text, knowing what was bound to be coming but also knowing if he ignored her it would only get worse:

Oliver? It's a simple question. Blink once for yes. Twice for no. Are we finally going to meet your new girlfriend? Your mother xx

Uh-oh. She was dropping the veiled interest and taking a more direct approach. This was serious.

He flicked a text back:

When your message flashes onto my screen it identifies you as my mother. There is also a little photo of you smiling at me at the top of your texts. You don't need to tell me who you are.

He added two kisses, because, well, she was his mother: *Ollie xx*

A pause while he watched three grey dots dance on his screen and then:

Not a single blink. How do I interpret that? We just want to see you happy. Your mother xxx

By happy, she meant married. As if you couldn't be otherwise. Although he knew just as many people who were married and miserable as married and happy.

How was he even meant to send a blink by text anyway? He rolled his eyes instead. Nothing confirmed as yet.

Before he could say 'Baa Humbug' her reply flashed on his screen:

When will you know? Your mother xx

I don't know.

If he told her the delightful Clarissa had moved on to a more malleable boyfriend his mum would be trying to arrange dates for him.

As if on cue another text arrived:

Is there something you're not telling us? Is it over? So soon? Again? Oh, Oliver.

He could feel the disappointment coming through the airwaves as her next text quickly followed:

Perhaps I should invite the Henleys over on Christmas Day.

I heard Arabella's back from her Indian ashram trip and
SINGLE. And stop rolling your eyes at me. Your mother xx

He couldn't help but laugh at that, despite his growing frustration. He tried to stay noncommittal. Apparently, according to his
ex, noncommittal was a strength of his:

Do NOT set any more dates up for me. Nothing's confirmed
re Xmas. I'll let you know when I know.

At the new store opening then?

Just a matter of weeks away. She clearly wasn't giving up. She
never gave up. She wouldn't give up until she was holding his first
child. Or maybe his second – his second set of triplets.

That was the problem; she wasn't giving up. He just needed to
appease her. Or ignore her. So, he chose the latter.

Realizing he hadn't finished his drink and grateful that the bar
staff were now shuffling the off-tune singers outside he sat back
down and resumed his contemplation of the whisky in front of
him. At some point the staff would shuffle him out too, but for
now he craved this brief peace and quiet, save for his mother's
infuriating but well-meaning texts and a muted conversation
between the servers coming from a little room off to the side of
the bar.

He could hear Paul, the guy who'd served him earlier say, 'Hey,
Vicki, are you OK to close up tonight? I promised Amanda I'd
get home early. It's our anniversary.'

'Of course,' a soft voice filtered through. 'You helped me out
by taking the early shift so I could teach my class, so I'm more
than happy to hang around here for the stragglers. Sara said she'd
stay on and help me clear up.'

Stragglers? Is that what he was now? Ollie looked around the bar at the three other solo drinkers – all male, all staring hopelessly into glasses of alcohol. He laughed to himself. Yeah, damned right he fitted that description; moving slowly. He didn't want to hurry because the sooner he went home, the sooner tomorrow would arrive bringing with it all his problems.

'So how did class go today?' he heard Paul ask the owner of the soft voice. 'Any more visits from the local cops?'

Police? Interesting. Ollie leaned forward to hear mystery woman's answer.

'Oh, that was all just a misunderstanding. Her brother gave her the iPad, Jasmine didn't know it was stolen.' A pause. 'Um. By her brother.' A rumble of soft laughter that sounded so free and bright had Ollie straining to see who the voice belonged to. It wasn't the other woman who worked here because she was now collecting glasses from empty tables and her accent was Cockney through and through. This Vicki woman was from somewhere else. South-west maybe, a tiny hint of something he recognized from holidays down in Cornwall. Laughter threaded through her intonation. 'We sorted it out. The police dropped the charges against her.'

'So, one of the kids you're teaching is harbouring stolen goods. Great. You really need to stay away from trouble like that, Vicki.' Paul came back into the bar and started to wipe down the counter with a dishcloth.

The woman followed. 'If I stayed away there'd be even more trouble for her, I'm sure. She's so talented. You should see her designs, they're stunning. Really fresh ideas. She could go a long way with the right guidance. I'm pulling out all the stops.'

'You're too good to those kids.' Paul frowned. 'Instead of

focusing on your own career you're spending all your energy on a bunch of no-hope teenagers who probably have never even heard the word *gratitude*.'

The Vicki woman turned and put her hands on her hips, giving Ollie full view of her face. *Wow*.

She was wearing a dress that looked like it had come straight out of the nineteen fifties; all slash neck and cinched waist in a fabric of cream and scarlet flowers. Her glossy, dark hair was loosely tied into a ponytail that was pulled forward over one shoulder. She had bright red lipstick on full lips – not smudged in the slightest, and the most intense dark eyes he'd ever seen.

In stark contrast her skin was pale, he wasn't sure whether it was make-up or natural and he didn't care. Oliver Russell had known a lot of beautiful women in his time, but she was next level. Quite simply, she was the most beautiful woman he'd ever seen.

That gorgeous red mouth curled into a smile, but a little frown appeared over her eyes. 'Paul, honestly, they're struggling in so many ways. They have so much hope and potential and no one else seems to care. If I don't help them then who will?'

'I'm just saying, be careful, that's all. Your heart's too soft, Vicki, you're going to get hurt.'

'It's a fashion design class for underprivileged kids, Paul. Not target practice in the 'hood. Trouble is, we're fast running out of opportunities for them to showcase their work. All the design schools have organized shows already and we're lagging behind. I'm going to have to be creative with my thinking.' Her eyes wandered over the bar and settled on Oliver, just for a moment.

Instinctively, he smiled. She gave him the faintest of smiles back and didn't look away immediately. A look of surprise flickered behind her eyes. Even from here he could see the flush of her cheeks as their gazes met and, as if someone had flicked a switch, a rush of heat hit him too. Interest. The flicker of awareness. Brief. So brief he checked himself; maybe he'd imagined it?

All too soon she dragged her eyes away. Swallowed. She turned to her workmate and took the cloth from his hands. 'Right. Well. Things to do. Off you go, Paul, we've got this. See you tomorrow.'

With that she bent to stack more bottles into a small fridge behind the bar, giving Ollie a front-row view of her graceful, slender neck, the gentle slope of her shoulders, the pearls of her spine trailing into that curve-enhancing vintage dress. Even the back of her was more interesting, more alluring than anything he'd seen in weeks. Months. *Ever.*

In his peripheral vision he sensed movement. As Sara put a fist-ful of dirty glasses next to him on the counter, she caught him looking at Vicki and grinned. Her eyes widened in something he could only interpret as mischief and he could almost read what she was thinking. Yeah, he was checking this Vicki out. *So sue me.*

But damn, the last thing he wanted was to make anyone uncomfortable. He drew his eyes away but there was something about her that made him want to take a second glance and keep on looking. She was stunning, had a gentle confidence about her, and was helping poor kids in her spare time… his kind of perfect.

Not that he was interested in perfect. Or anyone at all right now. He had far too much to do to save the family business to be distracted by a woman. Still, a guy could look, right?

Vicki was oblivious. Vicki? She was more a Victoria, he thought. Victoria smacked of gravitas and class and she had both in spades.

8

Sara was still grinning. She opened her mouth, no doubt to say some smart-ass comment, but right on cue his phone vibrated again. *Phew.* Saved by the ringtone. But sadly, saved by his mother was way more of a crush to his ego than being caught admiring a beautiful woman.

How about Jecca Forsythe? She's lovely. Just come out of a messy divorce, so I imagine she's keen to get dating again.
Your mother xx

The latest in the line of single women his mother kept parading in front of him. They were all perfectly nice women, all fitting his parents' ideal of what a Russell wife should be like; preferably the daughter of business associates to strengthen the Russell brand, clever, pretty but not showy, happy to support him in his business, keen for a family. But none of them made him feel... whatever it was he was supposed to feel. The kind of thing his grandparents had had. The laugh together, play together, grow together love. That wasn't something they shared in his Russell household. Loyalty, yes. Proximity... if necessary. Closeness, not so much.

No, Mum. Not Jecca. Or Arabella. Or anyone else for that matter. I can sort out my own love life, thanks.

Another ping on his phone. He didn't want to look, but he had to, because ignoring her wasn't working.

Well, from where I'm sitting you obviously can't. You need an intervention. I'm worried about you, Oliver. It's not good to be alone. Your father is so invested in your future, we both are.
We miss you. Your mother xx

Oliver read it twice and cursed while his heart crushed at the mention of his father. The reason for this most recent intense interest in his love life suddenly crystallized: his parents had so

much to worry about – too much – that they were looking for
a distraction. And why the hell not? They didn't have much else
to look forward to, so a marriage and babies and a rosy future for
their son was all they could hope for.

Annoyed at himself for his surly replies, and rightfully humbled,
Oliver flicked another text to his mum:

How is Dad?

A couple of moments passed, during which guilt shivered
through Oliver's gut. Then:

Oh, you know. The same. But his doctor says there's some
experimental treatment he wants to try.

That was where they'd got to, experimental treatment when
everything else had failed so far.

Give him my love.

His mother was trying, he knew, to forge a better relationship
between them all at this difficult time and he welcomed that, but
sometimes it could be suffocating. He'd tried I'm fine on my own.
He'd tried I'm not ready to settle down and none of it convinced
her he was OK. But now she wanted to meet this special woman.
Who didn't exist. Who'd got bored of waiting for commitment.

He didn't want to let his parents feel that bitter tang of disappointment, not again when they had so much to battle already,
but he didn't want his mother setting up surreptitious dates over
Christmas either, inviting the very nice but not for him Arabella or
Jecca or any other woman she believed would be a perfect match.

He wanted them to have something to look forward to.

What to do?

Oliver? We're so looking forward to meeting her. Your father
in particular.

So without thinking too much about the ramifications Oliver sent a text straight back:

OK. OK, Mum. I'll bring her to the opening day.

Oh! Ollie! Love. Ollie! Finally! See, that wasn't too hard, was it? I'm so excited. Your mother xx

He stared at the screen for a minute and let his actions sink in. Hell. He'd just lied to his mother about a non-existent girlfriend. Great stuff.

He took another gulp of whisky. He had time. Time to find a new girlfriend. Or time to think up another excuse to tell his mother on opening day.

Damn. Because if he didn't come up with a plan his mum would be hounding him then too. If only he could find someone who was open to a mutually beneficial arrangement of *pretend girlfriend* then he could get Mummy Dearest off his back.

'It's last orders.' That voice again. Vicki was close enough he could smell her perfume. A playful, flowery mix that made him want to lean closer and breathe her in. As she spoke her hands moved, fluttering over the glasses. 'Is there anything you want before I close the till?'

So many things but none of them would be found here in this bar.

Unless… Kind. Beautiful. *Perfect.* The germ of an idea started to form in his head. He looked across the bar into dark caramel eyes that swirled with fun and, if he wasn't mistaken, a little heat. 'Actually, yes. There is something.'

She smiled, holding his gaze in a way that made his gut curl in desire. 'Sure?'

'Will you marry me?'

* * *

Not again.

'Absolutely not.' Victoria tried to hide her smile as Mr Tall, Dark and Dangerous' hopeful grin withered under her death stare. Too often – because she was petite and kind of pretty – she'd been underestimated as being a push-over, but she had a backbone made of steel. She'd had to, just to survive. It served her well dealing politely yet firmly with alcohol-soaked guys. But this one was different, definitely a level higher than the usual punters.

'If I had a pound for every marriage proposal I got at the end of a boozy night I'd be a rich girl indeed. But a word of advice, mate – as proposals go it needs work. Next time, maybe do some sort of grand romantic gesture like… oh, I don't know, find out the woman's name before you ask her to spend the rest of her life with you?'

'I take it that's a no, then?'

He grinned and she had to admit that, in another life where she wasn't jaded and burnt by relationship failure, she might have found him a teeny-weeny bit attractive. There was something about his grey-blue eyes that made her want to keep looking at him, despite his ridiculous question. Something about the scruff of his messy hair that made her want to slide her fingers in and smooth it. She wasn't even going to think about his strong jaw and stubble. He was dressed in the usual uniform for people working in offices in the Chelsea area – dark suit, white shirt, brown leather boots. He'd hung his suit jacket on the hook under the bar, and sat with his shirt neck open, no tie, and sleeves rolled up. Dressed down for Friday-night drinks.

The linen shirt caressed well-honed muscles. Broad shoulders. A fine body. He had a crystal-cut voice that was as deep as the trouble he'd just got himself into. So OK, maybe he was extraordinary compared to the usual suited and booted or trendy wannabe King's Road hipster guys that came in after work.

Oh, and then there'd been that deep, low burn she'd felt as her gaze had clashed with his. Something totally elemental and primal. A prickling awareness over her skin. Something she hadn't felt in a long time, and she had to admit it was happening again as he smiled.

She shook her head. 'A definite no. Sorry, not sorry.'

'Way to break a man's heart.' He shrugged.

'Oh, I'm sure you'll survive. There are plenty of women looking for what you're offering.' Ignoring the tingles zipping through her, Victoria printed his bill and put it on onto a saucer. She pushed it towards him. 'Here's your tab. Sara will ring it up for you.'

Then she turned away and busied herself with wiping down the optics. But out of the corner of her eye she watched him scrape back his stool and take out his platinum credit card, pay, then stride confidently towards the door. She pretended not to be gaping when he turned and gave her a woefully sad smile and playfully tapped his 'broken' heart before he disappeared into the night.

When the door closed she felt her body sag on a sigh, as if she'd been holding her breath through the whole interaction. Wow. That connection when they first saw each other had been… weird.

Her friend Sara, standing next to her, gave her a nudge. 'Whoa. Victoria Scott, he is one hell of a hot dude.'

Yes, he is. 'Says the woman with the uber hot girlfriend.'

Sara laughed and raised her palms. 'Sweetheart, just because I don't work that way doesn't mean I don't know talent when I see it.'

Victoria allowed herself to enjoy the fizzy feelings inside her, just for a moment. Because it had been fun and playful but that's all it was. Then reality – fuelled by her doomed romantic history – slid into her brain, so she put those feelings in a box and closed the lid. 'Gorgeous, but drunk. He must be to propose to a stranger.'

'Hmmm.' Sara's mouth twisted. 'He nursed one Macallan the whole time he was here.'

'A cheap drunk, then.' Victoria laughed. 'That's even worse. What a blow to my ego.'

'Not at all. He seemed entirely in possession of all faculties, as you would agree, having not taken your eyes off him for the whole time it took him to pay and walk out the door. Maybe you should have taken him up on his offer?'

Victoria whirled round to look at her friend. 'What? Seriously?'

'Hypothetically speaking. At least, you could have chatted a bit more and seen where it could have gone… drinks, dinner? Bed?' She grinned and Victoria wasn't sure whether she was being serious or not.

Sara was relatively new to the bar and they'd started to develop a friendship that was fresh and fun, but with new friendships there was always that lag time of developing a bond, learning to trust, knowing what to say and what to keep secret.

With her tight group of old friends from Devon, Victoria always knew exactly what they meant, what they were thinking, what they were about to say even before they said it. They'd shared years of closeness, had been there for each other during amazing times, bad times and worse, and although they were all spread across the world now – and she missed them so much it made her heart hurt – they still talked as often as they could on group chats. They'd talk her off the ledge or encourage her to take the next step in anything she was considering, even dating, if ever she felt ready to do it again. Sara was great but Victoria knew it was going to take a little more time before she felt as close to her as she did to Zoe, Lily and Malic.

'Sara, he asked me to marry him, not go on a date. No drinks, dinner or bed. Just cut straight to the 'til death us do part stuff. No thanks.'

'He looked more like the for richer *not* for poorer type, though and he might have been fun, which is just what you need right now.' Sara appeared to be more excited than Victoria was over this. Which was strange, given that proposals did indeed come thick and fast at the end of a drunken night and normally Sara rolled her eyes and bit her tongue. 'You never know, he might even be The One.'

'I do know. He isn't.' There wasn't such a thing.

'Your loss' Sara shrugged. 'All I'm saying is—'

'It's time to mop the floors and then we can go home?' Victoria closed off this conversation about her hapless love life and looked at her watch. Her feet hurt from standing all day and her brain hurt from teaching lovely but demanding teenagers and then managing the bar into the small hours.

'On it, boss lady.' While Sara filled the bucket with hot soapy water Victoria looked at the empty seat where the hot guy had been sitting and something in her belly kind of imploded at the thought of him. Which was irritating, because even though her head could rationalize how someone good-looking could have a physical effect that was purely instinctive, her body was going along with it as if he was the answer to her recent sex drought. He wasn't.

'I'm not interested in The One who proposes to a random stranger in a random bar on a random Friday night in November. I'm not interested in anyone, you know that. I'm off men. Off relationships. Off getting my heart stamped on. For good. Right now, all I'm interested in is keeping this job so I can fund my design business and the night classes for the kids. Accepting marriage proposals or dating is lower on my to-do list than getting a root canal.' She hit the reconcile button on the till and frowned. 'And we're twelve pounds seventy-five pence down.'

'Ah, yes.'

She felt Sara's eyes on her. 'Ah, yes, what?'

Her friend nodded and her eyes grew sad as she leaned on the mop handle. 'Peter.'

'Oh, and here I was thinking you were going to give me a rational explanation as to why we're over twelve quid short' – Victoria shuddered at the mention of her ex's name – 'not bring *him* up. What about him?'

Sara's hand was now on Victoria's back, gentle. Supportive. 'He did a number on you, sure, but why you let that sleazebag have such an influence over you even now I don't know.'

'Er... because he taught me a very good life lesson: never trust anyone.' And never tell them your innermost secrets and doubts, because they'll use them against you when you least expect it.

'You were hurt, love. But you have to forget him and move on.'

'I am well and truly over him. To be honest, I don't think I ever really loved him, but just when I think I'm over all that – the expectation and the lost time – he parades his new fiancée in front of me as if he's just won the lottery and all I was to him was some sort of temporary booby prize.'

'Sleazebag. Although you do have a damned fine rack, girl-friend.' Sara laughed. 'And that is something I do know a lot about.'

'OK, enough already.' Laughing, Victoria caught a quick look of herself in the mirror behind the bar. Hair smooth, shiny and still in place. Lipstick also still in place. Cat eyeliner... perfect. Boobs enhanced by the dress she'd finished making this morning. Yes, she was looking good today. But she tried to look her best every day in the clothes she fashioned for herself – as a kind of walking showcase of her design talents. She wanted people to look at her clothes, to enquire about her dresses, maybe commission some vintage-inspired pieces.

And *he'd* been looking. She should probably take a proposal from a gorgeous man as a compliment, right? Just a compliment. 'I'm done talking about men. Past or present.'

'What about future?' Sara winked then laughed at Victoria's warning scowl. 'OK, OK, I get the message. No more men talk.'

Although, as Victoria finished closing up, her mind kept flashing back to the stranger's smile. The confidence in his stance. The way the linen shirt clung to his well-toned biceps...

And it occurred to her that she may be done *talking* about him, but she sure as heck wasn't done *thinking* about him.

Meet me in London © **Georgia Toffolo 2020**

Available now!

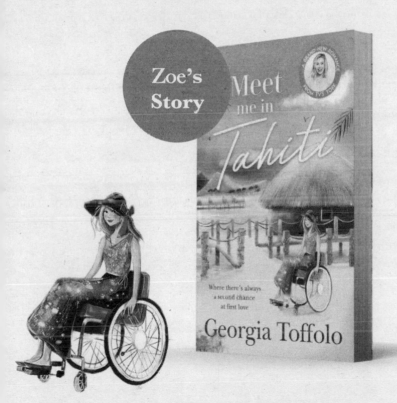

Keep in touch with...

Georgia Toffolo

Follow:

f ToffTalks

⊙ Georgiatoffolo

🐦 @ToffTalks

For all the latest book news from Georgia, sign up to the newsletter:
b.link/ToffNews

MILLS & BOON

THE HEART OF ROMANCE

LET'S TALK

Romance

Follow us:

f millsandboon

⊙ @millsandboonuk

𝕏 @millsandboon

For all the latest titles and special
offers, sign up to our newsletter:
Millsandboon.co.uk